FLETCHER WAS HERE

FLETCHER WAS HERE

Subtitle: A diary about a tiny baby's enormous strength, insurmountable struggles and the many lives he touched during his short life.

Lauren K. Wolfe

Author photo copyright through donation of their time to Now I Lay Me Down To Sleep.

This book is a publication and is available at special quantity discounts for bulk purchases for sales promotions, premiums, fund-raising or educational use. Special books or book excerpts can also be created to fit specific needs. For details, please email:
fletcherwashere@hotmail.com

Acknowledgments

I want to thank our families for their emotional, physical, and financial help, and for coming to assist us at a moment's notice. Friends from all over the world, including cyber-space, who provided relentless support through emails, telephone calls, letters, cards, care packages, food, and gift cards.

A special thank you to community pediatric palliative care organization for all your guidance and expertise; my OB and his partner and his entire office; Fletcher's primary nurse, who gave us the best possible care; and the NICU and staff who worked tirelessly to try and improve his health.

And much love to everyone who met or has heard about Fletcher and those who grew to care about him.

Saving the best for last, to my amazing children, who are my world and my joy, and remind every single day of what's truly important.

Table Of Contents

A Father's Perspective

I remember the three of us sitting together. Fletcher was in my arms and Lauren was next to me, stroking his sweet peach fuzz covered head. All the machines had been turned off and the nurses left us alone.

We were spending our final moments with our youngest son, Fletcher in a back of the neonatal intensive care unit (NICU). We both felt so numb; I don't think we were even crying. We just wanted to be with him and remember everything about him; how strong he was, how he loved to pull the tubes out of his nose, how, even at a little over four months old, his personality shone through.

After the machines were off and the ventilator tubes had been removed, Fletcher didn't even live an hour. As he exhaled his last breath, his body went limp and a little smile came to his lips. His pain was over.

We spent the next three hours holding him, kissing him, and talking to him. I remember thinking that somehow, if we just kept holding him and telling him how much we loved him, his brain would make his lungs work again. It didn't.

The funeral home representative came with a warm blanket and a little basket. We wrapped Fletcher up, put him inside, and he was taken away.

The next day, we went to the funeral home and made arrangements for his ceremony. It just felt wrong, like the whole world was out of balance. We decided to have him cremated because the thought of putting him in the cold ground forever was unthinkable. We wanted to keep him with us.

The day before the ceremony, the funeral director called to say the urn we ordered was too small. That was too horrible to comprehend. The director eventually remedied the situation and we had a very nice remembrance ceremony for Fletcher. The room was packed with family, friends, and medical staff. In his short time, Fletcher had touched a lot of lives.

Lauren has gained an impressive amount of medical knowledge because of everything she and Fletcher went through. In fact, the highly trained specialists that were dealing with Fletcher were regularly taken aback by just how much she knew. On several occasions, she was able to suggest alternative methods of care that they'd not previously considered. She's shown herself to be a top-notch researcher. I believe that without her input and constant monitoring of the doctors and nurses, Fletcher probably wouldn't have lived as long as he did. Even if he'd managed to live until July 29 without the benefit of her newfound knowledge, it would've been with multiple surgeries and excruciating pain.

The doctors wanted to perform a tracheotomy on Fletcher so badly they could taste it. Initially, they presented it to us that it was imperative in order to administer the necessary care to Fletcher. As we continued to listen and ask questions we realized it was really a matter of convenience for the doctors and nurses, and not a matter of life or death. They would no longer have to mess with tubes up his nose and masks over his mouth. Whether he could've even survived the operation was also of great concern to us. After numerous phone calls and several difficult meetings with all of the doctors and specialists, we were able to prevent the surgery.

We didn't have anyone to give us guidance while Fletcher was in the NICU. No one was there to help us filter through all the information and terminology that was thrown at us. We never imagined Fletcher would be in the NICU as long as he was. The longer he stayed in the NICU the more issues arose. It would've been easier to simply accept what the doctors said, and pray for the best, which was exactly what was expected of us but neither Lauren nor I felt comfortable doing that.

Sometimes there seemed to be an adversarial relationship between the doctors and parents. I'm not sure if this is because of the litigious nature of our society, or if the doctors just need to stay detached from the frequently emotional, and sometimes irrational parents. Either one of these reasons would be understandable, but I don't think they are the cause.

Before all of this happened, I'd never given any thought to the term "Practicing Medicine." Now I realize that it's an evolving science. The deeper we got into Fletcher's situation, the more I saw that the doctors had no idea what to do for him. So, as I look back on everything, I've decided that they were probably not adversaries, but deeply concerned, and frustrated.

I hope that as you read about our experiences, it won't make you fearful of having a baby. Instead, it should serve to enlighten and prepare you for what probably won't, but could possibly, happen. If I had read something like this previously, I probably would've handled everything much better than I did.

To any men who may read this, if you and your wife are trying to have a baby, or are expecting, I'd like to share a few things with you:

As soon as we realized that things were going badly with her pregnancy, and Lauren had to check into the hospital, I should've let go of my fear within a few days. Fear and anger have no place in a situation like this. Even if your wife is not sick while she's pregnant, she'll need more emotional support than ever. I wish I had admitted that the situation was bigger than I was. Caring for my other children, doing well at work, and being a consistent, loving spouse were the most important jobs I had. I think I did well with two of the three things. Spiritually, I was a wreck and not in any shape to be her emotional rock. Several mornings, after dropping our three children off at day care I literally vomited in the parking lot. I was sick, sad, angry, and scared. The last place I wanted our beautiful babies to be was in daycare. Lauren and I had always agreed that she would stay home and care for the kids. We never wanted them to be cared for by strangers, but that's what happened.

I should've reminded myself that none of this was her fault. That would've been the right way to look at it. I wasn't able to do that. In fact, I never even realized that I was so angry with her until after it was all over. Now I understand just how critical my mental state was. At the time, I downplayed it. I told myself that if the kids were happy, and safe, and my boss was satisfied with my work, then nothing else mattered.

That was a mistake. Instead of really talking to Lauren, and seeking out the support and understanding I needed, I filled the void with alcohol. That served to further shut me down emotionally, which was exactly what I wanted. But it was the opposite of what I should've done.

Something I'm proud of is the amount of time I spent with her in the hospital. Even though we didn't really talk a lot, I spent many hours just being there with her. I would bring her milkshakes and veggie burgers from the cafeteria, and she would help me with spreadsheets for work. That was good for us both, I think.

Now, it's about three and a half years since Fletcher's death. As I sit here in my rented apartment with no furniture, I certainly have regrets. I regret not being more mature about her desire to get pregnant for a fifth time. We should've been able to discuss it and work it out, without all the yelling and accusations. I regret not being more supportive of her when other people questioned her judgment, or motives. I regret all the anger and sadness.

I've included this in the introduction because we both hope that her book will help others to avoid some of the things we went through. Or, if these things can't be avoided, maybe they can handle them better than we did.

Overall, this was the scariest thing either of us has ever gone through. I don't think we'll ever understand why any of it happened. I also don't think we would change her decision to try for another baby, even if we could. Some things are beyond human control, and this was certainly one of them.

I hope you'll enjoy, and learn from Lauren's book. She's a great person and a wonderful mother. I'm still amazed that Lauren had the strength, stamina and determination to write this book. As difficult as it is for me to read, I know it was even harder for her to write. This is about her struggles during the pregnancy, and Fletcher's struggles to survive.

We love you Fletcher, and we'll never forget you.

Love, Daddy

Introduction

Fletchie, Fletch, Wolfman, Wolfie, Sugar Bug – these were all names of endearment given to Fletcher by the people who took care of him. He was a very popular boy! At any given time of the day, people stopped by to talk to him, pat him on the butt, or give him back his beloved pacifier.

Although he had more than his share of uncomfortable times, Fletcher had good moments that will be treasured by his family and me. His eyes wide open, sucking on his pacifier so hard it left a mark on his cheeks; while he was vibrating in that bouncy seat, just kicking his legs as hard as he could to make the seat move even more. He loved when his grandparents held him. He loved sitting in his little bathtub in the warm water. Once he stole a sweet moment with his mom and breastfed, if only for a couple of minutes. He loved looking at his buddy, the lamb, in his bed. He was so cute when his brother came to see him. Every single time he would settle right down, be quiet and stiff and just look at his brother like he was the whole world. And of course, all the times I got to snuggle, sing and talk to him are so special to me. We had a lot of deep, meaningful conversations.

The day he died, Fletcher had a few precious moments with his whole family around him. He could feel the energy of his brothers and sister, and the sweet, deep love of his parents.

It's impossible to know why Fletcher had to have such a short, little life, but it's unbelievable how many people were affected by it.

By April F., Fletcher's primary nurse

PART I – Fletcher's in There

CHAPTER 1

I should've been more careful about what I wished for.

Friday, September 21, 2007 5:08 AM
3 Weeks 5 Days

I'm pregnant! Lee had to get up at 4:30 AM to go to work, so I decided to take an early home pregnancy test. I expected it to be negative since I am still nursing Cassie during the day and I'm not even officially late. There was an obvious second line! It was positive. I'm so happy! It's been a long few months with me wanting to start trying for another child and Lee telling me that he doesn't want any more children. We've been fighting about it for months and, at times, I accused him of sabotaging my efforts to get pregnant. Our children mean the world to him so I hope his lukewarm response this morning will eventually grow into excitement!

Friday, September 21, 2007 2:33 PM
3 Weeks 5 Days

I called my obstetrician's (OB) to let them know my early pregnancy test was positive and to let them know I am spotting and have some side pain. Given my medical history, having persistent, sometimes debilitating pain during pregnancy is one of the scariest things I've ever been through. I hope it's because of scar tissue from my three previous cesarean sections (C-sections) and not because I'm having an ectopic pregnancy. I had an ectopic pregnancy a few years ago and had emergency surgery to remove my right fallopian tube. This pain feels similar to that. One thing that is keeping me hopeful, though, is that I've had this spotting for the last four months when I wasn't pregnant. I'm trying to just stay calm because there's nothing I can do at this point. Early blood work with my ectopic pregnancy came back abnormal, so my OB told me to come in and have blood work done.

Monday, September 24, 2007 10:00 AM
4 Weeks 1 Day

My latest obsession is with the old wives' tale "needle and thread trick" that I've done during each of my pregnancies. This has become my new obsession. Supposedly, threading a needle, touching the needle to the inside of the wrist three times and then holding the tip of the needle over the wrist can predict the number of children and gender. The needle moves in a circle for a girl and side to side for a boy and stops moving once it has shown the number of children you will have. Mine keeps showing boy-boy-girl (Spencer, Wesley and Cassie) and then I *think* boy, but sometimes it stops after three. Since the needle trick supposedly only predicts live births, this has me worried.

Friday, September 28, 2007 7:21 AM
4 Weeks 5 Days

Last night I started having terrible cramps. Lee went to bed and I stayed on the couch in our living room watching TV and tried to ignore the pain. All of a sudden a wave of excruciating pain came over me and I ran in to the guest bathroom and sat on the toilet. Within a few seconds I passed a clot! I'd never had anything like that happen to me before. I sat there shaking but finally got enough nerve to fish it out of the toilet. The mass looked like a grape; it was about one inch and squishy. I quickly dropped it back in and flushed it.

I convinced myself that it was the baby so I ran into the master bedroom and woke Lee. I cried to him that I just lost the baby! He was scared and asked if I kept the clot. I can't believe I flushed it! It didn't even occur to me to keep it. Lee was able to calm me down and said to call my OB in the morning.

There's no way I could sleep; so I stayed in the living room and watched TV most of the night.

The cramps continued but the bleeding stopped by the time the sun came up. I'll call my OB as soon as their office opens.

Friday, September 28, 2007 9:05 AM
4 Weeks 5 Days

I'm on my way to my OB's office for more blood work. My first blood work results were good, but my progesterone levels were a little low so my OB put me on supplements. My OB will get the results of this latest draw this afternoon and compare them to the first draw and also figure out if I lost the baby last night. It's going to be a long day and rather than sit around waiting, I decided to meet up with my friend and let our kids all play together.

Friday, September 28, 2007 3:25 PM
4 Weeks 5 Days

My kids and I had a nice day out. Lee offered to take the day off and stay with the kids, but I thought it would be best for me to get out of the house. Lee hasn't exactly been supportive so I didn't want his help and I was glad that my friend called to get the kids together and I didn't need to take him up on his offer. I've been so preoccupied and the kids are starting to sense my anxiety that the four of us needed this fun day together. I've been fussing at them for things that normally don't bother me, such as them leaving dirty clothes around the house, or not putting away their shoes. I'm definitely not acting like my normal self and they can tell something is wrong.

My OB office called and said my blood work came back normal and that my pregnancy seems to be progressing perfectly. He isn't sure what came out last night but is certain it was not the baby. My spotting and continuous, painful cramping has my OB concerned, though, so he put me on pelvic rest (which means no sex) and exercise restriction. I hate not knowing what my body is doing, but I just have to wait and see if the ultrasound next week will give me answers. I want to try to take it easy this weekend and think about something else, but I know myself and I won't be able to just put it all aside and have a nice weekend. I'll probably do a lot of Internet searches and take the kids out somewhere.

It would be nice to have a family dinner out, but I think Lee will be working.

Sunday, September 30, 2007 2:15 PM
5 Weeks 0 Days

I have been spotting all weekend, even though I've been in bed most of the time. My room is small, but has all the essentials I need at the moment: a television, computer, bathroom, telephone and most of all, my queen bed. I have a newfound appreciation for the pale blue walls because it seems to have a calming effect. I keep my nail polish kit under the bed and I've been taking it out and doing the needle trick all weekend but it's still not conclusive. I failed at not obsessing about the pregnancy this weekend. I called a few friends I knew that had miscarriages and asked them to explain everything they went through, in detail. I want to know exactly what to expect, just in case.

Monday, October 1, 2007 6:30 PM
5 Weeks 1 Day

I ended up going in for blood work again and although I'm still spotting, the baby is growing. I have no idea how this pregnancy is progressing normally! Usually an ultrasound can't show much until about six weeks but my OB knew I didn't want to wait until next week so he set up an ultrasound for this Friday. I know it's going to be a long week. I haven't really been discussing any of this with Lee because he still hasn't embraced having a fourth child. He's completely closed-off, but I don't have the patience to deal with him and this pregnancy right now.

Friday, October 5, 2007 2:05 PM
5 Weeks 5 Days

I had the ultrasound this morning and it didn't go well. Before the ultrasound technician even started, I began to cry. She tried her best to calm me down and once I stopped shaking and crying, she started the ultrasound. Even knowing how on edge I was, she didn't sugarcoat anything.

Even though all my blood tests came back normal, the ultrasound showed an abnormally shaped sac. She pointed it out to me and I saw exactly what she was talking about. She explained that most of the time, when the shape of the sac is irregular, it could be the start of a miscarriage. The technician also said the baby implanted very low. Here I was thinking the only thing I had to worry about was that the pregnancy wasn't ectopic. I had no idea that the shape of the sac and the place where the baby implanted was so crucial. I can't believe how naïve I am. She told me to meet my OB in his office and that he would explain everything in more detail.

My OB's first words were, "Aren't you excited?!" I asked him what he meant by that since the ultrasound was not good! He said that I should be happy to have gotten pregnant so fast while breast feeding and being 36 years old. He added that if this pregnancy isn't viable, I should be able to get pregnant again easily. I didn't want to hear what he was saying so I interrupted him and asked him to explain the ultrasound to me.

My OB said with the irregular shaped sac he would give this pregnancy about a 10% chance of viability. Usually a sac that is abnormally shaped ends up folding over or collapsing onto itself, causing a miscarriage. The only reason he gave me a 10% chance was because my blood work had been perfect and also because the ultrasound showed a yolk and fetal pole. He wasn't able to give me an estimated due date (EDD) because the ultrasound technician couldn't get a good measurement. Although I know my EDD since I know the exact date I ovulated, it would have been nice have the ultrasound confirm it.

My OB theorized that the spotting was because of low progesterone levels but couldn't explain why I am having so much pain. He tested me for urinary tract and bacterial infections but both tests were negative. The baby is implanted really low so maybe that's the reason for all the pain.

My OB is on call this weekend and said I could call him if there was any change in my condition. He told me to come back next Wednesday for another ultrasound and we'll go from there. He's going out of town next Thursday and didn't want me to have to wait another week if there's something wrong. If the ultrasound shows the baby hasn't grown or that the pregnancy is non-viable, he'll do a dilation and curettage (D&C) that day. I don't know how I am going to get through another week of not knowing. I'm so upset and wish I had answers one way or the other.

Lee has been extremely worried about me and wants me to talk to a mental health professional. I think I just need time. It's so hard to explain how I feel about my wanting this baby so badly, getting pregnant and then having this happen. He doesn't like how upset I've been for the last two weeks. I said that if anything happens to this baby I would want to try again right away. He asked, "Why would I put you through all this again?" He doesn't want me to get me pregnant again if this is the way I'm going to act! I know he's trying to be nice and said that I am his main priority, but all he did was make me even more anxious. All I heard him tell me was that if I lose the baby he doesn't want to try for another. I just need to calm myself down and not speculate about the future, which is extremely hard for a control-freak like me!

Sunday, October 7, 2007 10:22 PM
6 Weeks 0 Days

After the ultrasound Lee called his parents to see if they would come down and watch the kids so we could get away for a few days. He thought I needed a break and he definitely needed one. We ended up driving to a little beach town a few hours away. It was a beautiful place and we had fun discovering the local area. We sat on the beach, walked around town, met some locals, and ate at great restaurants. Although my heart was not completely in it, I tried to fake it and realized that being away did me a lot of good.

CHAPTER 2

I've learned more about pregnancy and possible complications than I ever wanted to know. Most of what I learned came from women I've never met, not from medical doctors.

Wednesday, October 10, 2007 12:25 PM
6 Weeks 3 Days

I had another ultrasound this morning. What a difference these last few days made! The sac is no longer irregular! I'm also measuring exactly on schedule with an EDD of June 1, 2008, which is the date that I had calculated based on when I ovulated. Most importantly, there was a heartbeat. The pregnancy is still high-risk because of the low implantation. My OB said the chances for a viable pregnancy are now about 50-50, rather than 10-90.

The ultrasound confirmed that the baby implanted very low, perhaps in my C-section scar. This can cause placental complications during pregnancy. I could have placenta previa, which is when the placenta is near or covers the cervix. Placenta previa might cause pregnancy complications and always results in a caesarian delivery (C-section). I'm not concerned about the C-section though, since I have already had three of them and would have another C-section regardless. The technician and my OB were much more concerned about the possibility that the baby implanted in my C-section scar. If that's the case, there is a high probability that I will have placenta accreta, which is when the placenta attaches too deep into the wall of the uterus. The most significant risk to the baby is prematurity. For me, it can cause bleeding during pregnancy and according to my OB, "It makes for a very messy delivery." There is a high likelihood of hemorrhaging during the C-section, which means I will most likely need blood transfusions during the surgery. Depending on how much of the placenta is attached, I might also need a hysterectomy. I'm hearing all this, but not comprehending all the dangers my OB is pointing out to me. I figure that there must be a lot of women who have placenta accreta and everything turns out fine for them. Also, since my OB is aware of these potential complications, he will be prepared and know what to do when the time comes. Time will tell. I'm very lucky to have three precious distractions; my two sons, Spencer, who is four and a half years old and Wesley, who will be three years old next month, and my daughter, Cassandra, who is 14 months old.

I'm still spotting and cramping which means I'm still on pelvic rest and not allowed to exercise.

Thursday, October 11, 2007 6:19AM
6 Weeks 4 Days

The Internet is amazing! I've been researching placental issues in pregnancy and the problem I'm having is being able to filter out the bad or irrelevant information in an effort to understand what is going on with my baby and me. I'm self-educating myself about things my doctors should be explaining to me. One commonality I've found is that in most cases the doctors were unaware of the condition beforehand. I believe that knowledge is power and since my OB and I know about the condition we can make modifications and adjustments during the pregnancy, and at the time of delivery. I've started a list of questions to go over with my OB as the pregnancy progresses.

Tuesday, October 16, 2007 2:26 PM
7 Weeks 2 Days

I was starting to feel more hopeful about this pregnancy and then I started bleeding over the weekend. It was mostly brown but there was some red and pink spotting, too. I'm still in pain but thankfully I'm not having cramps. I really think the pain is because of scar tissue, especially from adhesions.

During my last C-section, my OB said that my bladder was stuck to my uterus by scar tissue from previous C-sections. If this were any other pregnancy, I would be a complete disaster and think the worst but already this pregnancy is far from typical and my OB warned me that I should expect spotting and even some bleeding. I'm trying to accept the fact that these are normal symptoms for this pregnancy.

Friday, October 26, 2007 3:23 PM
8 Weeks 5 Days

Today is my birthday. I know I should be happy and thankful to be surrounded by my husband and children, but I had an awful ultrasound and OB appointment this morning and do not feel like celebrating.

Although the baby is continuing to grow, and is even measuring ahead of my EDD, there is a new, serious complication. I have a subchorionic hematoma (SCH) in the sac, which is basically a blood clot between the uterine wall and amniotic sac. In early pregnancy, the bleeding caused by the SCH can actually wash the baby away, causing a miscarriage. My SCH is considered large, but luckily it's located on the opposite side of the baby and far away from my placenta. My OB said this is less concerning than if it was on top of the fetus or near the developing placenta. My OB explained that the SCH is the cause of my bleeding. He also said that SCH's can be common in very early pregnancy and there's a chance it can dissolve after the first trimester.

The ultrasound technician was able to see my placenta and confirmed that it's low and covering my cervix. I officially have placenta previa. My OB thinks the baby implanted so low, perhaps in my C-section scar, that it caused a blood vessel to pop, causing the SCH. I'm thinking the clot I passed a few weeks ago was part of the blood vessel that ruptured. Even though the SCH is an added complication, I feel much better knowing exactly what is going on and why I am having these symptoms.

My OB didn't want to do the standard prenatal paperwork or blood work yet. He said he didn't want to waste my time at this point, which I took to mean that he didn't think this pregnancy would go on much longer. He also gave me the Rh immune globulin shot because I'm Rh negative but Lee is Rh positive, so the baby could be Rh positive. There's a chance fetal blood has mixed with my blood, and could endanger the baby and me so my OB gave me the shot. I usually don't get this shot until I'm about 28 weeks pregnant, but I also never bled during pregnancy. The antibodies in the shot last for three months, so I shouldn't need it again for a while.

Lee and I called our family members to update them on the latest developments. Rather than thanking us for keeping them updated, they berated and scolded us. After hearing about my appointment a few asked, "why can't your OB just do a D&C and you can start over?" I'm someone who struggles not to be a pessimist or see things in only black and white, so these comments were very hard to hear. My mom and my father-in-law both told us how irresponsible it was for me to get pregnant. My mom knew I wanted another child but asked Lee why he allowed this to happen. I guess she meant why did he go along with having another child. Lee told me he agreed with my mother and that he should've insisted we were done having children. Wow. There's no way to describe how alone I feel. I have my own husband going against me. Now I feel like this is my own personal battle to fight and I resent all of them for playing the blame-game and not giving me the love and support I desperately need. I guess our families' opinions wouldn't hurt me as much if I felt that Lee was here for, and with, me.

Friday, October 26, 2007, 8:00 PM
8 Weeks 5 Days

Lee and the kids surprised me tonight with a huge chocolate chip cookie cake for my birthday. I think the kids were more excited than I was! We sat at the kitchen table and they sang to me, helped me make a wish and blew out the candles. I love it. I know I should be grateful and happy for what I have. They reminded me of that. Even so, I'm sure it's no surprise what I wished for.

Sunday, October 28, 2007, 7:43 AM
9 Weeks 0 Days

I couldn't sleep for most of the night because I'm in so much pain. I'm also having brown, sludge-like discharge. It's a weird consistency and is simply gross. I've never seen or heard of anyone having this happen to them during pregnancy. I know from my past pregnancies that weird things happen to your body during pregnancy and that each pregnancy is very different, so I'm thinking this just might be a new symptom.

I took the laptop from the desk in our room and typed in "SCH" in the Internet search engine and found an active online community of women who had SCHs in pregnancy. I read through all the archives and heard happy stories and a lot of very sad ones. Reading through hundreds of posts, I was able to see which women were sincere and supportive, and which were only on the board to start irrelevant debates. I started a spreadsheet of the women who I found to be genuine and took notes on their pregnancies, symptoms, how far along they were when they got diagnosed with their SCH, if they miscarried or had their baby, and if so, how far along they were. I also noted if they were taking special medicines or were on any type of bed rest. I learned a lot; probably too much. I cried for most of the weekend.

This afternoon Lee sat down on the bed with me, gave me a hug and told me to stop crying unless I actually had something to cry about, and right now, he didn't think I had a reason to be so upset. He reminded me that right now the baby is growing and doing fine so I need focus on that.

Sunday, October 28, 2007 4:25 PM
9 Weeks 0 Days

I've been thinking about everything from the last OB appointment. The four positive things I am trying to focus on are:

1) The baby's heartbeat was well over 150 and measured perfect for my EDD.
2) The location of the hematoma is closer to the cervix, which is a little better than if it was closer to the fundus.
3) I read online that SCHs occur very often when the baby implants low. I wonder why the doctor didn't mention that correlation to me.
4) The brown sludgy discharge started up again, probably because of the vaginal ultrasound. I keep reading that this type of discharge is a good thing because it's most likely old blood and could possibly mean the SCH is dissolving.

I need to keep this list with me at all times, especially in those moments when I find myself focusing on the negative.

After studying my spreadsheet, I felt confident enough to start posting on the SCH board. I immediately got responses from a lot of the women, each with different stories to tell. I asked straightforward questions and they were brutally honest. There were a few women who ended up emailing me privately to give me personal support. One woman had the exact same pregnancy as I have right now and although she had her daughter two months early, she is a healthy and happy two year old. I know that medical doctors do amazing things, but there is something to be said about talking directly to other women who have been through exactly the same thing that you're going through.

Tuesday, October 30, 2007 8:54 PM
9 Weeks 2 Days

Most of the women on the SCH board were put on bed rest early in their pregnancies. I don't know how I would be able to do that with the three kids and Lee working two jobs. We have no family around. Spencer is in school for three hours a day but that's it. I chose to be a stay-at-home to be able to take care of my kids myself. I'm terrified that my OB will put me on bed rest.

I'm so overwhelmed with the what-ifs and the not knowing. I could be pregnant for one more week, or day, or hour, or minute, or I could be pregnant for about seven more months. I want answers now even though I know, rationally, that the only way to get answers is to just keep living through it.

This situation is especially difficult because my OB told me I'm not allowed to carry anything over 20 pounds. My daughter is used to me carrying her everywhere and she still sleeps in a crib. I hate having to tell her that I can't pick her up all the time. I still lift her to put her in the car seat and into her high chair. Lee has been getting her out of the crib for me, but at night I've been using a kitchen chair to help her into it. I'm trying to really take it easy but it's so hard because Cassie doesn't understand why I won't hold her anymore. This is all new for me too, because I am the main caregiver to the kids and I not only cherish it, but I take that role very seriously.

Monday, November 5, 2007 1:23 PM
10 Weeks 1 Day

I went in for my ultrasound today and the technician told me that the SCH has nearly halved in size, but it's still considered a large size. In spite of the SCH, the baby is growing and the heartbeat is a strong 155 beats per minute.

Usually in the first few months of pregnancy, most women are excited and trying to either hide her pregnancy or want people to know she's pregnant. She'll start shopping for cute in-between clothes; ones that aren't quite maternity size, but are made for growing waists. In my other pregnancies, other people could tell that I was pregnant from my facial glow, twinkling eyes, and never-ending smile. With this pregnancy, I'm just the opposite.

I'm in so much pain and feel as if someone took scissors, got inside me and started cutting through the inside of my pelvis and stomach. My teeth are constantly clenched as a way to tolerate the pain and my skin is ashen.

The ultrasound didn't show anything unusual so my OB still assumes that the pain is caused by the adhesions and scar tissue from previous C-sections being stretched by my growing uterus and stomach. My OB is very concerned about the very real possibility of me having placenta accreta or worse, placenta increta, where the placenta attaches even deeper in the uterus. He thinks either way, I will definitely have a hysterectomy because there will be no other way for him to remove the placenta after delivery. I don't think that has truly sunk in for me yet.

I have the nuchal translucency test (NTT) on the 21st, which is a special ultrasound that can detect any genetic abnormalities. I'm still taking it one day at a time, and so is my OB. At least at this appointment my OB did the prenatal blood tests and had me fill out prenatal paperwork.

Monday, November 5, 2007 11:07 PM
10 Weeks 1 Day

I've been posting on the online SCH group and told them about my latest ultrasound. I was asked if my OB suggested I go on bed rest, which he didn't. Everyone suggested I should put myself on strict bed rest or to stay in bed as much as possible. Almost all the women said their doctors didn't think bed rest was necessary and did not order it. There's conflicting data about the merits of bed with regard to SCH in pregnancy, yet most of these women ended up putting themselves on bed rest and said it definitely did help them. I feel like it's worth a shot.

I ended up calling my mother-in-law myself and asked if she could come down for the week. My mother works full-time and lives farther away than my mother-in-law, who doesn't work and could drive down if necessary. Amazingly, my mother-in-law said she would book an early flight and get here in the morning and stay through the weekend. My father-in-law will drive down on Friday and they'll leave together on Sunday. I'm excited for her to come. She always takes great care of the children when she's in charge and I know that, at the same time, she will take as great care of her son. She's a wonderful cook and cleaner so a lot will get done with her here.

I've also been thinking of putting Wesley in school two days a week. I think Cassie is fine hanging out at home all day since she's so young, but I feel so guilty about not doing much with Wesley. I know he misses Spencer and also misses socializing. I'm usually out all day with the kids, having play dates, going to the mall, museums, to lunch, or just exploring our neighborhood and parks. It was hard enough putting Spencer in school in the mornings but he's in pre-Kindergarten and it was time for him to go. I was looking forward to having Wesley and Cassie at home for a few more years and being able to do more fun things during the day before they have to be in school but it's not good for Wesley to be stuck at home all day while I'm on the couch or in bed. Lee and I need to talk about it some more, but as much as I don't want Wesley to go, I think it's for the best to have him go a few days a week.

Saturday, November 10, 2007 5:55 PM
10 Weeks 6 Days

Although my OB hasn't said anything to me about going on bed rest, I decided to stay in bed most of the time while my in-laws were here. Of course the kids wanted me to do certain things for them like tuck them in at night and singing to them, which I did. I'm curious to see if this is helping my SCH shrink and/or giving this pregnancy a greater chance of viability.

Saturday, November 17, 2007 7:49 PM
11 Weeks 6 Days

I took it easy all last week while my in-laws were in town but with no one here this week helping me, any type of bed rest is impossible. Even when I am trying to do as little as possible, I still do a lot! I drive 20 minutes to and from Spencer's pre-kindergarten every day. Even getting Cassie in and out of her car seat and the car is stressful. We no longer go out, have play dates, or socialize. Lee has taken over grocery shopping, laundry and household cleaning, but with him working two jobs and not getting home until after the kids' bed times, it's impossible to stay in bed for more than a few minutes at a time.

I'm feeling so torn! On one hand I feel so guilty that my body is not able to give this baby a better environment in which to grow and that I'm unable to stay on strict bed rest to make up for the bad conditions. On the other hand, I feel so badly that I am short-changing my kids by not being able to give them all my time, attention, or even providing basic care for them. I'm short-changing everyone and am starting to feel completely worthless and useless.

I keep telling myself this is not forever and that hopefully Lee and the kids understand. I know the kids are confused by my lack of 'mothering' them the way they are accustomed to, but hopefully one day they will understand. If I can find anything positive, it's that they are very young and won't remember most of this in the long run.

CHAPTER 3

I can't believe how calm I was while gushing blood during my pregnancy.

Wednesday, November 21, 2007 2:27 PM
12 Weeks 3 Days

This morning I had an appointment with my high risk OB (perinatologist). He performed genetic tests on me when I was pregnant with Cassie because I was 35 years old when pregnant with her. Doctors consider that advanced maternal age (AMA) and want to do more genetic testing because of the increased risk of birth defects in babies born to older mothers. Perinatologists usually perform these tests.

I had the NTT and accompanying blood test. Because of my SCH and bleeding, the blood test might not be conclusive but he still wanted me to have the test. The NTT measurement should be less than three millimeters and mine was well below that at 1.34 millimeters! With this low measurement, my odds of having a child with genetic abnormalities went way down from the average for a 35 year old. The blood test results will be back next week and my odds will be changed accordingly.

I got to see Fletcher and he was moving all around. He looked perfect! It's amazing to be able to see so much detail at only 12 weeks. I could see his fingers, toes, nose, face and ears. He even waved!

The ultrasound technician said she saw a small bleed in the sac near the baby's face and a large bleed by my cervix. She also said there might be more clots around the placenta but said that at this point in the pregnancy, there's no way to differentiate between the actual placenta and clots. She didn't take any measurements on the bleeds but said they were medium-sized. The low-lying placenta was also confirmed, but the technician said there's a small chance of it moving higher over the next few weeks.

The perinatologist told me that my pregnancy is extremely high risk. At this point, there's still no way to know what the outcome will be. He kept saying that it's wait and see. Usually at twelve weeks the risk for miscarriage greatly decreases, but not in my case. It's not fair. I should be breathing a sigh of relief, but instead I'm being told that this pregnancy is just as precarious as it was a few months ago.

After my perinatologist appointment, I went to my OB appointment. My OB said the same thing as the perinatologist; that we have to watch and wait to see how the pregnancy progresses. He said he'd schedule ultrasounds every four weeks in order to watch the placenta and monitor the SCH.

Wednesday, November 21, 2007 5:39 PM
12 Weeks 3 Days

I'm grateful to have access to great doctors and have health insurance, but I just spent three hours dealing with the insurance company. Before my perinatologist appointment this morning I checked my insurance website to make sure he was in my health plan network. When I got to the appointment they said they haven't taken my insurance in over five years! The perinatologist office asked me if I still wanted to have the appointment and if so, I would have to pay them cash. I had no choice because the NTT has to be done within a strict time frame in pregnancy and there's also no other perinatologist in the area.

As soon as I got home I grabbed the phone, went into bed and called the health insurance company. I was so upset with them and tried to calm myself down because I didn't need this added stress. I told the benefits coordinator that I checked the website and she also saw that my perinatologist was listed as in-network, even though she knew they weren't part of my plan. Since he was on their website, she told me it was their mistake and she would bill the visit, as well as any future visits as in-network and would immediately refund me the difference. What a relief! I guess the lesson learned could carry over to my pregnancy, too – not to freak out about something before I know how it's going to turn out.

Thursday, November 22, 2007 8:23 AM
12 Weeks 4 Days

Lee took the kids out for dinner last night and explained what was going on with the baby and me. He asked the boys if they had any questions and Wesley brought up all the blood he's been seeing. I've tried keeping things private, but it's hard with the kids coming in while I'm using the bathroom or changing. I had no idea he ever saw anything and his comment really upset us. Lee told him that I would be fine and the baby is fine, but that I need to take it easy so the baby can come in a few months.

Wesley said to Lee that he knows we're waiting for the baby to grow and come live with us, but he's not supposed to come yet! I can't imagine what a hard conversation that was for Lee. He must have handled it perfectly because all three kids came home and gave me a huge hug. I could see that they were much less concerned and stressed about the baby and me.

Knowing that the kids were relieved didn't make it easier for me to forgive myself. I mean, it's just not right for these three young kids to know half the things that they know. I want them to remain innocent and also oblivious. It's hard to know how much to tell them, especially when they ask so many specific questions. I just hope Lee and I are handling this right. Deep in my heart, I know that we are because kids are highly sensitive and feed off of their parent's emotions. Even when I try to fake being happy, the kids know that I'm acting. If I don't acknowledge what's going on, the kids end up acting out, fighting with each other and throwing tantrums. We've already seen a positive change in their behavior and more compassion towards each other.

I'm so proud of Lee. He's never been in this situation before, but he's handling everything like a natural. Our home has become beyond stressful, but he's staying positive and bringing that energy to the kids. I'm the one who needs to work on my outlook and attitude. I've been getting short-tempered and snapping at the kids, which gets them even more upset. Wesley keeps asking me why I'm mad at him. I'll try harder not to be so depressed and upset all the time even though it's hard not to be. I wonder how Lee makes it look so easy. He's leading by example, so I need to do the same. We also need to try to be a united front, rather than the kids seeing Lee as the rational and calm parent and me as the basket case. I need to try to come across as Lee's wife to him, rather than a helpless patient and then maybe we can start working through this together.

Friday, November 23, 2007 6:15 AM
12 Weeks 5 Days

I'm trying not to get too attached to this baby, which is impossible. I wish I could fast forward to 38 weeks pregnant! In the meantime, I rented an at-home fetal heartbeat monitor so I can hear the heartbeat every day. My stomach is growing and I need to get past my superstitions and get out my maternity clothes. I know that taking out the clothes won't make something bad happen, but I am not entirely convinced, either. In all my pregnancies, I waited until the last moment to take out and wear maternity clothes until I felt more confident about the pregnancy. I never started wearing maternity clothes early on because, irrationally, I felt that I could jinx the pregnancy. I have to admit that in this pregnancy, I am very thankful for my ultra-stretchy stretch pants.

Thursday, November 29, 2007 3:30 AM
13 Weeks 4 Days

All week long I've been having strong, painful cramps. Lee's been taking Spencer to school every morning this week so I could stay in bed and not rush out with all the kids. Even while trying to take it easy, however, my cramps have been steadily getting worse.

Last night at 8:30 PM, my cramps escaladed and suddenly I felt a huge gush. I knew it had to be blood. I was surprisingly calm, though, because the women on the SCH board warned me this might happen. I called my OB's office and they told me to head straight for the Emergency Room. Lee wasn't going to be home for another hour, so I had to wait for him to get home. I was torn between wanting Lee to come with me and having him stay home. We both decided it wouldn't be fair to wake up the kids, so I ended up driving myself to the hospital. The bottom line is that even if Lee went with me this is something going on within me, so no matter what happens, I'm the one who has to go through it. I know this is Lee's child too, but it's my body and regardless, I'm the one who's going to be poked, prodded and whatever else.

After two hours of waiting, the nurse finally called me back and asked me what was going on. I told her and she immediately paged the on-call emergency doctor. I warned him about the amount of bleeding, but it wasn't until he did an internal exam that he realized I wasn't exaggerating. I officially freaked out the ER doctor!

The doctor asked me to pee in a cup to see if I had a urinary tract infection. I asked him if my bleeding would skew the test results. He said it wouldn't, but then the results showed blood in my urine. He wrote me a prescription for antibiotics anyway and I told him I wanted to wait until I talked with my OB before I started taking any medicine.

The doctor sent me to get an ultrasound. The ultrasound technician said she hadn't done a prenatal ultrasound in over three years, which didn't fill me with confidence. When she started the exam, she told me she couldn't tell me anything and I would have to wait for a doctor to read the results. However, the picture was hard to interpret and because I told her I had had so many ultrasounds and knew what was going on, she turned the screen towards me and we studied it together. The SCH was no longer only pooled over my cervix. My entire uterus was now engulfed. I actually had to explain the image to her. The technician said she could get better images if I had a full bladder so she connected me to a catheter and filled my bladder. While we were waiting, blood was pouring out of me and I soaked through three pads. By the end of the scan, there was only a little blood left in my uterus and it was, once again, pooled on top of my cervix. It was fascinating to see exactly what was going on inside my uterus during an active bleeding episode. The technician checked on the baby and said he looked very healthy, in spite of everything. She shut the machine off and while I was being wheeled out of the ultrasound room, she told me "You just bought yourself a few weeks of strict bed rest." I understand the severity of the situation, but all I could think about was how glad I was that the SCH was clearly visible on the ultrasound. In that moment I was truly able to separate the baby from the pregnancy condition.

The ER doctor met me back in the exam room and said he couldn't tell where the bleed was coming from. He tested my hemoglobin levels and it was still a healthy 12 grams per deciliter (g/dl)! Normal levels are between 12 g/dl and 16 g/dl. The doctor said he had never seen anything like this before and that I should be prepared for a miscarriage. He said to make an appointment with my OB as soon as possible and added, "Don't go on any roller coasters or ride on any ATVs." I guess he thought he was being funny. He wasn't. It was an insensitive statement, but I think the ER doctor didn't know what else to say to me.

I had been in the ER for six hours. During that time I bled through 12 maxi-pads, had blood tests, urine tests and an ultrasound. I had all those tests and spent so much time in the hospital and there are still no answers for why this was happening. It's confusing enough for me, but when medical doctors tell me they don't know what's going on, that just makes things worse. I don't know what to think. If I'm going to lose this baby, I just want to lose him now. I can't handle this.

Thursday, November 29, 2007 8:45 AM
13 Weeks 4 Days

I called my OB's office this morning and explained what happened last night. My OB was very matter-of-fact and said that as far as he's concerned there's been no change in my condition. He said I should expect to have these bleeding episodes throughout the pregnancy but for now, he put me on strict bed rest for five days.

I'm very stressed out about having to be on strict bed rest. When I put myself on bed rest I felt like any time I spent lying down was good enough, but now that my OB has prescribed it, I feel like any time I'm not in bed, I'm harming my baby. Lee told me we would figure it out together but then told me I had to bring Spencer to school because he had an early appointment for work, so I am already not following my OB's orders.

Today is Wesley's 3rd birthday and I promised to make him a cake for his birthday and another one when his grandparents come this weekend to celebrate. I am trying to figure out how to get all the ingredients together and not have to stand up for very long. I'm wondering if this is even worth it. I was on modified bed rest and still ended up in the ER. I don't want to neglect my other kids and still end up losing this baby. I'm completely conflicted.

Friday, November 30, 2007 10:22 AM
13 Weeks 5 Days

The perinatologist office finally called with the blood work results from my NTT. My risks for Down Syndrome and other chromosomal abnormalities should be about one in 166 for my age. After adjusting the results from my blood work, my risk went down to one in 3,301. I'm so glad and very relieved. I hope this puts an end to my OB wanting to do an amniocentesis (amnio). An amnio under normal circumstances has risks, but with this pregnancy, I feel like the dangers would be compounded. My next appointment with the perinatologist is December 16th for a Level II ultrasound, which is similar to a regular ultrasound only more in-depth. Hopefully everything will look great and prevent me from needing prenatal genetic tests.

Friday, November 30, 2007 3:04 PM
13 Weeks 5 Days

Family is in town for the weekend to celebrate Wesley's birthday. I might ask my mom if she can take off work and stay through next Sunday. My mom works full-time and would have to take vacation days and pay to have her flight changed, but I'm still going to ask. She always says she doesn't get enough time alone with her grandchildren, so I can present it that way to her. It would be a lot easier to have my mother-in-law come down, but last time she was here she got bronchitis and said she wouldn't be able to help out for awhile.

Saturday, December 1, 2007 9:10 PM
13 Weeks 6 Days

I'm almost 14 weeks pregnant, but I barely look it, even though this is my fifth pregnancy, including the ectopic. Before my bleed last week I finally had a pregnancy bump. Now I don't think anyone could tell because my pooch is gone. I would be worried about this if I hadn't had confirmation from my ultrasounds that the baby is measuring on target.

CHAPTER 4

No one can say that I'm not committed to this pregnancy, but even the right choices aren't made easily.

Sunday, December 2, 2007 8:55 PM
14 Weeks 0 Days

While our families were here this weekend, we all sat down at the kitchen table and set up a plan for the next few months. With my increased pregnancy and health complications, the kids' routines have been dramatically changed. I've been trying to stay in bed as much as possible, and the kids have been stuck at home, bored and worried about me. Lee and his parents decided it would be best to put all three kids in full time school/daycare. Apparently, they had talked about this a few weeks ago, hoping not to have to do this until early January. My latest ER episode has everyone more concerned. They're worried about me being able to take proper care of Spencer, Wesley and Cassie. Even though I know it's the right thing to do, I'm devastated! I feel like a complete failure not being able to take care of my own children. I have to be honest though, and admit that a part of me is very relieved because it was making me nervous being alone with the kids until late at night. I'm thankful that my in-laws have offered to pay for the kids' school too, because without them, this would not even be an option. It really is all about what's best for the children and even though I don't think this is best for them, my in-laws and Lee do. They obviously had already made the decision and told me that they'll full-time school/daycare tomorrow. I need to remind myself that this won't be forever, even if it feels like it will.

Monday, December 3, 2007 2:43 PM
14 Weeks 1 Day

Lee dropped off all three kids at school this morning for their first full-day. My stomach is in knots and I feel like driving to the school and grabbing them and taking them back home. They shouldn't be there. They're too young. They have a stay-at-home-mom who doesn't work outside the home in order to keep them at home. But, I guess at this point, they really don't have a capable parent at home to watch them.

I hope Cassie and Wesley will make the transition well, but I'm so worried about Spencer, who's used to being picked up by 11:30 AM every day. I keep picturing his face when parent pick-up time came and went and his mommy didn't show up. The school assured me that he would be outside playing with the other kids and wouldn't even notice. When they called earlier they said that Cassie had only cried at drop-off, but then quickly found toys to play with. Cassie has mandatory naptime, which will be great for her. They tried to make Wesley go down for his nap, but he refused. He hasn't napped in a few months so I thought it would be a problem. The school was great and rather than force Wesley, and chance him disturbing the other kids, they decided to put him in Spencer's class during nap time in the afternoon and the boys were happily playing together.

I'm very fortunate to have found such an accommodating school, but even with them making such concessions, it doesn't change the fact that I'm an emotional wreck over them having to go away every day. I hope the kids can get through it and they don't hate me for this. I also hope that Lee can forgive me, and I can forgive myself.

Tuesday, December 4, 2007 9:24 PM
14 Weeks 2 Days

The kids and I survived the second day of school. I'm so proud of the kids for doing so well and adapting. Spencer told me it's a long day for him, but he has a lot of friends that stay too, and he loves that Wesley comes to his room in the afternoon. Cassie is sad and Wesley is not too sure about it yet. I know that I need to be more positive about the situation because they're definitely feeding off of my negative energy.

Even though I don't have to pick them up until 6:00 PM, I decided to pick them up by 4:00 PM every day. I have so much guilt and there's not much that can be done to ease it right now. I suppose getting them two hours early is the only thing I feel I can do right now.

Aside from dropping off and picking up the kids, and getting up for food and drinks, I've been very strict with my bed rest. As soon as I get home I grab my laptop and crawl into bed. I've been doing a lot of on-line holiday shopping since we're going to my in-laws for Christmas. They've been so generous with coming down to help and paying for the kids' school, so I want to make sure we bring amazing presents for them. I've been so surprised by how many stores give free shipping and have discount codes! A lot of items were less expensive than if I had physically gone to the store. I suppose it's nice to have this as a diversion and a way to feel a little bit useful right now.

Thursday, December 6, 2007 10:03 AM
14 Weeks 4 Days

I swear I'm having a nervous breakdown! I can't handle the stress that I'm putting on my family and I'm tired having to go through this alone. My heart breaks every morning when I drop the kids off at school. I hate having to admit that I'm incapable of taking care of my own children right now. Cassie and Wesley have been crying every morning and Spencer has been internalizing his feelings and anxieties.

I can't talk to Lee about how I feel because he's even more upset than I am about putting the kids in school full-time and I can tell he blames me for it. His response every time I try to talk to him is, "It is what it is! You're the one who wanted to have a fourth, so we have to deal with this," and then he leaves the room. I understand that he's angry and upset but I don't deserve all the blame. I'm a victim in all this just the same as him. I wish someone would tell me that they feel for me and are so sorry for everything I'm going through. I wish someone would tell me that it will all be okay; that the kids will adjust; that what I'm doing is the right thing, or at least not the worst possible thing and that I need love and support and taking care of the same as, if not more, than the kids. I'm driving myself crazy and there isn't anyone around me that can, or is willing to, calm me down.

I'm trying to be the calm and rational voice for myself. I've been repeating over and over that in the grand scheme of things, it really is a short time for the kids to have to be in daycare, that they're being socialized and are having fun being with tons of kids their own age. The kids are fine and I know that I need to give this baby a fighting chance. But, while I try to be positive, I'm still so torn and feel completely helpless and worthless, unable to take care of any of my children. It didn't help me to hear Lee tell me he's gotten physically sick this week after dropping the kids off every morning. I'm not sure why Lee decided to tell me that, unless he thought that would make me suddenly become well enough to take care of them. If that were possible, I would be doing it. The only thing that did was make me more resentful because he's letting me know how much he blames me for putting him through this. Hearing him say this only made me feel, once again, that I'm completely alone. I don't even have my husband on my side for support.

Adding to our stress is the fact that Lee's parents are generously paying for the kids' schooling since we can't afford it. This amazing gesture is making Lee even more upset. It's so tense at home. I know he's just worried about me, scared for the baby, and sad for the kids. I know that this new way of life is just temporary, but even so, it's still something we all have to get used to right now. I wish Lee would open up to me and talk rather than either avoid me or cut the conversation short with one-liners. I don't have the strength to fight with him, so I decide to let him be and rely on my close friends and my own inner-strength, which is slowly being chipped away. The best thing for me to do is focus on the baby growing inside of me. I believe it will give me all the strength I need.

Friday, December 7, 2007 10:17 PM
14 Weeks 5 Days

I had another big bleed a few hours ago. It was exactly like the one last week when I ended up going to the ER and wasting six hours on different tests and getting no answers or game-plans, only to have my OB tell me this was to be expected. So this time I decided to stay in bed and call my OB's office just to let them know what was going on. The nurse suggested I go to the ER if I need more than one maxi pad an hour. I explained that I've been going through that many off and on for days and don't want to waste another long night in the ER. The nurse obviously hadn't heard about my condition and was extremely upset that I wouldn't follow her medical advice. I told her if the bleeding became worse and I felt something change, I would go in. When I hung up the phone I couldn't believe that I was arguing with a nurse about not seeking help while gushing blood during pregnancy! That's so surreal to me, especially because when I was in my early pregnancy with Cassie, I had light spotting and drove straight to the ER within ten minutes!

I'm not sure if it's just me being callous or I'm feeling more relaxed with this pregnancy, because patterns are starting to emerge and it's comforting to know when to expect a bleed. My atypical pregnancy has become very normal for me.

Tuesday, December 11, 2007 9:45 PM
15 Weeks 2 Days

I had another night of gushing blood and it was still going strong this morning. This was the most blood I've lost so far during this pregnancy. I called my OB and he said to just expect this for the rest of the pregnancy. He was able to calm me down with his usual matter-of-fact demeanor. I spent all afternoon in bed, as usual, but this time was different. While lying there, all of a sudden, I felt…a flutter! I felt the baby! It was wonderful and reminded me why I'm going through all this; why all of us are going through this. There's a baby inside me!

Wednesday, December 12, 2007 12:22 PM
15 Weeks 3 Days

My ultrasound this morning showed the SCH grew to 5.5x5.8x2.8. I'm so frustrated because I've been on modified bed rest but the SCH actually got bigger. My iron level is now officially on the low side so now I'm on a high dose of iron supplements. He said that if I keep having major bleeding episodes and my levels drop anymore, I'll need a blood transfusion. I've never had a blood transfusion, but the thought of one is scary, mostly because of risks of contracting diseases and infections. I really don't want someone else's blood inside me, either. I hope the supplements avoid me needing one.

The OB is also very concerned about my placenta starting to penetrate my uterus and possibly even going through the uterus and invading other organs. I didn't even know that was possible! My OB told me it's very rare, but he can't rule it out. The only way to know for sure during pregnancy is to have a special type of diagnostic test called magnetic resonance imaging (MRI). The MRI enables doctors to look inside the body without having to do surgery. My OB said that he would probably order an MRI in a few months.

The ultrasound also showed an issue with the baby. The baby's bowel is echogenic, meaning that the bowels look bright and white on the scan, when it should look like a dark shadow. An echogenic bowel could indicate chromosomal abnormalities, or something as innocuous as the baby has been swallowing blood that has mixed in with my amniotic fluid. I really think it's the latter because it makes perfect sense, especially because there were no other markers indicating anything wrong with the baby. Unfortunately, my OB disagrees and insists that I have an amniocentesis. My pregnancy is putting my health in jeopardy and he doesn't want me to continue this pregnancy if there's any chance that this baby has a fatal disease. The only way to know for certain is through the amniocentesis. I really don't want to have the amniocentesis. Under the best of circumstances, the amniocentesis presents risks to the baby. In my situation, especially with the SCH, the risks are greatly increased. I respect my OB and know that he's looking out for me and the best interest of my family, but don't think that I could terminate the pregnancy if the choice was between the baby and me. I know that's very selfish since I have three little kids that need me. I just hope that there's nothing wrong with the baby so I don't have to make any life-or-death decision. I'm also terrified of having the actual amniocentesis. I hear that it hurts a lot. I know that should be the least of my fears, but I don't want to have that long needle stuck inside my stomach and uterus!

The ultrasound technician was able to see the sex of the baby and asked if I wanted to know. I haven't thought about the sex of the baby because I've been so focused on all the problems I've been having. Of course I wanted to know! It's a boy! I'm so excited to have another boy, but now am even more nervous. I know there is no way I'm carrying this baby to term and I've read and heard that boys' lungs take longer to develop than girls'. I don't need anything else to worry about in the pregnancy so I will try not to focus on that, which is easier said than done. There are certain things within my control, but the sex of the baby isn't one of them. I love boys and hate that I'm upset that this baby is a boy, but I'm only nervous for him, knowing that he's going to struggle more than if he were a girl. This is one time I must try and hope he's going to be okay.

Wednesday, December 12, 2007 1:49 PM
15 Weeks 3 Days

Despite all the pain and sleep deprivation, and knowledge that preemie boys have a harder time than girls, I'm elated, and re-energized, knowing I'm having another boy. As soon as I got home from my OB appointment I called Lee and told him, "It's a Fletcher!" Fletcher is a name we both loved when I was pregnant with Cassie, if she was a boy. I could almost hear Lee smile, but then he told me that he doesn't believe an ultrasound 15 1/2 weeks could possibly be accurate. He told me he'd believe it when I have the amniocentesis. Before hanging up with Lee he said, "Fletcher! That's a great name!" It was the first time in this pregnancy that Lee and I were happy and connected with each other. In that moment, there was no worry about pregnancy issues or my health, just pure happiness over having another boy who will become a part of our family.

Lee wants me to have the amniocentesis so I called my perinatologist and made the appointment for early January.

Sunday, December 16, 2007 3:12 PM
16 Weeks 0 Days

I don't know which I dread more, weekdays or weekends. Lee works at his second job on alternating weekend days. When he's not working, he's been taking the kids out. I feel badly that he doesn't have any downtime. I can see how tired he is and that he needs a break. When he's at work on the weekends, I feel guilty for not doing anything with the kids. They have a lot of toys and electronics but they don't feel like doing anything while I'm lying in bed. I was able to arrange a play date for the boys yesterday, so that was good for all of us. At least during the week the kids are with other kids. There's just something about the weekends, having the entire family home but everything being so tense, that makes me feel even worse for disrupting their lives.

Saturday, December 22, 2007 9:54 PM
16 Weeks 6 Days

I begrudgingly packed up and mentally prepared myself to go to my in-laws in Georgia, but would prefer to stay home. We're leaving in tomorrow morning for the seven-hour drive and I'm nervous. I'm scared of driving through very rural areas and being so far away from home and my doctors. I asked Lee if I could stay home but he said he wouldn't be comfortable having me alone in the house, especially if I had an emergency. I tried to argue that I could call 9-1-1 but Lee said he'd already thought about that and had visions of me lying on our bathroom floor, hemorrhaging and being unable to get to the phone. I can't blame him for being worried and insisting that I go with the family. At least my in-laws live less than a quarter mile from a full-service hospital.

I ended up checking with my OB to make sure it was okay for me to travel and he said it would be fine. He said at this point in my pregnancy, if something were to happen, the same steps would be taken regardless of what hospital I went to. I begrudgingly agreed to go, but in reality, I had no choice.

Monday, December 24, 2007 3:10 PM
17 Weeks 1 Day

The drive up to my in-laws was long and the roads were bumpy. I was so uncomfortable and nervous. I had two pillows between my legs and my stomach as cushions and I think that helped. I wish I had insisted on staying home. I don't feel safe being far away from my doctor and hospital. If something happens while I'm here, I don't know if the care would be the same as at home. In addition to being nervous about my medical condition, I'm miserable being here. I want to be in my own bed, with my own blankets, and not have to socialize or be around other people. Any time I get up I have to get fully dressed, which is a hassle too. My mother-in-law keeps asking me what I want or need, which is very thoughtful, but I don't want to be catered to; I just want to be left alone. My in-laws are very excited about the holiday and my kids can't wait either. I feel like I'm a distraction. It was a bad idea for me to come here and now I'm stuck.

Wednesday, December 26, 2007 5:45 PM
17 Weeks 3 Days

The kids had a great Christmas, which made it worth coming up here. Lee has to fly home tonight to go back to work. I want all of us to drive home together, but it wouldn't be fair to the kids to go home now. They're off from school for almost two more weeks and they would be bored at home, not to mention that I wouldn't be able to really care for them. My father-in-law said he would drive us back New Year's Eve and fly home the next day. I know it's the right decision but I am jealous that Lee gets to go home.

Monday, December 31, 2007 11:59 PM
18 Weeks 1 Day

What a long day. I know Lee's family was happy that my father-in-law offered to drive us home, but it was awkward. I'm a grown woman with my own family, but I felt like a child being told I couldn't drive home. That seems to be a common theme in my life right now and something I need to get used to, at least for the time being.

We left my in-laws early in the morning, but I started having painful cramps soon after so I had my father-in-law drop me off at my OB's hospital before heading to my house. At my last appointment, my OB said to go to his hospital next time I had an emergency, which I took to mean the ER at his hospital, so that's where I was dropped off.

This ER was less prepared for a pregnancy emergency than the one at my house, even though they have the Woman's Hospital attached. There was no ultrasound machine in the entire area and the staff acted as if they've never dealt with a pregnant person before. They said my severe cramps were most likely due to dehydration, but wouldn't give me an IV of fluids. They did check my hemoglobin level, which fell even though I'm taking a supplement. After four hours, the ER released me and said there was nothing they could do for me, but that I should try to drink more water and call my OB after the holiday. I was so upset and angry that I wasted my New Year's Eve here.

Once outside, I realized that it was New Year's Eve and wondered how I was going to get home. All the cab companies' phone numbers were busy with people needing rides to parties and there is no bus service near my house. I didn't want to bother Lee or my father-in-law because it was so late and I know they were watching the football game. It wouldn't be much of an issue if I had gone to the hospital near my house, but this one is about a half hour from my house. Part of me hoped that Lee would have insisted on coming to get me, rather than being fine with watching television and letting me figure out on my own how to get home. I was too tired to be mad or upset, especially since I'm the one who decided to go to the hospital and told him he didn't have to pick me up.

I'd been calling various taxi companies but there was either no answer or I would get a busy signal. I was finally able to get in touch with one cab company, who told me someone would come in 30 minutes. I went inside and got food from the vending machine, then went back outside to wait. After 45 minutes, I realized the cab wasn't coming and there was no answer when I called back. I tried not to panic and sat down for a few minutes to think about how I was going to get myself home. Just as I was about to call Lee, a cab dropped off a passenger. I ran to him and asked if he could take me home but he told me he had another customer waiting for him. I was about to start crying when he took out his cell phone and called another cab driver. He hung up and told me someone would come get me in 10 minutes. I decided to wait and see, before I bothered Lee, and, amazingly, nine minutes later the cab was there to get me. I was so relieved.

I got home at 11:40 PM, 17 hours after leaving my in-laws. I appreciated being back in my own home, especially before the New Year began!

Wednesday, January 2, 2008 11:12 PM
18 Weeks 3 Days

I finally got to see my OB this morning. It felt like it had been months!

My OB reprimanded me for going to the hospital ER the other night. He said that he told me to go to labor and delivery (L&D) at his hospital, not the ER at his hospital. I argued that pregnant women are usually turned away from L&D unless they are at least 20 weeks, but my OB said that L&D would've called him and I would've been taken care of properly. I wish I had understood that was what he meant! There's nothing I can do about it now, and even though the ER didn't do anything for me, I'm glad I didn't end up disrupting my OB's New Year's Eve by going to L&D.

Once we got that discussion out of the way, and I told him I understood that the next time I'll go to L&D, the rest of the appointment was routine. My OB listened to the baby's heartbeat, and checked my weight and hemoglobin levels.

Before leaving he made me promise me that I would go to tomorrow's amniocentesis appointment with the perinatologist. As much as I want to cancel it, I understand why he is insisting on me having the test. I assured him I would.

Since my OB doesn't want me going past 36 weeks, I'm officially more than halfway through this pregnancy!

Thursday, January 3, 2008 2:18 PM
18 Weeks 4 Days

I had the amniocentesis this morning, but not before I panicked and almost walked out without having it done. The perinatologist let me use his office to call Lee, but before he closed the door he told me the importance of having this done. Usually Lee usually defers to me when it comes to pregnancy tests, but this time he told me he wants me to have it done. He has had numerous conversations with my OB and the perinatologists, and understands why they are urging me to have it. The most compelling reason is because the pregnancy has become life threatening for me. If the baby has a condition that is "incompatible with life", the doctors told Lee that they would have a medical responsibility to terminate the pregnancy. Hearing Lee tell me this makes me realize just how serious my condition is, especially because all these doctors are profoundly pro-life. They're pro-life except when the mother's life is in jeopardy. Apparently mine is.

I hung up with Lee and told the perinatologist I was ready to have the amniocentesis. He brought me back in to the examination room. He put some weird goop on his hands and all over my stomach, and then put on special one-use gloves that came in a secured pouch. He set up the ultrasound machine, took out a huge needle, and asked me to hold my breath for a few seconds.

The preparations took longer than the test itself! The actual amniocentesis took less than five minutes, but it was awful. When the perinatologist inserted the needle, I heard a popping sound and felt some pressure and then a stabbing pain in my stomach area and uterus. I felt all my muscles seizing up and I wasn't able to breathe. A few moments later, when he took the needle out, I started having strong, painful cramps. My perinatologist was amazing and very patient with me during the procedure. I took the time to explain exactly what was going on, but it didn't do anything to alleviate any of the discomfort and fear I had.

He showed me the sample of fluid and it was a dark reddish and brown. I thought amniotic fluid was clear and he told me that of the thousands of amniocenteses he's performed, he's never seen amniotic fluid that color before. My perinatologist called the lab with me still in the room, to let them know ahead of time that this was actual amniotic fluid. I'm not sure why he wanted me in the room when he made that phone call, but it was an interesting conversation to overhear. The lab immediately asked if the perinatologist was sure that he performed the test properly, which immediately put him on the defensive. He explained about my SCH and pregnancy issues and the lab said they would make a notation in my chart and be prepared once the sample arrived.

The perinatologist told me, aside from the color of the fluid, that this was a success and at no time was the baby in jeopardy. He said that the baby moved out of the way of the needle to allow him get the sample. I'm glad he told me that after the fact because the thought of Fletcher being so close to the needle and possibly in danger made me nervous. He gave me the Rh immune globulin shot and told me to take it easy for the next few days. I told him I still had cramps and he said they might continue for a few days. He asked if there was someone to call to pick me up, but I told him I drove myself here and will be driving myself home. He wasn't happy about that, but told me once I got home that I should lie down for a few hours.

Thursday, January 3, 2008 11:25 PM
18 Weeks 4 Days

Once I got home I started leaking fluid that looked exactly like the amniotic fluid sample. I know there is a way to test for amniotic fluid leaking by using a PH strip. However, blood and amniotic fluid have the same PH level so the only way to know if I'm leaking amniotic fluid is to do an ultrasound.

I didn't know what to do, so I called my OB. He and the ultrasound technician said they would keep the office open for me to come in late this afternoon and do another ultrasound. In the meantime, I called Lee and started crying. He told me to stay in bed and he would come home and drive me to my OB's office. He also ended up calling my mom and asked her to stay here for the weekend. She was able to get a flight out this afternoon, so after Lee dropped me off at my OB's office; he went to pick up my mom at the airport.

At the ultrasound, my amniotic fluid level was normal. My OB thinks I was leaking serum. He ended up putting me on antibiotics just in case I develop an infection.

Tonight I am cramping a lot and am in so much pain. I hate amniocenteses! I'm glad my mom will be here this weekend so Lee can work. I hope she'll take care of the kids so I can be left alone. I know that sounds horrible but my brain is fried and I don't have it in me to be fun, loving, nice and motherly.

Sunday, January 6, 2008 5:28 PM
19 Weeks 0 Days

I took full advantage of having my mom here this weekend and am glad she'll be here for another day. I was surprised at all the cramping I had after the amniocentesis. It lasted through this morning. The rest of today has been great. The cramps have subsided and I haven't bled in over 12 hours; the longest stretch in nearly six weeks.

Monday, January 7, 2008 11:59 PM
19 Weeks 1 Day

I spoke too soon about feeling good. At 11:00 PM last night I started bleeding bright red and had severe cramps. I tried to wait it out but after a few hours with no relief, I woke up Lee and told him I was leaving to go to the hospital.

The hospital has a security checkpoint during off-business hours. The guard stopped me and asked whom I was going to visit and I told him I needed to go to L&D. He asked me again for the name of the patient I was going to see and I repeated that I needed to go to L&D. He was getting irritated with me and was about to ask me to leave when I started to cry. I told him that I'm pregnant and bleeding and have to go to L&D right away. He glanced at my stomach and I could tell he didn't believe I was actually pregnant. At this point I was sobbing and he didn't want to upset me any further so he gave me a pass. I know that I'm smaller than I usually am at this point in my pregnancies, but I can't believe the guard thought I was lying. Even if he didn't believe that I was pregnant, he could definitely see how distraught I was. Rather than give me a hard time, he should have called someone from L&D to come speak with me. It was humiliating and made me so angry to be treated this way, but I was thankful that he finally let me through.

I finally got to the L&D department at 3:00 AM and was hooked up to a monitor. The nurse told me I was having contractions every two minutes and gave me a terbutaline shot in my arm. Terbutaline is a medication that's used to help stop pre-term labor. The shot didn't work and the contractions were getting stronger, so she gave me a second dose. By this point, my arm was throbbing and the combination of exhaustion and medication made me jittery and nauseous. Thankfully, fifteen minutes later, the contractions completely stopped. The nurse wanted me to stay in the L&D room until my perinatologist office opened and someone could examine me. I had my own room, so I watched re-runs on television.

At 7:30 AM I was put in a wheelchair and taken up to my perinatologist office for an ultrasound. I saw a different perinatologist than my usual one, but he seemed to be familiar with my case. He said my ultrasound looked great. There was no blood floating in the fluid and the SCH looked smaller. My cervix was closed and long and my fluid level was perfect. The perinatologist said I had an irritable uterus, where my uterus contracts but does not cause labor. He explained that my uterus was already irritated by the SCH, and then sticking a needle through it really pissed it off! He was being nice but it just validated my reasons why I shouldn't have had the amniocentesis, which of course is too little, too late.

The perinatologist also told me to start asking friends to donate blood for me. It turns out my blood type is rare; only about one in 70 people have it and with my placental issues, I will definitely need a blood transfusion at delivery. He also told me I have to continue to take the terbutaline pill four times a day until I deliver.

Lee and my mom came to pick me up around noon. The look on their faces said it all. I could see that Lee was nearing his breaking point. The first thing he asked me when he entered the room was if I was okay to continue the pregnancy. I don't know if he didn't think I could handle the pregnancy or if he couldn't handle it. All I could think about was the conversation he and my mom must have had this morning. I wondered if they decided to try to convince me to terminate. I immediately told Lee there was no way I would end the pregnancy and that I was fine, just tired and ready to go home.

My mom didn't even ask how I was doing. She immediately lectured me about how irresponsible I was to get pregnant and then asked why I didn't terminate the pregnancy when I had the chance early on. I understand that she's scared for my life, but I wish she just say that because then I'd tell her that I'm also a mother and am just as scared for my child. I never had the chance to say any of that because as soon as she was done scolding me, a nurse told me I could leave.

I didn't want to go home with either one of them. Even though spending the night in the L&D wasn't fun, at least I was surrounded by people who want to save Fletcher's life, and who gave me the support I desperately needed. It's ridiculous that my mom and husband are acting this way.

Although I'm thankful to my mom for spending the weekend taking care of my kids and me, I'm also extremely resentful. Now, more than ever, I need her and my husband's love and support and I don't expect to be reprimanded for wanting another child! Thinking that the two of them were discussing this made me even angrier. I'm trying to remain positive and stay hopeful, but it's getting harder and harder to do with those closest to me being against me. I realized I'm going to have to get through the emotional part of this pregnancy alone.

Tuesday, January 8, 2008 5:00 PM
19 Weeks 2 Days

I contacted the local blood bank and they are in the process of setting up an account for me so that people can donate blood directly to me. It's a tedious process, but I figure I have time to get everything finalized. I've also been sending out emails asking friends what their blood type is to see if anyone is B negative or O negative and, if so, would they be willing to donate blood for me. My neighbor called and told me that her daughter is O negative and she would be more than happy to donate as much blood as she's allowed! I'm so happy to know that I have at least one person donating, just in case.

Wednesday, January 9, 2008 6:34 PM
19 Weeks 3 Days

I've been trying to stay in bed as much as possible, but get up to get food and drinks throughout the day, and to use the bathroom. I'm not allowed to take baths, but since I can't stay upright for very long, Lee bought me a hand held showerhead so I can sit down in the shower. Lee sweetly offered to get me a shower chair but I told him no. Those chairs are not for 37 year olds! I know he's trying to be helpful and, in his way, show support, but to me, this isn't the way to show it. It felt more like him telling me how worthless and weak I was. I hope I didn't discourage him from wanting to help me.

Thursday, January 10, 2008 9:12 AM
19 Weeks 4 Days

My mom left this morning. Even with her comments to me, I can't deny that she's been a huge help to the kids and me. The kids have been able to go out after school and play and I've been able to stay in bed and not feel like I am neglecting everyone.

The kids have bonded with her, which is something my mother has always wanted and complained about because she lives so far away. However, more than once she mentioned that this was not the way she wanted to get closer to them.

I know Lee has had mixed feelings about having her here. He knows the added stress she causes me when she makes negative comments and they have always had a tumultuous relationship. Regardless, Lee has been able to go to work without worrying about me. She has been making sure food is in the house when he gets home, and she's been able to see how great a dad he is with the kids. But most importantly, the kids have been taken cared of.

With my mom leaving today, I've come to realize that I need someone to be here helping me. I'm nervous about being alone with the kids, not just because I can't take them places, but because I'm so self-absorbed with my own issues right now. Even though most family members are worried, none are willing to commit to coming here to help more than sporadically for only a few days at a time. I'm tired of the constant lectures about me causing this situation. It upsets me, but since I'm so preoccupied with my life and simply trying to survive every day, I've been able to tune them out, but Lee is starting to get worn down by it. He's been telling me that our families have a point and that he never wanted another child and now his entire family life is being disrupted. He hates relying financially on his father and told me it makes him physically sick that his children are in full-time daycare.

There's so much tension and anger between us that could be alleviated with help from our families, but they all have made their opinions very clear. It makes me so mad that no one can put aside their disapproval to come help for a few months, even if their reason is only caring for my kids. I can't focus on this right now, but I can definitely feel the resentment building.

It's amazing to me that my in-laws and mom believe I've done something so horrible by getting pregnant. Lee's parents are acting as though I should be punished for simply wanting another child, and my mother has made her disapproval very clear. I'm very frustrated and angry. I hate being in the position of needing my family, asking for help and being lectured and told that this is all my own doing. What they're saying is preposterous, but I can't defend myself against such irrational arguments. I'm debating whether or not to resume my normal activities since there doesn't seem to be anything else I can do.

CHAPTER 5

People, especially those in the medical field, are starting to realize just how atypical my pregnancy is.

Sunday, January 13, 2008 12:11 PM
20 Weeks 0 Days

I had to ask Lee to take me to the hospital this morning. Last night I passed two golf ball sized clots and had bleeding that became heavier as the night went on. I didn't feel safe driving, so when Lee and the kids woke up, I asked him to take me to the hospital. We both thought I would only be a few hours, so he and the kids went to a nearby park. A few hours later he called to see if I was ready to be picked up, but the nurse said there were no immediate plans to discharge me. Lee was upset and wanted to see me and talk to the nurses, but I didn't want the kids to have to see me like this, so I told him to go home. I'm not sure why the hospital didn't let me go home this afternoon, and I hope Lee won't be mad if he gets home and then has to turn around to pick me up.

Sunday, January 13, 2008 7:39 PM
20 Weeks 0 Days

I haven't bled since this morning, but my OB wants me to stay overnight for observation. When I called Lee to tell him, I heard the boys ask when they were going to pick me up. We're all so sad that I won't be coming home tonight. I wonder what Lee is telling them? I hope I can go home tomorrow.

Monday, January 14, 2008 7:52 AM
20 Weeks 1 Day

I think the nurses thought I was being dramatic when I arrived yesterday, but after last night, everyone here knows the seriousness of this pregnancy. At 3:00 AM I had to page the nurse because I started bleeding and passing large clots. The nurse took her time coming in, but as soon as she saw the bed, she was visibly shocked. She ran to the bathroom and grabbed a handful of towels then tilted my bed so my feet were elevated. She started pulling out the clots while applying pressure, hoping to stop the bleeding. She paged another nurse to come help her, but the bleeding stopped before she arrived.

The nurse cautiously grabbed the fetal monitor to check on Fletcher. Thankfully, she immediately found his heartbeat. She told me how relieved she was because she had never seen anything like that in any pregnancy before. Even though the baby seemed to be okay, the monitor showed that I was having contractions three minutes apart. The nurse called my OB, who ordered two shots of the terbutaline and an hour later the contractions stopped. The nurse and I were both exhausted. She must have written a lot of detail in my chart and explained everything to my OB because when the day nurse came in, she told me I would be staying in the hospital for at least another two days.

Monday, January 14, 2008 8:32 AM
20 Weeks 1 Day

As soon as my perinatologist office opened, one of their technicians came with a portable ultrasound machine. The baby looked perfect! He was very active and kept opening and closing his mouth. He kicked the ultrasound wand each time she pressed down on my stomach! I loved seeing that he was safe and sound.

However, all the doctors and nurses are worried about all the bleeding. They have me on strict bed rest. I have to lie on my left side because that's supposed to give the best blood flow to the baby. I can only get out of bed to go to the bathroom.

I think Lee is relieved that I'm not at home. He doesn't have to worry about something happening to me, especially if I'm alone with the kids. I have to admit that I am relieved to be here because last night really frightened me. The nurse agreed and said for my safety and health, she is glad I'm here and not at home.

I do miss my babies though and wonder if they can understand any of this. I hope they know how much I wish I could be home with them.

Monday, January 14, 2008 12:45 PM
20 Weeks 1 Day

So having friends and neighbors bank blood for me was a great idea in theory, but not in reality. There's only one blood bank in the area that does directed blood donations. The blood bank needs to have a specific date when the blood will be used in order to set any aside. Any blood taken would only be good for a certain amount of days too. Since we don't have a date when I would need the blood, there's a possibility that the blood would expire and be wasted. I appreciate everyone who said they would donate on my behalf, but it seems I will have to rely on anonymous donors for my blood transfusions. When I spoke to some of my friends and told them the news, most said they would still donate blood for the blood bank for other people to use. I have amazing friends and now I feel like I have helped others too.

Tuesday, January 15, 2008 2:30 PM
20 Weeks 2 Days

I'm still in the hospital. It's amazing how time keeps passing and I'm not bored or restless. One thing that's been keeping me busy is filling out insurance papers. My insurance company requires pre-approval for any hospital stay and since I didn't get permission from them, they are telling the hospital they refuse to cover this hospital stay. I was able to talk with a manager at the company who listened to me and said if I apply now to have coverage retroactively, she would attach a personal recommendation and try to get it covered. She waved the deadline for me to get my paperwork in until I can get home and fax over the information. I could ask Lee to do it, but I don't want to give him anything more to do. He needs to focus on his job and since I am the one in the hospital, I'll deal with the insurance issues. I have the manager's direct phone number and I gave her the head of L&Ds information so that she can have all the information she needs to write her letter. With her help, I think I should be able to get this hospital stay covered. I'm glad I called the different departments, rather than simply accepting that they denied my claim. It would be easier if the insurance company would accept my claims right away so I don't have to waste time and energy on this, but ultimately I need this paid for so it's something I need to be persistent about and get done.

Wednesday, January 16, 2008 2:30 PM
20 Weeks 3 Days

A few hours ago my perinatologist ran into my room to tell me my amniocentesis results just came in and that Fletcher is a perfectly healthy baby. I was relieved to hear it, but deep down I knew it. My baby has been growing perfectly, even under all the stress, and my physical problems. My ultrasounds haven't showed anything abnormal (that couldn't be explained by the SCH). After he told me the news, he became serious and said the bleeding and clotting I've been having is not normal and the fact that he has no idea why this is happening has him even more concerned. He's unsure how long I will be able to carry the baby and told me that all we can do is to take it one day at a time. He told me that he discussed my pregnancy with the other perinatologists in his practice and they would permit me to terminate the pregnancy, but he said there's no reason to end the pregnancy at this point. He stressed that my health is deteriorating and continues to be more dangerous each day the pregnancy progresses, so there could come a time where we would have to discuss ending the pregnancy. I know how hard it was for him to tell me this because he and his partners are pro-life. I remember when I was pregnant with Cassie, he told me that all the prenatal tests were done for informational reasons only, not to end the pregnancy based on the results, and now he is one of the doctors giving me permission to terminate. I am pro-choice but feel it's a personal decision. Even though I am pro-choice, and my health is in danger, I will continue the pregnancy until the doctors insist I have to deliver because they feel my life is in immediate danger.

My perinatologist said he's certain I'll need a blood transfusion soon because my hemoglobin levels keep dropping. He told me that his wife and a woman in his office are universal donors and can donate blood for me. I appreciated his offer and hated to explain to him that wouldn't be possible. I figured that he would have had some patients over the years that needed blood banked, but apparently I'm the first in his all his years in practice; that both shocked and frightened me. It made me nervous to learn that my high-risk pregnancy doctor never treated a patient going through this.

As he was leaving my room, he told me he was very proud of me and that I should continue to stay strong. I realized that was the first time anyone has said that to me. I really needed to hear that, but I wished it came from my family. At this point, however, I'll take the support wherever I can get it.

Wednesday, January 16, 2008 10:00 PM
20 Weeks 3 Days

I can't decide if it's better for my family and me to stay in the hospital or go home. Lee is feeling overwhelmed with working full-time and having sole responsibility of the kids. He told me last night that he had to quit his second job and he was very angry about it. He loved working there and resented having to quit. I told him they would probably rehire him when this was all over, but he cut the conversation short and said he didn't want to talk about it anymore. I'm trying to be supportive and I want him to vent his frustrations to me, but at the same time I don't want to constantly be blamed for everything.

After talking with Lee, my mom called. She said she's concerned for me and I should seriously consider terminating this pregnancy. She said she had a long talk with my in-laws and they all agreed that Lee and I were so irresponsible to get pregnant, and my father-in-law said Lee agreed. They all said I was stupid for getting myself into this situation. Lee and I have always wanted our parents to bond, but this isn't how we wanted it to happen. I can't believe Lee would agree with them, either. This is our life and family and we should be allowed to have as many children as we want without having to ask our parents. Do they think I knew this was going to happen? How could I have known? This is not something I had the foresight of knowing about ahead of time. I'm not sure why they are treating me this way, but it's definitely not helping.

After my mom told me this, she asked if she could visit this weekend and I said no. I don't want her hovering and being negative when I am trying so hard to stay calm and hopeful, which, even under the best of circumstances, is very hard for me to do.

I'm so lonely and feel abandoned. I'm fighting for my child and wish my family would show me compassion. Instead, everyone is telling me how much I've messed up. I want to scream that I didn't know this would happen and that I am scared and feel alone and would love to have support. I take full responsibility for wanting another child and what's so wrong with that? I thought wanting and having children was a reason for joy and happiness. It should be.

I could handle my mom and in-laws if Lee would stick up for me, and us. It seems, for now, I'll have to get encouragement from my doctors, nurses, and friends.

Thursday, January 17, 2008 6:00 AM
20 Weeks 4 Days

I'm still in the same L&D room. There are no windows and nothing but a TV and my bed in the room. I think the doctors are afraid to move me because I'm still so unstable. I'm passing clots and gushing blood a few times a day. I think everyone expected me to have lost the baby by now.

At least the room has an Internet connection through the TV. I'm able to read my emails, but for some reason I can only respond in the subject line, so friends have been getting some strange emails from me. There's a group of women I befriended on-line when I was pregnant with my oldest, over five years ago. We have been there for each other over the years, even though we all live in different states, and some in different countries. Even though I've only met a few of them, I feel like they are my true family, especially in trying times. I can always email or call any of them, any time of day, and know I'll get unconditional love and support. I'm very grateful to have contact with them.

Thursday, January 17, 2008 4:39 PM
20 Weeks 4 Days

I was moved to a different room on the L&D floor. It's a lot bigger and has windows! There's a view of a pedestrian bridge linking different parts of the hospital. At this point, I'll take whatever view of the outside world I can get! I guess my other nurse wrote notes in my medical file about me not sleeping, so tonight's nurse told me I have to take a sleeping pill. I argued with her and I know it sounds crazy for me to be worried about taking a sleeping pill during pregnancy considering I'm on so many other medications, but I am. We compromised and I agreed to take half of the pill.

I had a conversation with my mom and told her it would be nice if someone in the family would be supportive and understand that this is hard on me too! I think she heard me because as we were about to hang up, she told me that she didn't understand why this was happening to me and said she was so sorry I was going through this. I'm not sure if she was being sincere, but I gave her the benefit of the doubt and thanked her.

Friday, January 18, 2008 12:59 AM
20 Weeks 5 Days

Lee spent the day with me today while the kids were in school. He's a mess. He hasn't been sleeping and isn't able to concentrate at work. I tried to tell him how great he's doing, but he didn't want to hear it. He's just very angry, tired and concerned for Fletcher and me. There's nothing I can say or do for him and that frustrates me. Lee said the kids are very confused and don't like me not being at home. Wesley seems to be having the toughest time. He needs to talk to me on the phone every morning on the way to daycare and every night before bed.

Lee left and picked up the kids and everyone came to visit me tonight. They've only been here once since I was admitted. The hospital is over 35 minutes away, and after a long day, it's too hard on everyone to visit more often.

Lee said it took 20 minutes to get to my room from the parking lot so that by the time they got to my room, tonight, they were ready to leave! I could tell that the boys had a hard time seeing me stuck in the hospital bed, and the only thing Cassie wanted to do was jump on me, which made me nervous. Lee and I decided it would be better for the kids to call more often than come visit.

Friday, January 18, 2008 6:45 AM
20 Weeks 5 Days

I had hoped to be discharged this weekend, but I just had an awful night. Just after midnight I started having strong contractions that were three minutes apart. It took a few hours and three different medications to get them to slow down. My OB's partner was on call and ended up writing me new orders, one being that I now have to use a bedpan for the next twelve hours. There's no chance of me going home anytime soon.

My OB is back in town this afternoon and I can't wait to see him this weekend and hear his thoughts.

Friday, January 18, 2008 8:33 PM
20 Weeks 5 Days

I was moved from L&D up to the antepartum floor a few hours ago. My OB's partner said I didn't have to use the disgusting bedpan anymore. I guess they feel I've stabilized enough to leave L&D, but not enough to go home. I love the new room though. It's huge. The room was converted from a two patient room to a room for one, but they left the two television sets. I can watch two shows at a time or the kids can watch a show and Lee and I can watch a different one. There's a dining table and four chairs, so the kids can come here and we can have a family meal together! There's also a couch for family to just sit and relax or Lee to come and take a nap. The entire outside wall is a huge window. I can see cars, the sun, moon, stars, and people walking around. It's amazing how this change of scenery has lifted my mood. I called Lee and asked him to come with the kids tonight so we could all have dinner together. I hadn't seen them for almost a week! Lee wasn't sure if the kids would be able to handle seeing me in a hospital bed, but as soon as the kids came in the room, they were so happy. They all rushed to hug and kiss me. Then they noticed the room had a huge couch and started jumping on it. I pointed out the two television sets and they thought that was great! It was loud and chaotic, and perfect! It was a very fun evening, considering the circumstances, but saying goodbye was hard on all of us. I hope Lee will bring them back over the weekend.

Saturday, January 19, 2008 6:50AM
20 Weeks 6 Days

My OB came by late last night and said I might be able to head home today if I had a good night. Unfortunately, my night was awful. However I'm noticing that if I don't bleed for a few hours or days, the next day I usually have a bad episode. I guess the blood is pooling inside me and at some point I'll have another long night of gushing. The doctors are more concerned with the pain and contractions caused by the bleeding, than the bleeding itself. My OB is pretty sure I just have an irritable uterus, but wants to make sure the contractions don't continue and cause preterm labor. Since there's no way to stop the bleeding, his focus is to stop the contractions. He's having me take a terbutaline pill every six hours around the clock in order to give my uterus a rest. I hope this will work because nothing else seems to be and I'm becoming extremely discouraged. I was having such a great day yesterday. I felt great up until 10:00 PM, when all of a sudden, without warning, I was in severe pain, bleeding and having contractions yet again. The pain feels like someone is stabbing me with a huge knife, from the inside out. The only way to ease the pain is to stop the contractions. It took over an hour for the medicine to stop them and another hour for the other pain to subside.

My OB told me to expect to be here for at least a few more days. Thankfully he changed my orders so my IV line can be taken out. I'm also allowed to take a quick shower, too. I'm so excited to have the needle out of my arm and be able to clean myself. I don't want the hospital staff to think I'm too comfortable here. Even with my improved room, IV out and being allowed to shower, I just want to go home! I miss being around Lee and my kids. I hate being away from them.

Sunday, January 20, 2008 8:15 AM
21 Weeks 0 Days

The nurses take my blood pressure every four hours around the clock. High blood pressure in pregnancy can signal problems, but low blood pressure can also be worrisome in my situation because it can signal internal bleeding. My reading at 3:00 AM was so low, 70/48 (normal for me is about 90/70), that it set the alarms off. The nurses called my OB who told them to take another reading in two hours and then call him back if it was still low. My reading at 5:00 AM was a little higher so I hope they didn't call him. My OB must be pretty annoyed with me right about now.

Monday, January 21, 2008 11:31 AM
21 Weeks 1 Day

I had another horrible night last night. I swear that my bed looked like a murder scene. I called the emergency buttons and when the nurse came in, her face turned pale and she said she would be right back. She ran out of the room and came back in with two other nurses. Two nurses lifted me in to a chair and cleaned me up while the other changed the sheets. Another nurse was called in to put me on the machine to check on the baby. Thankfully there was a strong heartbeat.

My OB was in the hospital when he got the call and came to check on me. He said that since I didn't have any contractions with the episode, he said he would still discharge me today. The nurses were all shaking their heads, obviously disagreeing with that decision. I'm torn. Although I am ready to be home, be with my family, and sleep in my own bed, a part of me is afraid of having a bad episode at home that might lead to labor. I'm only 21 weeks along and don't want to be in the hospital for another three or four months. Being in the hospital didn't stop the episodes, so I might as well be home and if something does happen, I can go to a nearby hospital that is less than ten minutes away.

The next goal for me is to get to 26 weeks, and be given the steroid shot. During pregnancy, if there's a possibility of having the baby before 37 weeks, the corticosteroid betamethasone shot is given. It's been shown to speed up lung development by increasing the production of surfactant in the lungs. Surfactant lubricates air sacs in the lungs, and prevents the sacs from sticking, which helps babies breathe on their own. My OB also said that there's some research that these steroids could help prevent brain hemorrhaging, which is another serious issue that can cause brain damage.

He increased my terbutaline dose from every six to every four hours. I hate this medicine. The side effects are horrible. It has been causing me to have heart pounding and palpitations, hot flashes, dizziness and headaches, just to name a few. The only reason I can handle taking this is because the terbutaline seems to be keeping away the contractions.

The nurses made Lee promise that I would be as strict in my bed rest at home as in the hospital. We both agreed that I wouldn't leave my bed except to go to the bathroom and to take a quick shower. I know I can do that, but I hope that Lee realizes that's all I'll be able to do.

Monday, January 21, 2008 9:55 PM
21 Weeks 1 Day

As soon as Lee walked in my hospital room to pick me up, I started bleeding. I hated to call the nurse because I didn't want her to tell me I couldn't go home. She called for my OB, who, luckily, still discharged me. He said unless a new symptom starts up, or the bleeding doesn't stop within a few hours, I might as well be in my own home.

Lee drove straight to the kids' school for us to surprise them and pick them up. I felt like a celebrity walking through their school. I was touched by how compassionate the teachers were. They all came rushing over to me, hugged me, and said how happy they were to see me. They followed us while we went to each classroom.

First we went to pick up Wesley. He looked up at me but it didn't seem to register to him that I was his mom! He froze for about five seconds before realizing I really was there. He came running up to me and gave me the biggest hug. He crashed into my stomach, which hurt, but I didn't care. He held on to my hand very tightly while we walked in to pick up Spencer. Spencer saw me right away and sort of backed away for a second. I could tell he was overcome with joy but didn't want to seem too excited. He asked if I was going home and I said yes! He smiled and grabbed my other hand while we all walked to Cassie's room. She was outside playing and I got to watch her for a few seconds before she saw us. She was playing with a few other little girls, which I was relieved to see, but also gave me a pang in my heart because I could see that she was getting so big.

Cassie turned and saw us and came running over. She wanted me to pick her up, but I couldn't do, and immediately her smile faded. Lee helped her up to me, though, and we got to cuddle.

The car ride home was very loud! Each child talked over the other, telling me all about their day. Unfortunately, I didn't hear a word of it because I kept thinking that I was so happy to have us all together, even when doing something as mundane as driving home from school pick-up.

Tuesday, January 22, 2008 9:00 AM
21 Weeks 2 Days

It is so great to be home, even though I'm stuck in bed. I love being surrounded by my family, my things, my cat, my own bed, pillows, and blankets. I appreciate not having the IV in, not having to give blood every other day, and not having the nurses come in every few hours to take my temperature and blood pressure! I was thrilled to be able to hug and kiss the kids goodbye this morning as they left for school. I don't like that they still have to go to school, but we're all getting more used to it.

I have to admit though, that I'm freaked out being home because I'm still bleeding a lot and I don't have the option of pressing a button and having a nurse, or my OB, come check on me. I still think it was the right decision to leave the hospital, if for no other reason than to preserve my sanity and mitigate loneliness caused by being away from Lee and the kids.

I'm not naïve enough to think I'll be home for the rest of my pregnancy, so I spent most of the morning pre-paying monthly bills and faxing the medical paperwork to my insurance company.

Wednesday, January 23, 2008 6:30 AM
21 Weeks 3 Days

Lee was up all night coughing and hacking up tons of mucous. It's obvious he's sick. I asked him how long he's been coughing and he said at least a few weeks. I told him as soon as the doctor's office opens I'm calling and making him an appointment. He cannot get sick!

Wednesday, January 23, 2008 7:45 PM
21 Weeks 3 Days

I was able to get Lee in this afternoon to see the doctor. It turns out that Lee has pneumonia. I guess I was discharged from the hospital at the perfect time. I have to admit it's nice that someone else has to go to the doctor for a change! I do feel guilty that Lee's been so busy worrying about the kids and me that he's been neglecting his own health. I hope the medicine he's been prescribed works fast.

Thursday, January 24, 2008 9:45 AM
22 Weeks 4 Days

I called the insurance company this morning to make sure they've received my paperwork. After being on hold for over 45 minutes, the agent told me that they had received my fax, but my case had been closed because I missed the deadline to send in the paperwork. I started to get upset, but somehow explained my situation to her without crying. She was so empathetic and promised she would personally take over my case and get this taken care of immediately. She gave me her full name and her direct phone number. She said she would call me back sometime next week. I'm skeptical but hopeful this will be taken care of because I need the hospital stay to be covered by insurance.

Monday, January 28, 2008, 9:35 AM
23 Weeks 1 Day

The insurance agent called me first thing this morning to let me know that not only has the insurance claim gone through, but that it's been made retroactive from the beginning of the year and will continue for the rest of my pregnancy. If I end up back in the ER, L&D, or antepartum, I don't have to get authorization. I'm grateful to have this stress taken away from me. The agent said she would be happy to continue to deal with me directly, but that typically she works with the hospital administration department in these situations. They obviously dropped the ball, and I'm very grateful for this wonderful agent and to be able to deal with her directly going forward.

Thursday, January 31, 2008 12:34PM
22 Weeks 4 Days

I had a wonderfully quiet past five days, which abruptly came to an end yesterday. I was having so much pressure and pain that I went to see my OB. I apologized to him and said I hated to bother him. He was genuinely taken aback by my comment. He said I was right to come in because my pregnancy is anything but normal and that this pregnancy is so serious that he wants me to come in as often as I needed. He said that he has a patient like me once every ten years, explaining just how rare this pregnancy is for both of us.

After examining me, he said everything seemed to be okay and thought the pain and pressure was just typical pregnancy stuff. He was pleased that I gained five pounds since leaving the hospital. I've been having a hard time gaining weight even on the hospital's 2800-calorie diet. I thought that being on bed rest would cause my weight to skyrocket since I'm not expending any energy or burning any calories at all. I guess this baby is taking everything from me! Since I got home from the hospital, I've added nutritional high-protein, high-calorie shakes to my high-calorie diet and, thankfully, they seem to be helping.

I have an ultrasound scheduled for tomorrow morning. I hope everything looks good and the baby is growing on target.

The outing completely wore me out. I got home two hours later and was happy to climb back into bed.

Thursday, January 31, 2008 6:41PM
22 Weeks 4 Days

As soon as I got home from my OB appointment, my pain got even worse and I started having contractions. Thankfully they only lasted a few hours, went away on their own, and didn't cause any bleeding. It's crazy because now I get upset when I don't bleed because the longer I go without having a bleed, the worse my episode will be once I finally do. It's a bizarre way to have to live and is making me an emotional mess.

The needle trick is showing a fourth child and that it's definitely a boy.

CHAPTER 6

The hospital is now my home away from home.

Friday, February 1, 2008 10:38 PM
22 Weeks 5 days

I'm such an idiot for starting to feel positive about this pregnancy. This morning's ultrasound showed that my amniotic fluid was low. The amniotic fluid index (AFI) is an estimate of the amount of amniotic fluid in the uterus. A normal AFI should be about ten centimeters and mine was seven. This is the first time my AFI has been low.

So now there's another problem with this pregnancy! The technician called in my OB and he said that he's not ready to 'evacuate' my uterus just yet. I gasped and became hysterical. My OB mentioned taking the baby out now because my AFI was low? I couldn't believe it. I've endured so much and could not understand that because of this one bad ultrasound there was talk about delivering the baby! My OB calmed me down and said that there is no reason to end the pregnancy right now but that having low fluid indicates that there could be a rupture or tear in my uterus. If that is the case then there is a high risk of infection to the baby, which could ultimately kill him. Also, without proper amniotic fluid, the baby's lungs will not grow properly and he will not be able to survive outside once he is born.

My OB scheduled another ultrasound in a week and said we might have some decisions to make. I broke down and said I didn't want to leave the hospital. I didn't want to go all the way back home and sit there wondering and waiting for an entire week. All this stress is too much for me to handle and now, with a new, possibly fatal symptom, I was terrified to go back home.

My OB said he would admit me after I went to see the perinatologists to get a second opinion. Before leaving his office, I was given another Rh immune globulin shot and a blood draw to get a complete blood count (CBC) and my hemoglobin level. I didn't know if my OB just wanted to make sure my white and red blood counts were normal, or if he was preparing for my C-section.

Lee had stayed in the hospital cafeteria doing work while I had my OB appointment, so I called him to see if he would meet me at the perinatologist office. We were called back as soon as Lee got there. As soon as the technician started the scan, she stopped and called in all four of the perinatologists. They all agreed that my fluid was low, but that wasn't even their greatest concern.

They all said I had placenta percreta and were extremely concerned that my placenta could attach itself to my bladder. With placenta percreta, I could also hemorrhage at any moment and die within minutes. If I actually went into labor, odds are that neither the baby, nor myself, would survive. All the perinatologists agreed that I needed to be admitted to the hospital for the duration of my pregnancy.

The perinatologists then got on their phones and called different departments in the hospital. One called antepartum to have me readmitted, one called the blood bank to get me on their list, one called the urology department to let them know about my condition, and one called my OB to update him. They also scheduled an MRI to find out where my placenta is in relation to my bladder. Everyone in the woman's wing of the hospital is on notice; everyone now knows my name.

After the appointment, Lee came with me to check in at L&D intake, but then he had to leave to go back to work. I called my mom to let her know what was going on. She was understandably upset so I tried to reassure her, which wasn't easy to do since I was in a complete state of shock and dismay. Luckily, I couldn't stay on the phone long because the nurse was waiting to put me in a wheelchair and take me up to the antepartum floor. She put me in a small room that only had enough room for the bed and a chair. I asked if the large room I had been in before was available. The nurse remembered me from a few weeks ago and told me she would see what she could do and a few hours later she was able to get me moved to the larger room.

When the nurse left, the cafeteria employee came with my lunch, which was a huge plate of spaghetti and garlic bread. It was as if I was in a hotel and room service brought me my lunch, when in actuality, I didn't order this lunch and I don't want to have to be here. I was left alone for a few hours and I just sat in my bed and cried.

Saturday, February 2, 2008 5:45 AM
22 Weeks 6 Day

I don't know how I got through yesterday. I was never alone for more than a few minutes though, because the nurses were in and out of my room for most of the day. One nurse started me on two different IVs, one was a saline fluid for dehydration and the other was a mix of two different antibiotics as a precautionary measure to ward off any infection that could occur because of my possible uterine rupture.

Every four hours a nurse technician takes my temperature to make sure I don't have a fever, which could be a sign of infection, and also to check my blood pressure. If my blood pressure gets too high, it could be a sign that my body's going into distress. If it's too low, it could signal internal bleeding.

The perinatologist ordered non-stress tests (NSTs) for me every morning. The NST is a non-invasive way of monitoring the baby's heart rate and movements. There are two belts that are wrapped around the stomach. One belt measures the baby's heart rate and the other checks to see if there are any contractions. The NST usually lasts about thirty minutes and displays a graph showing how the baby's heart reacts to his movements, and/or to contractions that might be occurring.

I will have blood drawn every third morning at 4:30 AM to check on my white blood count (if high it could signal infection), red blood count and hemoglobin levels (for anemia). An hour ago I had my first blood draw. What a way to greet the day.

This is so much to take in all at once. I am terrified. I want to make this pregnancy last at least another five weeks but can't imagine living this way for that long.

Saturday, February 2, 2008 11:58 AM
22 Weeks 6 Day

My OB is very concerned about Fletcher and me. He thinks the low fluid is due to placental issues, and the perinatologists agree. Because he thinks my placenta isn't working properly, he feels this pregnancy can go either way. After being pregnant for over five months, hearing this completely devastates me.

Lee and the kids came to visit an hour ago. It's exhausting trying to be mommy and patient at the same time. Wesley is very worried about me being here in a strange place and being lonely without him so he brought me his monkey stuffed animal. He said that now I wouldn't be alone, especially at night. He's so precious and made me realize how thankful I am to have him, Spencer, and Cassie. He reminded me why I'm fighting so hard for their brother. Children are life's most wonderful and marvelous joys!

Sunday, February 3, 2008 9:23 AM
23 Weeks 0 Days

I'm not doing well. I'm exhausted and starting to feel sorry for myself, so I've been trying to focus on any positives. Fletcher is doing great. He's measuring a few days ahead and weighs 1 pound, 4 ounces. My hemoglobin levels have increased from 9.4 to 10.4, too. I haven't had any contractions at all and NST results are normal.

My OB came to see me this morning. He told me he isn't as worried about the placenta invading my bladder as the perinatologists. That gave me comfort because my perinatologists believe my placenta can start growing into my bladder at any moment. My OB reminded me that at my very first ultrasound, he thought that percreta would be an issue during the pregnancy. He said he'd come up with a game plan and deal with it when it's time to deliver the baby. He didn't think the MRI would be necessary but since the perinatologists insist I have it done, he told me to do it.

He said that if I make it to next weekend, I'd receive the first round of steroids. If I make it to 28 weeks, I'll have a second round. I just want to make it to 30 weeks and my OB told me to take it one day at a time.

My OB wants me to stay in bed as much as possible, so I am no longer allowed to walk to the bathroom. I now have a commode next to my bed. It's hard enough to get out of the bed with my IV lines, the IV poll, my hospital gown, and my lack of balance from being on bed rest, so although I think the commode is gross, it's a lot easier than having to walk in to the bathroom.

Monday, February 4, 2008 11:09 AM
23 Weeks 1 Day

Lee decided to spend the morning with me. A few minutes ago a hospital physical therapist came in to tell me how important it is to exercise while on bed rest in order to avoid blood clots, as well as to maintain muscle strength and tone. She handed me a guide showing women doing leg extensions, ankle twists, and arm stretches. I was very polite to her, even though I could see Lee in the corner of my eye holding back his laughter. The exercises she was telling me to do were absurd. They were more like muscle stretches – the kind you do in bed when you first wake up in the morning. When she left the room, Lee and I had a good laugh. I know her job was to teach me how to loosen my muscles, but she successfully relieved a lot of tension in just those few moments! For that reason, I feel she did her job well.

Monday, February 4, 2008 3:00 PM
23 Weeks 1 Day

The ultrasound this afternoon showed that my fluid level decreased. There were only three small pockets of amniotic fluid rather than it filling the entire sac. The largest one was in front of the baby's face and measured 3.94 centimeters. The other two pockets were by his foot and near his back, both measuring 1.9 centimeters. So although my AFI was about seven centimeters, the number is misleading because it was a total of three small pockets rather than one large area. The perinatologist said he was glad to see the pocket of fluid by the baby's mouth. The fetus needs to continually breathe in amniotic fluid in order for the lungs to develop normally. I told him that I saw urine in the baby's bladder so I thought that meant he was sucking and swallowing, which meant he was also breathing in fluid. The perinatologist said we were talking about two different things. He agreed that seeing fluid in his bladder was a good sign but only because it showed the baby was swallowing and that his kidneys were functioning properly, but that it had nothing to do with his lungs and their development.

The baby was breech, which made me feel better. I think with my low lying placenta and all my bleeding, that it's better for him to be as far away from that area as possible. There's no medical reason to think that way, but it does bring me comfort.

The perinatologist put in orders for me to have an ultrasound every other day. He wants to do a biophysical profile (BPP) test each time. The BPP measures the health of the baby by assigning points of either zero or two to the baby's muscle tone, movement, breathing, and the amniotic fluid, and sometimes the results of the NST, resulting in a maximum score of 10.

I really don't want to go up to the perinatologist so often, for a lot of reasons. The main one is that I have to get in a wheelchair and use the public elevator. I'm on the third floor and the perinatologist office is on the 18th floor. I sit in the wheelchair with the IV bag hanging on the back, wearing my see-through gown, getting stared by the people coming on and getting off the elevator. The stares don't bother me as much as me hating to be in this situation. Then, once I get to the office, the nurse wheels me directly to a back, narrow hallway where other patients have to squeeze past me. I'm their worst pregnancy nightmare, and living my own. If I have to be in the hospital, I want to remain secluded in my hospital room.

Tuesday, February 5, 2008 7:27 AM
23 Weeks 2 Days

My typical day here goes something like this:

4:00 AM – blood draw (every third day); blood pressure and temperature check; terbutaline pill

7:30 AM – each nurse shift is 12 hours, with the shift changes at 7:00 AM and 7:00 PM. The day nurse usually checks in around this time. I'm given my iron pill and stool softener. I always ask if the blood work is back. Some nurses tell me the number right away and others make me wait until my OB comes to tell me.

8:00 AM – blood pressure and temperature check, terbutaline pill

8:15 AM – housekeeping comes to mop the floor and take dirty linens.

8:30 AM – breakfast (and after about an hour they come to get the tray)

9:00 AM – someone from the cafeteria comes to get my menu for the next day's meals.

9:15 AM – NST for 30 minutes

10:00 AM – iron pill

Mid-morning –I usually see the perinatologist around this time.

11:00 AM – the nurse technician comes in to change my sheets.

11:30 AM – lunch

12:00 PM – blood pressure and temperature check; terbutaline pill

On Tuesdays at 2:00 PM – cafeteria employee brings around a dessert cart full of cake and fruit. Otherwise, I call the nurse to bring in my boost and other snacks and sandwiches Lee has kept in the fridge for me.

4:00 PM – blood pressure and temperature check; terbutaline pill. Every three days the IV line is changed out.

5:15 PM – dinner

8:00 PM – an hour after nurse shift change. The new nurse checks in and nurse usually will close my blinds; blood pressure and temperature check; terbutaline pill

10:00 PM –nurse checks in on me and offers me a sleeping pill, which I usually decline.

12:00 AM - blood pressure and temperature check; terbutaline pill. I usually get my longest stretch of uninterrupted time between midnight and 4:00 AM.

The day nurse usually gives me a sponge bath. I hope I can take a shower soon.

Either my OB or his partner comes in to check on me once per day. There's no set time, so it could be anytime – day or night.

When I'm given an IV of fluids, the bag needs to be changed every few hours around the clock. It's hooked up to an alarm and once it goes off, I call the nurse to come. Sometimes I'm lucky and it corresponds to a time the nurse is already scheduled to come in, but most of the time I have to call her in.

My OB has ordered Lee to come one afternoon a few days a week to take me outside. There's a patio area on the other side of the floor and Lee wheels me outside. Both Lee and my OB think the sun will be good for me. Aside from getting Vitamin D, they think that feeling the warmth of the sun will help improve my outlook, but I hate going outside. I don't enjoy being wheeled on to a slab of concrete that overlooks the hospital parking lot and the main street below. I hate seeing people and watching life go on around me. It's easier to be stuck in my hospital room, away from life going on around me. I don't need to go outside and be reminded of it.

My commode is supposed to be changed at least twice a shift, but usually I need to call someone to come in to change it. It's so gross. I compromised with my OB that I can walk to the actual toilet for bowel movements. This way I feel like I have a touch of dignity left.

I'm exhausted just thinking about my daily routine!

Tuesday, February 5, 2008 4:43 PM
23 Weeks 2 Days

The morning nurse said she scheduled my first round of steroids shots for Friday and Sunday. It's funny to hear that I have something scheduled on a weekend because in 'real life' it's nearly impossible to have medical procedures done on a Saturday or Sunday.

I've been so depressed and completely stressed. I only sleep a few hours a night and don't do much but watch TV. The nurses have tried to get me to read, do crossword puzzles, or teach me how to knit, but I have no patience or motivation to do anything. I promised the nurses I would change my attitude, but it's so hard when all I keep thinking is that any minute I could hemorrhage or the baby could stop breathing, or that I could continue with this pregnancy a few more months only to have the baby be stillborn. On my good days, I tell myself that the baby and I have already beaten so many odds and that we'll both continue to do so. On my bad days, I question why I'm living in the hospital, away from my family, when there's a good chance I'll lose the baby. It's a daily battle.

Tuesday, February 5, 2008 7:51 PM
23 Weeks 2 Days

The night nurse came in and removed my IV. My OB said to stop giving me IV fluids because the extra fluid is diluting my blood and drastically lowering my iron levels. I'm scared to stop the IV fluids. I don't want to become dehydrated, which could cause contractions. The nurse set up a system for me to follow to make sure that doesn't happen. She brought me two large pitchers covered with white paper, and a thick black marker. I have to write down the times that I finish each of them, which should take less than three hours per pitcher. She told me to drink at least five pitchers in twelve hours.

Wednesday, February 6, 2008 10:11 AM
23 Weeks 3 Days

The hospital prints out every doctor order, test result, and medication given, and puts it in a patient's chart. My file is already quite thick. The only times I see the chart is when I'm going to my perinatologist office. The nurse usually has me hold it on my lap while she pushes the wheelchair. This morning I went to open it to see the morning's blood results and the nurse snatched the file from me! She said it's a state law that a patient is not allowed to look through his or her own medical files and I could be arrested! She said that the law is in place to protect the patient because a patient wouldn't know how to interpret the results and could misread the information. Only medical staff is allowed to look in any patient file. To me, this is not only absurd, but also completely unacceptable! All the information is about me and I should have the right to read through it, but right now there's nothing I can do about. At least I'm educated enough to know what questions to ask and get the nurses to look up the answers for me, but I am so annoyed that I can't look for them myself.

I made the nurse look up my blood test results before continuing on to my appointment. She told me that my white blood count (WBC) increased from 10,000 (normal) to 12,000 (a little elevated). Anything over 10,000 is considered high and could signal an infection, but she said that no one was worried about it. She explained that it's normal for the count to fluctuate, which is why they take my temperature every four hours and repeat the WBC test every few days. They look for a trend over a few days. I think I'm supposed to have another blood test tomorrow.

Wednesday, February 6, 2008 1:09 PM
23 Weeks 3 Days

I had a bad ultrasound this morning. My amniotic fluid has decreased another two centimeters so my perinatologist put in orders for me to go back on IV fluids to see if that would help increase the fluid. I'm still on the IV antibiotics so it's easy to re-attach the saline bag, but now I'm concerned about my iron levels and what my OB thinks. At least I don't have to worry about drinking all that water, which has been harder to do than I thought.

The nurse did another blood draw this morning and thankfully my white blood count fell to 6,000. What the nurse said yesterday was exactly right and I'm no longer going to be upset over one number.

I've been having very bad heart palpitations, dizzy spells, and hot flashes for a while now. Lately, these bouts have been getting worse and more frequent. I complained to the nurse today and she decided to do a blood glucose test since gestational diabetes can have similar symptoms, but the test came back normal. She has been my nurse a few times, including when I was admitted in January, and is very familiar with my situation and pains. After reviewing my chart she said that, in her opinion, the likely culprit is the terbutaline. My attacks seem to peak two hours after I take the pill, and subside a few minutes before my next dose. I have to take these pills every four hours so there is a very small window when I have no symptoms. I guess it's just something I have to learn to live with for the next few months.

Another frustrating hospital rule deals with outside medication. Right before I was admitted to the hospital, I filled a prescription for 100 terbutaline pills. I asked the nurse if I could use them since I won't need them after this pregnancy. She told me it's illegal to bring in outside medication to the hospital, even if the nurse dispenses them. It's so frustrating because each hospital terbutaline pill costs much more than I paid for the entire prescription. It's such a waste of medicine and money. I'm so sick and tired of these stupid hospital policies!

Wednesday, February 6, 2008 11:43 PM
23 Weeks 3 Days

The morning nurse told me that a medical technician would be taking me for my MRI sometime this afternoon, but he didn't come get me until 9:00 PM. Apparently, there was a bad accident and a few emergency MRIs needed to be done. It's not as if I had anything else to do, but I was anxious all day thinking about the test and as the day dragged on, the more nervous I became.

The MRI machine is in the basement of the hospital's other wing. I was placed on a gurney and wheeled all over the place. I was twisted and turned around corners, through hallways, and in and out of three different elevators. I felt like I was in a maze. Twenty minutes later we got down to the MRI waiting area. The medical technician left me alone in the cold, dark waiting area for another 30 minutes. It was pretty creepy and I was thankful when the MRI technologist finally came to take me to the MRI room.

He put me in a wheelchair and took me to the machine. The room was huge and had a lot of different television sets and desks. There was a glass wall with a door, and once the technician helped me up to the MRI bed, he went into the other room. All I could see were a lot of lights blinking. The technician switched on the machine and the bed started moving. Even though I'm not claustrophobic, I was very glad that he stopped before my head was inside the tube. I kept my eyes closed the entire time, but wished I could have put my hands over my ears. The machine was unbelievably loud. It sounded like a dryer filled with boots; there was loud banging almost the entire time.

I'd expected the test to take a few minutes, but the test took over an hour! The technician said it took so long because the perinatologist ordered over 100 different pictures; the most he's ever seen ordered for a pregnancy MRI.

I was brought back to my room at 11:30 PM. I had the same night nurse as last night. She's been an antepartum nurse for over 20 years. Even though I just had my IV line changed yesterday, it was put in too close to the inside of my elbow and every time I bend my arm, it causes me throbbing pain. This nurse offered to change it for me and I am so glad I let her. The IV line went in smoothly and it no longer hurts to move my arm. I hope she'll be on duty the next time it needs to be changed.

Thursday, February 7, 2008 9:22 AM
23 Weeks 4 Days

I'm throwing myself a pity party. I wanted another child and now my entire family is suffering. My selfishness has completely disrupted my husband and children's lives. It's very hard on all of them not to have me at home. Lee told me he was up all night with Cassie because she has a high fever. He got her in to see the pediatrician and she has an ear infection, which is completely my fault. I blame myself because the boys never got ear infections because they were home with me. I feel like the only reason Cassie has an ear infection is because she's in daycare and the only reason she's in daycare is because of me.

I wish Lee's parents or my mom would come down and give him a break, but my mother-in-law told Lee it would be awhile before she's well enough to help out again. The last time she was here she was completely worn out and overwhelmed. When she got back home, she ended up getting bronchitis. My mom wants to come back but works full-time and is having a hard time getting time off and finding reasonably priced airfare. I'm so disappointed in everyone. My in-laws are able to drive here and my mother-in-law doesn't work. I understand that my father-in-law has his business to run, and my mom has to get her employer's permission to take vacation time, and my mother-in-law wants to regain her strength, but all those excuses seem to pale in comparison to what I'm going through. It doesn't matter what I think because there's nothing I can do about any of it.

Friday, February 8, 2008 1:54 PM
23 Weeks 5 Days

Last night, I was in excruciating pain and had major bleeding. I wasn't sure I would make it, physically or emotionally, but I did, and today's another day. I'm still alive and so is the baby. I really want to make it another 30 days, which doesn't seem like a long time, but when I have episodes like last night it seems like forever. Lee's been so supportive and told me that if I am unable to continue with the pregnancy, then I shouldn't. I keep telling myself that as long as Fletcher is fighting, then I need to fight, too.

I'm going to try to take a nap today since I only slept for about an hour last night. At least the IV antibiotics will be finished this morning. Now the nurse will only have to come in every four hours to give me my terbutaline pill rather than every two hours to change out the antibiotics bag.

The MRI results came back this morning. I officially have placenta percreta, but as of right now the placenta is near my bladder and hasn't invaded it yet. However, the odds of the placenta growing through my bladder increase as the pregnancy continues. The technician also wrote that I have Oligohydramnios, which is the medical term for having low amniotic fluid.

I had my first steroid shot of betamethasone this morning. This shot is given in two doses, 24-48 hours apart. If I make it another four weeks, I'll probably have another round. Supposedly after 32 weeks, they are no longer helpful. The shot was given through the muscle in my upper leg and it really hurt. I could literally feel the liquid going through my leg and within seconds my entire body started to sting. I felt dizzy and flushed for quite a while afterwards. I know it's a small price to pay, but I am not looking forward to the second injection on Sunday.

Friday, February 8, 2008 7:17 PM
23 Weeks 5 Days

Tonight when the cafeteria brought my dinner, the nurse came in and asked if I was given the special menu. I had no idea what she was talking about, so she explained that the cafeteria allows long-term patients to order from the daily specials menu. Since I don't eat meat, I've been rotating among macaroni-n-cheese, cottage cheese, pizza, and breakfast-for-dinner foods. Lee's been bringing me nutritional shakes and specialty sandwiches to break up the boredom. I can't believe this is the first I'm hearing about the special menu, but I am excited about it! I know Lee will be too, because he can stop running food to me during the week. Since the main cafeteria is closed on the weekends, the nurse said I could start ordering from this menu on Monday.

Saturday, February 9, 2008 10:28 PM
23 Weeks 6 Days

What's the saying about taxes? I'm in the hospital fighting one of those certainties (death), but there's no way around the other one. I know the government doesn't accept any excuses, so Lee brought me our tax documents and I spent most of the day doing our taxes and filing them online. I'm glad they're finished because I don't know one day from the next what's going to happen, and the taxes are now one less thing to have to worry about.

I also asked Lee to bring me my pedicure box, which is filled with everything I need to give myself a pedicure. I try to give myself a pedicure once a month because that's my one girly guilty pleasure. Needless to say, right now my feet are a mess. As soon as I finished our taxes, I did my toenails and it perked me right up! My toes look great. My OB and nurses all commented on my bright red toes throughout the day, too! It's amazing how little things can really change my outlook.

I'd forgotten about the travel sewing kit in my pedicure box. I did the needle trick for the last time. Again, it predicted a fourth, male child. I decided to finally retire the needle and thread.

Sunday, February 10, 2008 1:56 PM
24 Weeks 0 Days

I had an extremely rough weekend and came close to calling my OB and asking him to deliver the baby. Along with massive bleeding, I was in so much pain. Thankfully, two doses of pain medication helped.

My OB made his rounds this morning and put things in perspective for me. He explained that he doesn't want to deliver the baby right now because if the baby were to be born, he would most likely not survive and if he did survive, he would have major health issues and struggles, including brain injuries, hemorrhaging and heart and lung troubles. He said that while I'm here, when the baby starts showing signs of fetal distress, or if I get an infection or start to hemorrhage, then he would deliver the baby immediately. Obviously, there is a real risk of losing the baby in utero, but we're hoping that we'll know he's in distress and deliver him before that would happen. He did say though, that it would be better for the baby to pass inside me than to have to deliver the baby at 24 weeks. It was a morbid conversation, but I appreciate his honesty.

He said he would let the nurses know that I can have pain medicine up to every four hours, as needed. He wants me to keep the baby inside awhile longer, but also wants me to be as comfortable as possible. I'm glad he reminded me that I'm enduring this for the sake of the baby and that I need to sacrifice my comfort for a little while longer.

I had the second steroid shot this morning. This one hurt even more than the first, probably because I knew what to expect this time.

Monday, February 11, 2008 9:13 AM
24 Weeks 1 Day

I've been off the IV fluids since Friday and have been diligent about drinking water. Since I no longer need IV antibiotics or fluid, I begged my OB to take out the IV needle for a few days. Having a needle stuck in my arm full-time is so uncomfortable. The nurse told me she wants to keep it in place in case I needed to be rushed into surgery. It's faster for the medical team and safer for me to already have the IV needle in place. I understand what she's saying, but I've had enough IV lines

changed to know that it takes less than a few seconds to put it in. I saw
that the nurse wasn't going to budge, so I waited for my OB to make
rounds and pleaded with him. I'm beyond grateful that he agreed to take
it out for a few days.

My insurance company has given my case to a third party mediator. This
group talks to a nurse every week to find out what tests have been done,
which doctors I have seen, and what progress I've been making. Part of
their investigation includes speaking with me to corroborate what the
nurses said. Every Monday morning an employee from the mediator's
office calls and questions me. I guess there's a lot of medical fraud, but I
dislike having to talk to this agent, who at any time could tell the
insurance company to stop paying for any claims she deems
unnecessary. It seems odd to me, but I'm relying on my insurance to pay
a large portion of my medical claims and help me negotiate my financial
responsibility, so I will continue to keep them informed.

Monday, February 11, 2008 3:57 PM
24 Weeks 1 Day

I had my ultrasound this morning and the technician couldn't find
any measurable fluid. She called in the perinatologist to look at the
screen, and suddenly Fletcher moved and a small pocket of fluid
appeared. Although we were all glad to see the little fluid, I feel like
we're deluding ourselves and there's still no telling what's going to
happen with the baby. At least right now the baby is not in distress
so I have to focus on that, which is what the perinatologist advised
me to do.

I asked the perinatologist about doing an amnioinfusion on me. I read
about it on the computer this morning. The procedure involves having
saline injected into the uterus to replace amniotic fluid. It's typically
used in a full-term delivery after the woman's water breaks. It's
controversial because the outside fluid greatly increases the risk of
infection and the possibility of causing a uterine rupture, especially in
mothers who have had previous C-sections. My perinatologist said the
amnioinfusion is not an option for me for a few different reasons. I've
had three C-sections so there's a huge danger of causing a rupture and
that the added fluid only last a few hours. He also said that I have no
problem making fluid; the issue is keeping it in my uterus.

Monday, February 11, 2008 7:58 PM
24 Weeks 1 Days

I can't believe it, but I just called my OB and asked him to hook me back up to the IV fluids for the next few days. I've been drinking over four pitchers of water a day, but don't feel like it's making much of a difference. Last week, my AFI crept up while on the IV and fell when it was stopped, so I just want to see if it makes a difference at Thursday's ultrasound. My OB said he would put me back on the IV for two days even though he doesn't believe there's a correlation between the IV fluids and amniotic fluid. I really hope this proves him wrong.

Tuesday, February 12, 2008 8:59 AM
24 Weeks 2 Days

My OB came in this morning and sat and talked with me for 20 minutes. He said since the umbilical cord blood flow to the baby looks good, he's hesitant to blame the placenta for the lack of fluid and is convinced I have pPROM, preterm premature rupture of membranes. At first he and my perinatologist weren't convinced I had ruptured, but now they are certain. They know I'm making amniotic fluid (from seeing fluid in baby's bladder, watching him swallow, and all the pads I am growing through every day), but because there is no fluid in the uterus, there is a rupture. So now I have another official diagnosis.

Tuesday, February 12, 2008 7:15 PM
24 Weeks 2 Days

I know that there's very little that can be done to lighten my mood, but I had hoped the specialty menu from the cafeteria would help lift my spirits. I obviously had too high expectations and lost sight of the fact that this was still a hospital cafeteria. The food is nothing out of the ordinary. It's nice to have a soup option and add fried shrimp once a week, but I'm still going to have Lee bring me outside food whenever he's able.

Wednesday, February 13, 2008 9:15 PM
24 Weeks 3 Days

I had another horrible night of bleeding and passing clots that continued throughout the day. My OB and perinatologists were concerned and decided to order my first blood transfusion. My hemoglobin level was only a little low, but my OB wants to start building up my blood reserves for my C-section and hysterectomy, and the perinatologists want to replenish all the blood I've been losing.

I didn't know what to expect, but the blood transfusion was very anticlimactic. The nurse came in with a bag that looked just like the IV fluid bag, but was reddish rather than clear. She hooked it up through my existing IV and opened the valve on the tube, and the blood started to flow. The nurse stayed in my room for the first 15 minutes of the transfusion. At first I thought she stayed to help calm my nerves, but she explained that sometimes patients have bad reactions to the blood so she needed to monitor me. The entire transfusion took about an hour. I swear I already feel a little better; more energetic and alert. I'm definitely less pale.

Thursday, February 14, 2008 1:32 PM
24 Weeks 4 Days

One of my favorite day nurses came in this morning and asked if I've showered since being admitted. I told her that I'm still not allowed to shower and am grateful for the sponge baths and complained how my hair was a complete mess. She told me she'd be right back and came in with a wheelchair. I climbed in and she wheeled me into a janitor's closet that had a large utility sink. She told me she was going to wash my hair! She positioned the chair up against the sink and gave me the best shampoo and conditioning treatment I've ever had! What an amazing woman. I'm so thankful for her.

Thursday, February 14, 2008 9:16 PM
24 Weeks 4 Days

Today I had another bad day of gushing blood, which probably negated any benefits I received from the blood transfusion. Along with the bleeding, I had excruciating pain that got so bad I doubled-over in my bed and could barely breathe. I was able to call for the nurse and by the time she came in, I was hyperventilating and about to pass out. The nurse quickly brought me a hydrocodone pain pill and within 10 minutes I was pain free. I wonder what's going on inside of me. I hope it's not my placenta invading my bladder, or my uterus starting to rupture. I have to think that because the pain pill worked so quickly, that it's nothing as dire as that.

I had almost forgotten that it's Valentine's Day! Next year's holiday won't be nearly exciting, but should be much better!

Friday, February 15, 2008 2:03 PM
24 Weeks 5 Days

The ultrasound today showed no amniotic fluid at all, but Fletcher is still hanging in there. The perinatologist and the ultrasound technician were extremely negative about today's appointment. They told me I should get prepared to deliver the baby in the next few weeks, even though Fletcher didn't seem to be in distress. They said it looked like the placenta was attached to my bladder and they didn't want it to start growing into it. As soon as I got back to my room, I called my OB to hear his thoughts. He was very upset about the comments made by the perinatologist and his staff. He told me the only thing I should focus on when I go to the ultrasounds at my perinatologist is to make sure the baby isn't in distress. My OB said he, Lee, and I have the final say in any decisions about this pregnancy. Once again, my OB came through for me.

Even after yesterday's blood loss, my hemoglobin level rose this morning to 11.2. The nurse still went ahead with my scheduled second blood transfusion because they want to continue to build up my reserves. When the transfusion was finished, the nurse did a double take and told me how much better I looked; that my cheeks actually looked rosy. I've had no bleeding at all for over three hours and hope to have a break for at least a few more hours, or maybe even a few days, and allow this transfusion to really make an impact. My body could really use a break.

Friday, February 15, 2008 5:35 PM
24 Weeks 5 Days

I dread the weekends. I know Lee and the kids are going out together and I'm here alone. I also know that whatever they have planned, Lee has to go out of his way to make a special trip to come see me. The kids don't want to stay for more than a few minutes because Lee usually has something fun planned for them, and having to come to the hospital just delays it. It's also a scary place for them. I'm stuck in bed wearing a gown and don't look very good.

I usually don't get any phone calls or emails because all my friends are out with their families. There's nothing to watch on television either, so I usually surf the Internet or watch news programs.

If I can make it another nine days I'll be 26 weeks along. Nine days seem both so close, and an eternity away, but survival rates dramatically increase between a 24 and 26 week-old preemies. Of course, I need to go further than that, but my OB wants me to set small goals.

Saturday, February 16, 2008 11:09 PM
24 Weeks 6 Days

I've had a great day! The transfusion went well yesterday and now my iron levels are staying over 11. Even my blood pressure has increased and is now within the normal range, rather than being so low. My OB also switched my anti-contraction medication from terbutaline to nifedipine because the terbutaline started to affect the baby's heart rate. I've been complaining about the terbutaline side effects for weeks, but it wasn't until the baby started becoming negatively affected that they switched it. Another example of who is calling the shots! Nifedipine is a medication primarily used to treat angina and high blood pressure, but has been clinically proven to relax the uterus, preventing contractions. There are far less side effects than the terbutaline and I only have to take it every six hours, rather than every four. The main side effect though, is that it lowers blood pressure. Since my blood pressure has been low, I'll be even more closely monitored.

Lee's been taking me outside during the week while the kids are in school, but today he decided to have us all go outside together.

The kids loved the patio and having me outside watching them. It was the first time I enjoyed sitting outside!

Saturday, February 16, 2008 11:50 PM
24 Weeks 6 Days

The pain returned in full force today. It seems to come out of nowhere and feels like someone is stabbing and slicing me from the inside and tearing me apart. The nurse wanted to see if acetaminophen would bring me relief, but I ended up having to take hydrocodone. Thankfully it worked fast and I was even able to take a three-hour nap.

Sunday, February 17, 2008 8:24 PM
25 Weeks 0 Days

I had another long day of bleeding and gushing fluid. At 2:45 PM, I had another round of sharp, intense pain. I was given the pain medicine but this time it took over 20 minutes to stop the pain. At 6:30 PM, I had major heart palpitations and started having trouble breathing. By the time the nurse came in my heart rate was back to normal and I could breathe just fine. The nurse wanted to check and make sure the baby was fine. It took her over 15 minutes to find the baby's heartbeat but thankfully she did. I feel like these episodes are becoming more frequent and intense and that scares me.

Monday, February 18, 2008 9:25 AM
25 Weeks 1 Day

I had to call the insurance mediator this morning. The company sent a nasty letter to my house and Lee brought it to me over the weekend. They wanted doctors' notes, nurses' notes and lists of medicines I'm taking, as well as other items. The woman who wrote the letter was away from her desk, so I was put through to the mediator's assistant. She was extremely apologetic and said this is a new mediator and she inherited my case, and went after me without reading through her predecessor's notes. She told me to disregard the letter and that she would have her new boss call me personally to apologize. I hope I didn't get anyone in trouble, but am glad I called and said that I didn't appreciate receiving such an aggressive, bullying letter.

Tuesday, February 19, 2008 11:27 AM
25 Weeks 2 Days

The AFI today was 1.7 centimeters. I know my OB said to only be concerned with how Fletcher's doing, but I still want to know the AFI. When I went back to my room I asked the nurse to tilt my bed to see if it would help keep in my fluid. I'm desperate.

I'm getting irritated by people telling me "whatever is going to happen is going to happen" whether I'm anxious and nervous, or whether I can relax and be positive. It's easy for them to say since they aren't the ones going through this, or putting a burden on their family.

Tuesday, February 19, 2008 11:45 PM
25 Weeks 2 Days

I needed two pain pills to alleviate my pain this afternoon. When my OB did his rounds today, I asked him to give me one good reason why I shouldn't insist on having the C-section right now. He was very calm, patient, and understanding and told me that I was doing great. He reminded me that I'm in the safest place for Fletcher and me, and until the baby starts showing signs of distress there's no reason to deliver him. He said he wrote in my chart that whenever the pain is too intense, the nurses could give me up to two doses of pain medication at a time.

I asked him where he thought the pain was coming from. He hypothesized that the severe pain is from the baby, who is sitting very low in my uterus, kicking my placenta, which then bumps into my internal organs. That makes sense because the last two times the nurse came to check the baby's heart beat, it took her almost fifteen minutes to find it. She finally found the heartbeat extremely low, right near my pubic bone. Being able to visualize what's going on inside me should help me tolerate the pain a little better.

Wednesday, February 20, 2008 9:29 PM
25 Weeks 3 Days

Tonight I learned not to call for a nurse during shift change. Although the new shift is supposed to start at 7:00 PM, I don't think they plan on dealing with patients until well after that time. I had to call the nurse because I had another huge bleeding episode and needed help, but it was 6:59 PM. The nurses were not happy! Both the day and night nurse barged in to my room and yelled at me to put on one of the pads next to the bed. I told them I was wearing two pads and they aren't enough to contain the blood. They finally looked at the bed and saw what was happening. They immediately became more sympathetic and helped me get cleaned up. The night nurse sat with me until I re-stabilized. Now I'll be paranoid and hope I don't get a pain attack or another bleeding episode during shift change.

Thursday, February 21, 2008 8:55 PM
25 Weeks 4 Days

Lee has been bringing the kids to visit every four days. It's nice to see them, but so sad and depressing when they leave. Lee has been totally amazing. He takes phenomenal care of our children, and the house, all while working full time. He also finds time to visit me by himself every few days. I'm in awe of him and so thankful. My mother-in-law is finally coming back tomorrow for a week. Then my father-in-law and my mom will come to town on Friday for the weekend to celebrate Spencer's fifth birthday. I'm thrilled that Lee will have help and maybe he'll be able to take some time for himself.

Friday, February 22, 2008 4:56 AM
25 Weeks 5 Days

I passed huge clots all night. This time there were crazy looking things mixed in and I somehow convinced myself it was part of the baby's brain. I'm really starting to lose it. The night nurse assigned to me was completely useless. When I called her in to help, she brought me some pads, said there was nothing she could do for me, and turned to walk out of the room. I told her that most nurses check on the baby's heartbeat after these types of episodes, but she said she didn't know where the machine was and walked out. I ended up calling the head nurse. She apologized and explained that this nurse was actually a postpartum nurse so she didn't know how to deal with my issues. She said she would be my attending nurse for the night. She also explained that the odd looking things were just old clots. She got the machine and checked the baby's heartbeat, which was perfect, and then cleaned me up. These episodes continued for the entire night and I am exhausted.

Friday, February 22, 2008 6:17 PM
25 Weeks 5 Days

The growth ultrasound this morning was good, except there was no fluid at all. The good news is the baby was moving and had a full bladder, which means amniotic fluid is being made and stays by his mouth long enough for him to drink it. The ultrasound technician and the perinatologist were shocked to see how well Fletcher is growing. He's in the 53 percentile for weight at 1 pound, 14 ounces. The technician couldn't take any other measurements because without fluid, there's very little contrast in Fletcher's body parts, preventing accurate measurements.

My OB had another antepartum patient with low fluid and who was as far along as me. She ended up going into labor on Wednesday and her baby is doing pretty well. Now my OB is getting worried about me because he had been comparing our pregnancies for the last few weeks. He called the neonatal intensive care unit (NICU) to have one of the NICU doctors, the neonatologist, come speak with me. It was not a pleasant conversation. She explained to me that preemies are highly susceptible to brain hemorrhages and lung problems and that there's nothing the medical community can do about it. In babies born under 30 weeks, the risk of bleeding in the brain is very high. Even with today's advanced technology, there isn't any way to prevent or treat them. The same is true with preemies lungs. If the baby is born with unstructured, undeveloped lungs, there's no real treatment. The doctors can only give steroids and hope the baby's lungs grow on their own, but there are other parts of the lungs, such as alveoli, that they don't have any medication to assist in making work properly. Lung transplants on preemies are very rare and even if the transplant works, most develop complications after surgery and do not survive. Because my baby has had no fluid for so many weeks, the neonatologist said that there is a high likelihood that my baby's lungs will be 'incompatible with life'.

She explained that many preemies have a condition called Bronchopulmonary Dysplasia (BPD), also known as chronic lung disease. It involves abnormal development, inflammation and scarring of the lungs. She said some preemies outgrow it, some have long-term health problems and, in some cases, some die from it.

The fact that my baby will be premature and has been without amniotic fluid for so long at a critical point in his fetal development, there is a high chance of he will have BPD, but there's no way to know how he'll be affected by it until he is born. The coupling of BPD with hypoplastic lungs makes for a dire outcome. She said there was no way to know anything until the baby is born, but the longer the baby is inside me, the best chance the baby has.

What a brutally honest discussion.

Saturday, February 23, 2008 2:18 PM
25 Weeks 6 Days

I'm finally allowed to take a shower! My OB said I could have one per week. I can't believe how excited I am! I called Lee last night and asked him to bring my shampoo, conditioner, and body wash in the morning. He said he and the kids would be here early, but the clock on the wall showed 10:30 AM, and he still hadn't come. I was getting annoyed and was about to call him when they finally came. The clock read 10:50 AM. I asked him why he got here so much later than expected, especially because he knew I was waiting to take my first shower in over three weeks. He asked me how much earlier I wanted him to come since it was only 8:15 AM and he was pretty proud of himself for getting the kids up and out of the house so early. I pointed to the clock and told him it's actually 11:00 AM. He said that the clock was wrong, but I told him there was no way it was wrong because the clock is centrally hard-wired throughout the hospital. He ended up handing me his cell phone and, I couldn't believe it! He was right that it was only 8:15 AM. The nurse came in and told me that the hospital clocks go haywire every so often. I was so upset to realize how out of touch and completely dependent I am on the things within the walls of my hospital room. As someone who needs to be in control of her surroundings, this seemingly innocuous episode was devastating to me.

As soon as Lee and the kids left, I called the nurse in to help me get ready for my shower. The nurse wrapped up my IV line, put in the shower chair, padded it with towels, and put the emergency button within reach. It was ironic that I needed the shower chair, which I wouldn't let Lee buy me when I was first put on bed rest. I turned on the shower and let the water fall all over me. There wasn't much pressure, but I didn't care. It was hot and I was getting clean. I used my shampoo and it was the first time in awhile that I smelled like 'me'. I took a long shower, but got out sooner than I wanted to because I thought the nurse would get nervous and come check in on me. I got dressed and went back to bed feeling, and smelling, much better than I had in weeks.

Sunday, February 24, 2008 10:37 PM
26 Weeks 0 Days

It was a long weekend as usual, with more of the same old same old. Unbelievably, my hemoglobin is 11.7! My OB said he thinks it's so good because the IV fluid has been stopped and now my blood is more concentrated. I guess that makes sense. My WBC rose to 11,500, but again, no one is concerned.

The baby had two heart rate decelerations on today's NST. All the previous NSTs have been perfect so now I'm even more worried about my sweet baby boy. I hope this doesn't mean he's in distress. I'm actually looking forward to my ultrasound tomorrow morning.

Monday, February 25, 2008 11:11 PM
26 Weeks 1 Day

This morning's ultrasound showed that Fletcher was having premature ventricular contractions (PVCs), which is when the heart skips a beat and then resumes beating normally a few seconds later. The perinatologist did not think it was a big deal. He explained that PVCs are not unusual and most people have them at some point. However, when I got back to the room and the nurse performed the NST, it showed clusters of heartbeat decelerations. My OB's partner came to my room after seeing the results and put me back on the monitor while he observed. The baby's heartbeat sounded like, "thump......thump.......thump thump....thump......thump." It was very slow and irregular. My OB's partner stopped the test and immediately sent me to L&D. The head nurse thought there might be a cord compression issue and put me on oxygen and pumped me with IV fluids at a fast rate of a bag every fifteen minutes. After 45 minutes and three IV bags, the baby's heart rate was back to normal. The L&D nurse also thought the nifedipine medicine was beginning to affect the baby's heart rate, which she said was more superficial than it causing an actual heart defect. I know that one of the side effects I've been having is an irregular heartbeat, so it makes sense that the baby is also being affected. My OB's partner isn't sure if that's true, but says even if that is the case, the benefits of the nifedipine far outweigh the risks right now and he's not going to change the medication.

The L&D monitor also showed that I was having contractions every two minutes. After the IV fluid flush, they slowed to 10 minutes apart. Both L&D and my OB's partner feel that the contractions are still benign and due to an irritable uterus. At some point, however, these false contractions can cause real labor, so they still want to try to stop them.

I have to spend the night in L&D on oxygen and continuous IV fluid, at a slower rate, at least. I think I've gone to the bathroom six times an hour! Each time I have to walk to the bathroom since my commode is still in my antepartum room. I miss my other room. The L&D room has no windows, dim lighting, and the bed is hard and uncomfortable. I'm used to the other room. I hope there's something on television tonight because I doubt I'll get any sleep.

Tuesday, February 26, 2008, 10:26 PM
26 Weeks 2 Days

I'm still stuck in the L&D room. Lee brought me a computer and I've been researching BPD, hypoplastic lungs, pPROM, and oligohydramnios. It seems there's a very low survival rate for this baby. I wonder why no one here is telling me that. Why should I even stay here? Why shouldn't they just take the baby out right now? Of course I do know why. It's because nothing is certain until the baby is born. I have to fight and think positive, but it's becoming increasingly harder to do, especially now that I have names of diseases to research and actual numbers to analyze. I have to remember that every case is different and I'm here to give my son a chance at survival.

A nurse manager from the antepartum floor came to tell me that I no longer have to speak to the insurance mediators because they're getting all the information they need from the staff. I'm glad that I no longer have to be in the middle of the insurance issues. I have enough to deal with and am glad to get rid of that responsibility.

Wednesday, February 27, 2008 9:43 PM
26 Weeks 3 Days

I was brought back up to my antepartum room this morning. It's sad that this room feels like home now.

I'm still having contractions every 10 minutes and have started to lose my mucous plug, which could signal the start of labor. The ultrasound today showed that my placenta was touching my bladder. There's no way to know if it just resting on my bladder, or is starting to grow in to it. My perinatologist told me to look for any blood in urine. If there's any trace of blood, the baby will be delivered right away because that means that the placenta has invaded my bladder, which is very dangerous for me. The hospital urologists have been put on notice about my situation, along with the blood bank, all on-call OBs, and gynecology oncologists, who assist with hysterectomies.

Thursday, February 28, 2008 5:10 AM
26 Weeks 4 Days

My contractions have finally slowed and I've only had two since last night. When my OB came yesterday, he told me that sooner or later these contractions would result in actual labor because my body is starting to build up a tolerance to the anti-contraction medications. I feel like delivery is imminent, but would love to make it through the weekend, or next week, or another month! I just keep thinking that the next time I have contractions that I'll have to be rushed in to the emergency room and have this baby. I wonder if it'll be the next time, or time after that, when my contractions won't respond to the medications.

Thursday, February 28, 2008 11:00 PM
26 Weeks 4 Days

Today was my seventh wedding anniversary and Spencer's fifth birthday (he was the greatest anniversary present ever!). My in-laws are in town so tonight Lee brought in my favorite Chinese food for us to celebrate and have some time alone together. Unfortunately, my contractions started up again. They were less than two minutes apart and were very strong! I was taken to L&D and wasn't allowed to have any food or liquids just in case they'd have to perform the C-section tonight. I told Lee he didn't have to come, but he wanted to sit with me. At first, he didn't want to eat since I wasn't allowed to, but I insisted he should. He was able to enjoy the food and I was happy to have him here with me.

The L&D nurse came in and did the NST. She said the results looked like that of a 35 week fetus and everything with Fletcher looked perfect! I was given a terbutaline injection, another round of forced IV fluids, and another Rh immune globulin shot, and I also had blood work done. Four hours later I was stable again. As soon as Lee knew the baby wouldn't be delivered tonight, he went home and I was allowed back to the antepartum room. Lee had left me my Chinese food and I ended up eating my anniversary dinner alone.

Friday, February 29, 2008 3:35 PM
26 Weeks 5 Days

When my OB came down to do rounds, I asked him to deliver the baby today because it's leap year. I told him that if Fletcher didn't survive, I would only have to think about his birthday once every four years. My OB rolled his eyes and told me that was ridiculous. He told me to have a great weekend and he would come see me first thing Monday morning.

This is going to be an even harder weekend for me. My mom, her boyfriend, and Lee's parents are all in town for Spencer's birthday party.

I've never missed one of my children's birthdays. I'm glad Spencer has family surrounding him, and I know he's getting lots of love and attention, but I won't be with him. I think he'll be so busy that he won't miss me, but I will miss him.

My friends know how upset I am about not being at Spencer's party, and that being in the hospital so long has started to take its toll on me, so they've been sending me cards directly to my hospital room. A woman from the mailroom actually came and delivered a stack of mail to me!

My mom and her boyfriend came to see me straight from the airport and saw the pile of cards. She borrowed scotch tape from the nurse's station and hung up them on the wall in front of my bed. Looking at the wall decorated with all the encouraging, supportive, and loving cards made me smile, and I know they'll help me through this weekend and all my dark moments.

My mom didn't stay long because she was tired from the trip and wanted to get to the house to see the kids. I wasn't in the mood for company anyway so it was just as well.

Saturday, March 1, 2008 2:35 PM
26 Weeks 6 Days

I have been up on studies that have been done on women who have pPROM before 26 weeks and the outlook for the baby is very grim. Some of these women actually make it to 34 or 35 weeks but the baby doesn't make it because the lungs never develop. I'm feeling so distraught. I'm just not doing well.

Saturday, March 1, 2008 6:00 PM
26 Weeks 6 Days

Tonight is Spencer's birthday party at a local kid arcade. I think 22 people will be there to celebrate. I hope he'll have a blast. I know he doesn't like being the center of attention so I hope he doesn't get too overwhelmed. I wish I could be there with him. This is also the first time I haven't made his birthday cake. I hope he doesn't hate me. I hate me. I hate this for me. I hate this for him. I hate this.

But I know why I'm doing this and Spencer is surrounded by love, family, friends and fun. It'll be perfect for him. I need to try to focus on Spencer because all I keep thinking is that I'm here I am in a hospital room, in pain, and uncertain if all this sacrifice by all of us will result in a healthy baby capable of surviving outside the womb.

Saturday, March 1, 2008 9:54 PM
26 Weeks 6 Days

I've been watching the clock all night, visualizing Spencer's birthday party. I hope everyone showed up. I can see him playing his favorite racing games, being cheered on by his best pals and everyone giving him high-fives. I usually make a birthday cake but obviously this year I didn't. I hope he likes the cake he has. I wish I could've been there to sing to him, but I know he has plenty of voices singing loudly! I wonder what he wished for and if he was able to blow out all the candles. I can't wait to hear about all the presents he received.

As the night went on I was getting more and more anxious and wanted to hear from someone, anyone! Finally, at 9:00 PM, my mom called me and said that Spencer had a great time and he was beaming all night. As soon as we hung up, Lee called and reiterated what my mom told me. He put Spencer on the phone and he was so animated! He said that his party was fun and started telling me about the friends that came and all the different gifts he received. The party sounded like a complete success and Lee told me that everyone is now blissfully exhausted. I'm sad that I couldn't be there, but so happy that Spencer had a blast, which is the most important thing.

Sunday, March 2, 2008 2:22 PM
27 Weeks 0 Days

My mother-in-law was so thoughtful and ordered a second birthday cake for Spencer to bring up to the hospital. Although my in-laws had to leave early this morning, my mom, her boyfriend, Lee and the kids came to the hospital with candles and plates and I got to sing happy birthday to Spencer. It meant so much to me to be able to sing to my son, even if it was no longer his official birthday. Spencer told me he had the best birthday because he got to have two cakes!

Sunday, March 2, 2008 10:55 PM
27 Weeks 0 Days

Another frustrating thing about being in the hospital long-term is that there are so many different nurses working part-time that I rarely have the same nurse twice. At the beginning of every shift, the nurse comes in my room and asks routine questions. I always have to explain my situation in detail and watch their expression change from concern to disbelief, as if I'm exaggerating or being overly dramatic. I hate having to tell my story over and over again and wonder why the previous nurse doesn't leave detailed notes in my chart so I don't have to repeat it all every time I have a new nurse.

Tonight's nurse was extremely rude and condescending. Not only have I been here for over a month, but also I'm very well versed in my condition. After telling her about my MRI results, she left to read my chart and then came back and told me I was wrong. She said that the MRI showed that the placenta was just previa and that I was mistaken if I thought it was anything worse. I figured it wasn't worth fighting with her so I dropped it. When she came back to give me my medicine, she handed me two identical pills instead of just the one that I normally take. I asked her why I need double the dose I normally take and she told me this is the dose I have been taking. She said that maybe the pharmacy changed manufacturers and I need two pills for the same amount. I told her they both look exactly like the pills I've been taking for months and I refused to take more than the one. She told me that I was within my right to refuse medication, but that I would be doing great harm to the baby and myself if I didn't take it. I told her to check with the pharmacy and find out for certain why I need two pills. She left to check on it. When she returned she apologized to me, saying that she found out that the manufacturer accidentally packed two pills in one bag and I was only supposed to take one. I thanked her for checking on it, but I really just wanted to scream, "So which would have harmed me and the baby more?" Surprisingly, she said that she went and re-read my chart and saw that my MRI results did indeed show percreta. I thanked her again for double-checking and joked that I wish she had been right and that the others were the ones who had misread the MRI!

I realized how lucky I am to be alert and aware of my condition and all the medicines I have to take. Even with the slew of nurses here, the bottom line is that I'm ultimately responsible for Fletcher and me.

Monday, March 3, 2008 5:36 PM
27 Weeks 1 Day

Two nursing students were in the ultrasound room with me today. I told them they picked the right patient to observe, because I have numerous rare issues together in this one pregnancy. They asked what was going on in my pregnancy and I started to explain about my placenta issues, but neither student had ever heard of anything other than placenta previa. I ended up explaining placenta accreta, increta and percreta to them. I felt like I was their teacher! Either they have a lot to learn, or I've learned too much!

The ultrasound showed a small pocket of fluid, which was surprising since I've been leaking through one maxi pad per hour every day. The perinatologist also saw a little space between the placenta and bladder, which was great news! They don't think the placenta and bladder have attached yet, but feel that it could happen in the very near future. They want me to pay close attention to exactly where my blood is coming from, especially when I'm going to the bathroom. If I have any thought that the blood could be coming from my urethra, I'm supposed to immediately call a doctor in to examine me. If it does turn out that the blood is indeed from that area, there's a very high chance that the placenta has begun to invade my bladder, and Fletcher would have to be delivered within a few hours. I have no idea how I'll be able to differentiate blood coming from my vagina or urethra, but the perinatologist assured me it would be quite obvious if there were blood in my urine.

I told the perinatologist about my obsession with researching fetal lung development issues in preemies born in similar situations. One main struggle is my not being able to know if his lungs will function properly until after he is born. He sensed my frustration. I'm in the hospital having all these tests continuously performed on the baby and me, and I want a definitive answer before he's out of the womb and introduced to room air and oxygen. The perinatologist looked me right in the eyes and said "Look, you had a choice to terminate or continue the pregnancy. Either choice would have been medically justified. You chose to continue to carry the baby, and I would have made the same choice as you did. You have to look at it like this: you took this baby from 100% chance of not surviving, had you chosen to terminate, to giving this baby at least somewhat of a chance." He also said, "It's not the ideal odds, but it's still better than the 100% terminating option." I know what he's saying is true, and even now, I feel like I made the right decision. Even though rationally, I know the choice was the right one for me, it doesn't make it any easier to live through every single day with the uncertainty of not knowing if Fletcher will ever survive outside once he is born.

Tuesday, March 4, 2008 11:29 AM
27 Weeks 2 Days

Having an IV needle in my arm for over a month, and needing it changed out every few days, has left it full of bruises and lines. Not only are these track marks unsightly, they're painful. The IV is kept in place by two rows of medical tape. Unfortunately, every time the IV line is changed, the tape has to be ripped off. The tape clings to my arm hair and pulls it out, so in addition to the bruises, my arm is basically hairless, too. When the area becomes hairless, the next time the tape needs to be pulled is even worse and causes bleeding and scabs. At this point the nurses know to stay away from this area for at least a week.

It's also so painful to have the IV line. Sometimes I change my lying position or grab for an item and the line gets caught on the edge of the bed or bed desk and it tugs at the needle. My entire arm throbs for a few minutes and is so uncomfortable. Being attached to the IV pole is also a hassle. Getting up from the bed to go to the commode or to sit while they change my sheets can take me a while to do. It's completely awkward and clumsy. All I really want to do is not get the needle ripped out of my arm and cause the IV pole to fall over with my solution in it. Being in the hospital is hard enough without adding all this equipment sticking in me, on me, over me, and next to me!

Wednesday, March 5, 2008 1:38 PM
27 Weeks 3 Days

I'm supposed to have my next round of steroid shots this weekend and I'm not sure I want to have them. The more research I do, the more I read about differing opinions. Some studies say it's imperative to repeat them, some say that the second round of shots doesn't seem to make a difference, and some say that it's actually harmful for the baby to repeat them.

My main perinatologist said there's no question that I'll have to have them. My OB said he has read all the differing studies too and isn't sure what to recommend, so he called a few colleagues to get their advice. My OB's honesty and willingness to get outside input, as well as allowing me to make the final decision, is why I trust him so much. I think he's an amazing doctor!

Thursday, March 6, 2008 7:59 PM
27 Weeks 4 Days

I've been having contractions and heavy bleeding all day. The nurses gave me a terbutaline shot which was able to slow down the contractions. She noticed that my breathing was very shallow so she checked my oxygen levels, which were well below the minimum normal level of 90%. She had to put me on oxygen, which immediately made me feel more comfortable. I have to stay on the oxygen for at least two days.

I have my scheduled ultrasound and a growth scan on the baby tomorrow. I'm not sure I can handle the wheelchair ride up there much longer. I've reached a new level of exhaustion and I don't think my body can handle this pregnancy much longer.

My OB came by this afternoon and told me he thinks I should have the second round steroid shots. He said all his colleagues agree that it's the right thing to do; not just for Fletcher's lungs, but also to possibly prevent brain bleeds in preemies. He's convinced me that having them done is the right decision. He also took me off the oxygen.

Friday, March 7, 2008 11:42 AM
27 Weeks 5 Days

This morning's ultrasound was officially the last one of my pregnancy. Fletcher was clearly in distress. Because I'm not even 28 weeks along, the perinatologist scheduled the surgeries for Monday morning so I could have the second rounds of steroid over the weekend.

At the ultrasound, Fletcher measured under the fifth percentile, a huge drop from the growth scan two weeks ago. His heartbeat was irregular and his limbs looked very stiff, which is a side effect from being without fluid. The perinatologists all agreed that not only is it time to deliver because of his issues, but also because my body is steadily starting to shut down. It's a relief to know my exact delivery date, but even after months of complaining, I'm not ready to deliver him yet. I'm not ready to find out if Fletcher will live or die. I'm not ready for him to leave the safety of my womb; the one place it doesn't matter if his lungs are functioning properly or not.

My perinatologist called my OB during my appointment and my OB said he would meet me in my hospital room. After the perinatologist hung up with my OB, he kept me in his office awhile longer, going through the scan results with me and the other perinatologist. By the time I got back to my room, my OB had left to go back to work. I need to talk to him and hope he'll come sometime today.

I'm so afraid and nervous. I called Lee crying and he canceled all his appointments and said he was on his way to sit with me this afternoon. He called his parents and asked them to come down as soon as possible to watch the kids for the next week. I really can't bear be alone right now. I'm having heart palpitations and my body won't stop shaking. I can't shut off my mind. I don't feel ready to face what could be. I can't wait for Lee to get here and I can't wait for my in-laws to come, too. There's no way I can be alone this weekend.

Friday, March 7, 2008 9:46 PM
27 Weeks 5 Days

The hospital has chaplains that help counsel patients who want spiritual support. Apparently, one of the nurses thought I needed to speak with one after this morning's ultrasound. The chaplain came to my room and I didn't want to be rude and send her away, even though she was quite pushy. She said that the hospital feels like I could benefit from talking to her, but the first thing she wanted to discuss with me was about the Now I Lay Me Down To Sleep (NILMDTS) organization. I already know all about this amazing organization of professional photographers who volunteer their time to take pictures of babies that are either stillborn or aren't expected to live more than a few hours. I was so enraged that this chaplain would come in to my room uninvited, and tell me that my baby would need NILMDTS! I was livid. I thought she was supposed to provide love, support, and be a positive influence. How dare she talk to me about this as soon as she met me and before the baby's even born! I told her I didn't appreciate her coming in my room a few days before I was about to have my baby and assume he was going to die! Before kicking her out of my room, I told her how completely inappropriate she was and hoped that in the future she would be more tactful with other patients.

I had another steroid shot this afternoon. I'm still in shock over the ultrasound this morning. I'm going to try to put my mind on autopilot because otherwise, I get too upset and can hardly breathe. I still haven't spoken to my OB. Hopefully he'll come in tomorrow.

Saturday, March 8, 2008 7:45 AM
27 Weeks 6 Days

After yesterday's ultrasound, my perinatologists called the nurse's station and told them that since my condition has deteriorated they must immediately notify my OB of any change in symptoms between now and Monday. They must have frightened them because the nurses kept coming in every hour to check on me.

We gave one of the nurses a scare last night. Lee brought the kids to see me and when they first came in, Spencer said he had to use the bathroom. He accidentally pulled the emergency nurse cord without us knowing. A nurse came running into the room, looking terrified. At that moment, Spencer came out of the bathroom and we all realized he pulled the cord. Luckily the nurse was more relieved than angry! The good thing is that I'm now very confident that a nurse will respond quickly in a true emergency.

After consoling Spencer, we ended up having a very nice family night. I loved having Lee and the kids here with me. We had dinner together and then watched a hospital TV channel that shows different beach videos.

Lee's parents drove in late last night, which is such a relief. Lee can now spend all weekend with me and the kids will have fun with their grandparents.

I'm so glad the kids don't realize how nerve-wracking all of this is. I think all the adults are doing a great job shielding them. Lee broke down crying last night, which made me feel so bad since he's been holding it all together this entire time. I think the anticipation of Monday has gotten to him. I hate that I've put him through all of this. Having a baby should be a wonderful and happy experience. Instead, Lee is crying, afraid of losing both his son and his wife. It just isn't right.

Saturday, March 8, 2008 11:47 PM
27 Weeks 6 Days

My OB's partner is on call this weekend and he came to see me this morning. He spent some time talking to me about what to expect on Monday. My C-section, hysterectomy, and bladder reconstruction (if necessary) are scheduled for 10:00 AM. I have so many questions but don't feel like asking him. I'm waiting until I can speak directly to my OB. His partner said he would come see me Monday morning, before the surgery. I'm extremely anxious and, aside from Lee, my OB is the only other person who can calm me down right now. I can't believe he isn't going to talk to me this weekend!

This afternoon, a nurse from the NICU took me on a tour of the NICU. Due to privacy laws, I was only allowed to stay in the front part of the NICU, but that was enough for me. I heard loud beeping machines and alarms going off. I saw teeny-tiny babies with wires attached to them, connected to different machines. Some babies were in cribs, but most were in incubators. The incubator is like a plastic bassinet with a plastic cover. It keeps the babies in a sterile environment, which helps them avoid infection, as well as maintain their body temperature. The incubator also mutes noise and by throwing a cover over the top, can shut out light. I was secretly glad not to have a detailed tour because I don't even know if Fletcher will even make it to the NICU. There's a good chance that he'll be stillborn, or die within minutes of being born, so even though I was in the NICU for less than five minutes, the images stayed with me and I was up crying most of the night.

Thank goodness Lee is sleeping here tonight.

Sunday, March 9, 2008 8:49 PM
28 Weeks 0 Days

My OB just came to see me! I started fussing at him for waiting so long to see me, even telling his partner that he wouldn't speak with me until tomorrow, just before the surgery. He asked me how I could believe that. He said he had waited in my room for me after my perinatologist appointment on Friday, but I took too long and he had to get back to his office. He wasn't worried about it because he had planned to see me this weekend, but today was the soonest he could get here. I'm just so relieved he came in tonight.

My OB discussed all the different scenarios that could play out during the C-section and hysterectomy. He said he spent the weekend thinking about the best way to do the surgeries. I love that he took the time to think about everything and prepare for anything.

He said he isn't planning to use general anesthesia in either of the surgeries unless something unexpected happens, so I'll be awake the entire time, which should be about 1 ½ hours. He's already called the blood bank and they'll be sure to have bags of blood in the OR. His partner will assist him, and the urologist will be standing by in case there's an issue with my bladder.

Lee and I asked him about the possibility of hemorrhaging. He said that is a real possibility because of the placental issues, but he'll be prepared if that happens. He said he would not let me bleed out, even if he has to physically clamp down on the blood vessels until the bleeding stops, even if it takes hours. He repeated that he'd have all the necessary tools at hand in the OR for any situation that may arise.

He explained that a nurse will draw blood at 4:00 AM and bring the sample to the blood bank. The blood bank will then match my blood and have the correct pints ready in the OR. At 8:00 AM, I'll be taken down to L&D and will have two additional IV lines put in, one in case I need a blood transfusion, and another in case I need medicine, including general anesthesia. The surgeries are scheduled for 10:30 AM. A neonatologist and NICU nurse will be in the OR and will immediately bring Fletcher to the NICU as soon as he's born. Of course my OB assumes the baby will be born alive. I'm trying to be hopeful, but am also trying to prepare for the worst. The problem is that every time I think Fletcher won't live, my body shakes and I start to hyperventilate. My OB told me to stop thinking and take a sleeping pill to get my body and mind well rested. I know I won't, but do feel much less anxious knowing that my OB has thoughtfully planned out and prepared for tomorrow.

Monday, March 10, 2008 1:52 PM
Fletcher's Birthday!

Welcome to the world Fletcher William Wolfe! He was born at 12:25 PM, weighing 2 pounds, 3 ounces (980 grams) and 13.39 inches long (34 cm). Welcome Fletcher, my little guy! I'm so happy to meet you! I love you so very much!!

PART II – Fletcher is Here

CHAPTER 7

Fletcher's birth was just the end of my pregnancy, not the end of our struggles.

Monday, March 10, 2008 2:52 PM
Fletcher's Birthday!

Fletcher William Wolfe was born at 12:25 PM, and came out not only breathing, but also crying and screaming! His APGAR scores were eight at one minute, and nine at five minutes. These are great, especially for a 28-week preemie. APGAR a rating score used to evaluate a newborn baby on five criteria, which are on a scale from zero to two. The five values are then summed up, with 10 being the highest possible score. I feel so calm and peaceful.

Monday, March 10, 2008 7:15 PM
0 Days Old

My surgeries were scheduled for 10:00 AM this morning. I had blood drawn at 4:00 AM, and waited around until 8:30 AM, when I was brought down to L&D. My OB ended up having to do a few unscheduled surgeries and didn't get to my room until after 11:00 AM. At 11:15 AM, the anesthesiologist came in and told my OB that he would feel more comfortable putting in a central venous line (CVC) in addition to one regular IV line, rather than the four regular IV lines that were initially planned. The CVC is a catheter line that's placed through a vein in the neck. It's a safer and quicker way to administer medicine, fluids, and blood, than a typical IV line through the arm. It also allows for monitoring special blood pressures and gives the anesthesiologist more control over the patient in an emergency situation. My OB said he didn't think the CVC was necessary, but told the anesthesiologist he could use it if it made him feel more comfortable. My OB left to prepare the OR and the anesthesiologist attempted to insert the CVC. The first time he missed and I got a shot of pain throughout my neck. The second time he missed and the line came through my throat. I had to wave to the nurse in the room to stop him! By the fifth failed attempt, I was in so much pain I begged the doctor to stop. The nurse came over and saw my neck and immediately told the anesthesiologist to leave my room. The nurse was livid when she saw that my neck was completely swollen, bruised and bleeding. She called in her supervisor, who immediately called in the anesthesiologist's supervisor and reported him.

My neck was throbbing so I didn't notice the pain of the nurses putting in four IV lines in my arms. They told me he was the only anesthesiologist on duty so he was still going to be the one in the OR with me. I knew I still needed the spinal to numb me before my C-section, and insisted someone else do the procedure. The nurses and their supervisor agreed, but said it wouldn't be easy to convince him to allow his assistant to perform the spinal. I was terrified at the thought of him poking through my back and spine and the nurses said they didn't blame me and to not worry because they would come up with a plan.

A few minutes later, the anesthesiologist and my OB came back in my room so my OB could go over what would happen in the OR. The anesthesiologist kept interrupting my OB and disagreeing with him. They ended up getting in to a heated argument and my OB asked to speak with him privately. I could hear them outside my room, but a few minutes later my OB came back in and said I shouldn't worry. He promised me that he was the one in charge and had the final say in the OR. My OB said he ended up conceding some aspects of the surgery. My OB told me that it's important for the anesthesiologist to feel comfortable and in control, especially if something unforeseen should occur.

As I was being wheeled into the OR, the nurses told the anesthesiologist that it would be fine for the assistant to do the spinal so he could focus on more important things in the OR. The doctor kept saying that he didn't mind doing the spinal. All of us were getting nervous. They had to figure out a way to make the anesthesiologist go along with this decision. The anesthesiologist was still prepping his area so the nurses called over his assistant, whispered something to her, and then asked her out loud to begin the spinal. The anesthesiologist looked up and, thankfully, said it would be fine for her to do it since he was still organizing his tools. I could tell that the nurses were as relieved as I was!

Once the spinal took effect, a nurse brought Lee into the OR. He sat next to me and held my hand. A few minutes later, I heard my OB tell his partner, "This is a first!" Lee asked what was going on and apparently there was no safe place for him to cut into uterus and get the baby. My uterus was attached to my bladder and cervix, and was encased in scar tissue from my previous three C-sections. He said that my placenta was attached to my bladder, but he was able to manually remove it without causing damage. The placenta had also grown out of the uterus and was piled on top of my cervix and looked like ice cream on top of a cone. This was another first for my OB.

My OB had to detach my uterus and take it out with Fletcher still inside. He basically performed a hysterectomy while the baby was still inside! Lee stood up to watch. He narrated while my OB lifted out my uterus, placed it on my stomach, and then 'filleted' my uterus until he opened it enough to get Fletcher out. My OB also said that my uterus had no fluid in it at all and Fletcher was completely dry. He said it was definitely the right time to get the baby out.

Fletcher cried as soon as he was born! All these months of not knowing and he came out screaming! It was the moment I'd been thinking about, every second of every day of my pregnancy. A wave of emotion came over me and I started to have convulsions and my upper body started to shake uncontrollably. The nurses made Lee leave the OR and the anesthesiologist gave me medicine to calm me down. It made me feel woozy and out of it. I don't remember much after that. My OB closed me back up, slathered the surgical glue around the cervix to stop the bleeding that started once the placenta was removed, and told the anesthesiologist to transfuse two bags of blood.

My OB finally saw the cause of all my pregnancy complications. Fletcher had actually implanted on the top of my cervix, rather than fully inside the uterus. As the pregnancy progressed, my placenta developed and grew on top of my cervix and partially in my uterus.

Under the same conditions, most pregnancies would have ended in a miscarriage, but Fletcher was determined!

I was brought back to the L&D room at 1:30 PM. Lee and my father-in-law were there waiting. They were able to go see Fletcher while my OB finished my surgeries. They told me how great he looked and how strong he seemed. I was glad that Fletcher wasn't alone after his birth, but was so tired and drained that I fell asleep while they were talking.

Monday, March 10, 2008 7:15 PM
0 Days Old

I woke up around 2:30 PM and felt very uncomfortable. It seemed like my stomach was getting bigger. Even Lee even noticed. My blood pressure monitor kept going off, indicating that my blood pressure was falling below normal limits, and by 6:00 PM, my blood pressure was consistently reading 50/30, and I was in a lot of pain. My stomach was getting stretched out and looked larger than it had during my pregnancy! The L&D nurses were starting to panic and called my OB to come back to the hospital.

Tuesday, March 11, 2008 5:54 AM
1 Day Old

My OB came in and out of my room all evening, but by 11:00 PM, my pain became intolerable. My blood pressure dropped to 40/19, my hemoglobin was only four, and my potassium levels were well out of the normal range. It was clear to everyone that I was internally bleeding. At this point, my OB was ready to take action. He came in my room and Lee and I asked him what the plan was. He sat down on a chair next to my bed and told Lee that someone with blood pressure this low should be unconscious and was amazed that I was not only lucid, but having an intelligent conversation with him. Lee responded by asking my OB, "Don't you know who you're dealing with by now?" My OB chuckled but then became serious. He took a few deep breaths, let out some curse words and said to me, "I didn't want to have to do this but we need to get you back in to the OR." At that point, another medical team came in and started to prepare me for surgery. The same anesthesiologist as earlier came in the room and said that now I definitely needed a CVC line. I told my OB to make sure I was completely under anesthesia before he tried to put that line in. The last thing I remember was being wheeled into the OR and hearing my OB asking if anyone knew where the staple remover was.

It turned out that I was hemorrhaging. My OB had thought one spot started leaking through the surgical glue but when he reopened me, my entire cervical area was gushing blood. Placenta percreta does create an unstable environment but usually the surgical glue is strong enough to stop the area from internal bleeding. Since my placenta had attached itself to so many different places, there were more areas vulnerable to hemorrhaging. My OB ended up cauterizing the area, suturing parts, adding medical mesh and more medical glue before closing me back up. I had lost so much blood that I needed 12 pints of blood and four bags of platelets and plasma. The average human body has about 15 pints of blood, so I basically lost almost all of my own blood. The hospital blood bank ran out of B negative blood and plasma, so they substituted O negative for the blood and had to give me a mixture of negative and positive plasma.

I came out of the anesthesia while I was being wheeled back to my L&D room. It was around 12:45 AM. I saw my father-in-law and asked him why he was here since I remembered him leaving the hospital early afternoon. He said he came back to sit with Lee. Apparently the nurses told Lee that he needed to have a family member sit with him while I was in surgery. My situation was life threatening and they suggested Lee have family with him for support, just in case.

My OB stayed in the hospital the rest of the night, even though he wasn't on call. He came to check on me every few hours. The nurses told me that if I had a different doctor, I would've been put in the intensive care unit (ICU). Things were really, really bad.

All night I was in a medical daze. I remember being woken up by alarms going off. The anesthesiologist was able to put in the CVC line, as well as six different IV lines. Every time I moved I would press up on one of the lines and an alarm would go off. I was put on an oxygen mask and sometimes would knock it off. Without the oxygen, my oxygen saturation levels would fall drastically low causing another alarm to go off. Needless to say Lee and I got no sleep and I kept the nurses very busy.

The day nurse from the initial surgery called to check in on me and when she heard about the second surgery, she ended up calling in every few hours during the night and changed her shift to be back at work today to take care of me.

Tuesday, March 11, 2008 9:43 PM
1 Day Old

My OB came by tonight while on-call. I told him I was having pain at my incision site, even though I am on pain medicines. He was surprised to hear that since he went out of his way to get me a special type of pain pump, one that isn't used very often for C-sections. The pain pump he put in is a device with a reservoir containing local pain numbing medication that gets continuously pumped to a targeted area through a tiny tube. My OB took one look and apologized to me because no one had ever turned on the device. I hope it starts to work soon.

Wednesday, March 12, 2008 7:30 AM
2 Days Old

I'm still not able to breathe without the oxygen mask, and even then it's a struggle. Last night, I was given an incentive spirometer, which is a handheld device used to improve lung function after being put under general anesthesia. It helps lungs expand and measures how well the lungs are being filled with air when taking breaths. The level ranges from 500 to 4000. My initial goal was 200 and the first time I used it I couldn't get past 100. I've also been having stabbing pains in my chest and each time I inhale it gets worse. A nurse examined my chest and realized that I have a collapsed lung. My lungs were weakened by the general anesthesia. She told me to keep using the spirometer and add coughing exercises in between because coughing will clear out my lungs and help to avoid infection. The spirometer is hard to use, but not painful. Trying to cough, however, is excruciating. Each time I try to cough if feels as if the staples in my stomach are being ripped and torn out. I promised the nurse I will continue to try because I don't think I can handle having a lung infection!

Despite everything, my body is showing signs of healing. My latest blood work showed that my potassium, white and red blood counts, and hemoglobin are nearing normal levels. The nurse told my OB that I was stable enough to be brought up to the postpartum floor. My OB had the hospital keep my antepartum room available for me. It was both odd and comforting to be back in this room. I lived here for so long while pregnant and now I'm back in the room, no longer pregnant, and recovering from my surgeries.

Wednesday, March 12, 2008 9:30 AM
2 Days Old

This morning I was finally able to get out of bed and be helped into a wheelchair to go down to the NICU and see Fletcher. I can't believe he's two days old and I haven't had a chance to see or hold him yet!

The NICU is an intimidating place. It's so formal, especially compared to the newborn nursery. There are so many rules and regulations! No one can even be in the waiting room without being on a list and signing in. My nurse had to sign in for me because all my IV lines kept getting in the way. While she was signing in, I was given a number that corresponds to Fletcher so when I call to check in on him, I have to give the nurse that number in order to get any information on him. Obviously, all this is done to protect the baby, but it's so frustrating when all I want to do is go straight to my baby.

After the sign-in area, all cell phones must be shut off. I hope I remember that going forward. There are lockers with gowns in them to put on over your clothes to keep germs off of the baby, as well as optional facemasks. There are two industrial sinks supplied with stacks of special hand scrubbers, which are pre-filled with bright pink soap and include a fingernail stick. There are signs above the sinks that give step-by-step directions explaining that you must remove all jewelry, including rings and watches, and then scrub your hands, fingers, and up to your elbows, for at least three minutes. There are timers that you turn on and they automatically start counting down while you scrub.

I tried to stand up when we got to the sink area, but I was so weak that I had to immediately sit back down. It didn't matter though, because my arms still had three IV lines in them so I was only able to scrub my fingers. Even that was impossible because my oxygen tank and the nasal cannula tubing were too short and didn't allow me to get out of the wheelchair.

The nurses saw how sick I was and took pity on me. They knew I wouldn't be able to get out of my wheelchair or stay more than a few minutes, so they allowed me to go back and see him.

I was told not to look at the other babies in the NICU, but of course it's hard not to when you have to pass them. Every baby was so tiny! It was shocking to see how small they were! They all looked like real babies, just smaller and with tubes and needles stuck in them; and, of course, surrounded by machines and alarms.

As I approached Fletcher's incubator, I was shocked to see that those little babies I just passed were huge compared to mine! Although he was tiny, he was beautiful! The NICU nurses told me that he already has a very large and strong personality. It's standard procedure to put preemies on the ventilator as soon as they're brought in to the NICU. It took four nurses to get him intubated so he could be put on the ventilator and then an hour later, Fletcher ripped the tubing out! Rather than re-intubate him, the nurses monitored him and realized he didn't need to be put back on the ventilator. The nurses are saying he is one feisty little boy!

The neonatologist did end up putting Fletcher on the continuous positive airway pressure (CPAP) machine for the first day to make it easier for him to breathe since his lungs are so under-developed. She explained that the CPAP doesn't actually breathe for the baby like the ventilator does; it uses pressure to keep the baby's air sacs open in the lungs. They were able to take him off the CPAP early this morning and now he's breathing on his own.

I was taken aback by just how small he was and by his transparent skin. But I was pleasantly surprised that he had fingernails and a lot of hair on his head! Even though he looks like a miniature version of a full-term baby, he is anything but. Because a preemie, especially a micro-preemie born at 28 weeks, has very delicate skin and is so fragile, I was not allowed to touch him. Technically he should still be in-utero where he doesn't have to eat or breathe, maintain his own body temperature, or deal with lights, loud noises, and being touched. Therefore, the NICU has to take over for him. Even his delicate skin is too fragile to touch. So my visit with Fletcher was basically me looking at and talking to him. As I was observing him, I could see traits of my other kids in him, which made me smile. He has Spencer's lips, Wesley's eyes and hair color, and, from what the nurses told me, Cassie's spunk!

After 10 minutes I was exhausted and needed to get back to my room. I hoped to take a nap, but when I got back to the room, a lactation nurse was waiting for me. She brought me an electric breast pump and told me I could to start pumping. She gave me the tubing for the machine, as well as a huge bag of bottles to store the breast milk. The NICU feels strongly that breast milk is best for the preemies and provides all the bottles for the entire time the baby is there. I breastfed each of my other children until they were over a year old, but right now my body's in bad shape and the thought of having to pump my breasts is extremely unappealing. Of course Fletcher's health and growth are my biggest concerns, so I took the tubing and bottles and thanked her.

My lungs are slowly improving. I'm able to cough without causing myself too much discomfort, and I've been nearing the normal range with my spirometer. The nurse said she'd take away the spirometer tomorrow if I can get within the normal range. I know that won't be a problem for me.

I can use the hospital's electric pump while I'm here, as well as in the NICU, but I also need something I can use at home. This is all new to me because I never pumped or used bottles with my other children. I launched an Internet search to find electric breast pumps to rent and found that the closest place is 45 minutes from my house. Since I won't be able to drive for a few weeks, I was at a loss. I called an out of town friend to complain and get advice, but she told me she couldn't talk and would have to call me back. Five minutes later a mutual friend called to let me know she had packed up her portable electric pump and was on her way to the post office to send it overnight to me. I have amazing friends!

Thursday, March 13, 2008 8:58 AM
3 Days Old

The NICU uses weight as an indicator of how well the preemies are doing. Fletcher gets weighed every night and so far, he's doing great! The day after he was born, he dropped down to 1 pound, 11 ounces, but now he's back up to 2 pounds. The weight loss had made such a dramatic impact on his appearance. His ribs were protruding and his arms and legs were nothing but bones. Thank goodness he gained back five ounces! Although he's far from a chunky baby, he looks so much better.

This morning I was allowed to put my hand in his isolate and lightly stroke his face. Fletcher reached for and squeezed my finger! Wow. The nurse then opened the top of the isolate and I was allowed to stroke his hair and lean in and kiss him! The moment my lips touched his face I felt a rush of his energy pull through me. It was the first time I was able to physically show my love to my son. I wanted to lift him to my chest and rock him, but I knew I couldn't do that. When I leaned back after kissing him, Fletcher's eyes were fixed on my face. We stared at each other for a few moments and I started to cry. Fletcher is here and I'm so in love with him, and I think he knows it. He might even love me, too.

The nurses are still saying that he has a temper and is very headstrong. He tugs on his tubes, pulls off his diaper, and cries when he's hungry and has to wait until feeding time to eat. I love hearing about his personality. He's so amazing!

Many preemies have blood drawn frequently their first few days in order to monitor their blood chemistries. Since their systems are immature, it takes a long time to replace the blood, so many preemies need blood transfusions. Fletcher had his first one last night. I know it's routine for preemies, but it still makes me upset that he has someone else's blood running through him. He has the same blood type as Wesley and Cassie, but of course they're too young to be able to donate for him. Even if they could, I don't think the NICU allows families to do that. If Lee or I shared Fletcher's blood type, I would ask about it, but since we don't there's nothing to do but accept strangers' blood.

The most amazing thing is that Fletcher's no longer on the CPAP! He's still on oxygen, but by nasal cannula. It's set at 35% oxygen, which is relatively low for a newborn preemie (room air is 21%). I'm on a higher oxygen percentage than that!

The NICU has a team of four neonatologists; each does three-week rotations at this hospital's NICU. I've only spoken on the phone to the neonatologist in charge of Fletcher, so I hope to meet her in person soon.

Thursday, March 13, 2008, 2:45 PM
3 Days Old

My mom flew in today. She said she would stay in the hospital with me and let Lee's parents continue to take care of the kids. I'm actually relieved to have her stay with me because I'm still so limited in my movement. I need help getting to the bathroom, washing the breast pump, tubes and anything else besides lying around! It's also nice to have her in charge for a while. I've been the one responsible for me since being admitted, and now that I'm physically and mentally so weak, it's nice to have someone else call the shots and be in control of my well-being.

Just before my mom came, the nurse took me off the oxygen. I'm glad because I already look pretty beaten up and if she saw me on oxygen as well, that would make her much more concerned.

Thursday, March 13, 2008, 11:45 PM
3 Days Old

I've been on a liquid diet since Sunday night and am desperate for real food! My OB said that once I pass gas I could eat solids. I finally did late this afternoon and immediately called the nurse in to ask if I could order food. She told me that the hospital cafeteria serves new moms a congratulations meal, so I went ahead and ordered it. I don't know if it was because I hadn't eaten in so long, or if the entrée was truly amazing, but it was one of the best fish dishes I've had in a long time! I felt fine after eating it…for about two hours. Around 8:00 PM, I started to have sharp stomach pains and as soon as I called for a bowl, I became violently ill and threw up everywhere. My poor mom had to deal with this an hour after she got here!

The nurse had to call my OB because what I regurgitated was actually a mixture of the food, blood, and waste products. My OB was so concerned that he immediately sent me for an x-ray.

When I got to the x-ray room, the technician told me I had to lie completely flat on a hard, metallic table. It was excruciatingly painful. The technician was very kind and went as fast as possible. The pain pump kept getting in the way but he said he got the pictures he needed so he didn't have to repeat them.

The x-ray showed an Ileus, which is an intestinal blockage. Apparently, although I passed gas, my body was not ready to digest solid food. My OB reprimanded me for eating too much too fast, but I thought my body could handle eating. I was wrong. My OB put me back on IV fluids and I'm not allowed to eat or drink for a few days. He said that if the blockage doesn't pass on its own I would need surgery to remove it. I physically and mentally can't handle another surgery, so this better clear up on its own.

Friday, March 14, 2008 2:00 PM
4 Days Old

My milk came in today! I've been pumping out about four ounces, or 120 cubic centimeters (ccs), per session, but Fletcher is only taking two to three cubic centimeters at each feeding. The NICU said they can store some of my breast milk in their freezer, but most will have to be kept in my freezer at home. I'll have to drive up a few times a week to bring them milk.

Preemies sucking reflex usually doesn't mature until the gestational age of 34 weeks, so they are fed through an NG tube. The tube is put through the baby's mouth, down his throat, and into his stomach. When it's time to eat, the tube is attached to a machine that slowly dispenses the breast milk. It will be over a month before Fletcher will be able to suck, swallow, digest, and breathe all at the same time. The NICU has a speech therapist that works with preemies to help them learn to suck, swallow, use their tongues, and breathe during feedings. She will start working with Fletcher in the next few weeks to speed up the process.

Saturday, March 15, 2008 12:14 PM
5 Days Old

My nurse took out the pain pump this morning. It was so bulky and uncomfortable. I wish she took it out days ago. I never noticed a difference in my pain, even after the device was turned on.

As soon as she took out the tubing for the pump, blood started spewing out of my stomach! The nurse called another nurse to bring in towels and bandages. She bandaged up the spots but 20 minutes later the bleeding was so bad that my OB was called. My OB wasn't concerned. He said that that I had so much blood in my stomach from internal bleeding that he was unable to get it all out and pulling out the tubes gave the blood an outlet. He said it might take awhile longer for all the blood to get out and to keep medical supplies nearby.

My OB put in an order for me to have my IV line taken out and for me to be put on a liquid diet. If all goes well, I'll be able to eat solids and then hopefully be discharged.

Sunday, March 16, 2008 4:44 PM
6 Days Old

Fletcher has jaundice, which is very common in preemies. Preemies' livers are immature and unable to remove bilirubin from their bloodstream, causing excessively high bilirubin levels. Phototherapy, or light treatment, gets rid of the excess through light waves that absorb through the skin and into the blood. The bilirubin changes into a compound that is excreted through urine and stool. Because the lights are so bright, the baby has to wear a tiny eye mask to protect the eyes.

Fletcher seems to really enjoy these treatments. Today he was smiling while basking in the warmth of the lights. He will continue the light therapy for the next few days.

Monday, March 17, 2008 8:45 PM
1 Week 0 Days Old

I was discharged from the hospital this afternoon. If I didn't have to leave Fletcher, I would've been ecstatic to get out of there. Leaving without Fletcher was so emotionally painful. It's horrible to give birth to a child in the hospital and have to go home without him. I know he's being well taken care of, but I can't stand that I'll be over 30 minutes away from him and have to plan out when I'll see him. I'll call in as much as possible, but obviously that's no substitute for physically being with him.

I was wheeled outside and Lee was waiting with the car. I couldn't believe I was leaving. It had been over seven weeks since I was outside, aside from the hospital patio, or in a car.

There was so much noise from all the cars driving by. I was intrigued with all the people walking around, going about their business. As Lee drove away from the hospital, I became overwhelmed with the thought of having to start taking care of myself again. Even though I didn't like having the nurses in and out of my room all the time, I grew accustomed to them. I know I'll re-acclimate quickly, but it will still be an adjustment.

When I walked through the front door, the kids all ran up to me. I could see that they were not only happy to have me home, but also very relieved. I was so tired from the car ride that I had to sit down as soon as I walked in the house. I sat on the floor while the kids ran all around me showing me their schoolwork and talking over each other. They began telling me all about school, friends; just everything and anything that came to their minds. As I was listening, our cat came running up to me, sniffed for a second, and then jumped up on my back and gave me a huge hug and kiss! We all laughed. It's so very nice to be home.

A few minutes later, I went in to my bedroom and lied down in my own bed. It's amazing to be home, but at the same time, it breaks my heart that I had to leave Fletcher at the hospital. I've called the NICU three times already. It's not the same as being under the same roof as him and that's going to take some time to get used to.

Tuesday, March 18, 2008 8:02 PM
1 Week 1 Day Old

My OB sent me home with a prescription for painkillers, but I wanted to try and get by with only ibuprofen a few times a day. Unfortunately, my body is so sore and beaten up that I finally asked Lee to fill my prescription.

The kids have been so sweet to me. I've been getting so many hugs and kisses. I love and cherish it.

I called the NICU twice during the night. The nurse told me they've increased Fletcher's feedings to 15 ccs, which is almost half an ounce! I haven't been pumping as much as I should, but am getting five ounces per session, so I have plenty of breast milk for Fletcher. I hate pumping because it reminds me that I don't have Fletcher here with me and if he were, I wouldn't have to pump. Waking up during the night is especially hard. It's one thing to be woken up by the baby and get to cuddle together, but it's another thing to have to set an alarm clock every three hours and sit on the couch alone to pump. I also make sure to pump every three to four hours during the day. I'll continue to pump to ensure that Fletcher has plenty of milk.

My mom drove me up to the hospital today to see Fletcher. She had to use valet parking because I needed a wheelchair. Most people who use the hospital's valet service are much older than me, so I got plenty of angry looks when I got out of the car. I hate having to get in a car in order to see my son.

I'll never get used to the NICU. Every time I visit him, I have a knot in my stomach. It's completely different than the baby nursery, which is filled with healthy and strong babies. The anxiety of not knowing what to expect is overwhelming. I've already seen too much - mothers walking in while nurses and neonatologists were trying to resuscitate their babies, parents leaving the NICU sobbing, and alarms going off causing staff to rush to the baby's side.

When my mom and I saw Fletcher, he was awake but calm and quiet. The nurse said he was doing very well. When we approached Fletcher, he was lying on his stomach with his head towards us. I said "Hi

Fletcher!" and he lifted up his head and turned it away from me! I was so amazed by his strength that it didn't even bother me.

The NICU provides bottles to breastfeeding moms, as well as private pumping rooms. I brought 20 two-ounce bottles filled with breast milk, but the NICU didn't have room for them. I have to take them back home, freeze them, and bring them back as needed. The nurse gave me a lot more empty bottles, too, and told me she knows I'll make good use of them!

We didn't stay at the NICU very long because I was exhausted and needed to go back to bed.

Wednesday, March 19, 2008 9:17 AM
1 Weeks 2 Days Old

I called the NICU and Fletcher's nurse told me that last night they needed to increase his oxygen pressure to 45%, but by this morning she was able to decreased to 32%. He has also gained weight and is now 2 pound, 6 ounces! However, the nurse told me Fletcher is having bradycardia (brady) and apnea episodes, which are typically referred to as As and Bs. A brady is a slower than normal heart rhythm. In preemies, a heart rate is termed bradycardia if it falls below 100 beats per minute. Brady and apnea episodes are common in preemies until they're around 33 weeks gestational age. The nurse said that Fletcher is 'just acting his age', but hearing that he's having issues made me nervous.

I hope I can convince my mom to drive me to see him this afternoon. She thinks I need a day in bed and since I'm not allowed to drive yet, I probably won't be able to see Fletcher today.

Thursday, March 20, 2008 4:14 PM
1 Week 3 Days Old

Fletcher is now eating 17 ccs of breast milk per feeding. The nurse took out his IV today so now he only has the NG tube and the oxygen cannula. I was able to see him last night. He had an apnea and brady spell while I was there. It was really scary to watch. One second he was looking right at me and cooing, and the next, his eyes rolled back, he went limp, and an alarm went off. The nurse waited to see if he would recover on his own, but he didn't. Amazingly, all she had to do was pat his back and his breathing and heart rate went back to normal.

The NICU physical therapist started working with Fletcher today. Fletcher has contractures in his arms and legs, which means he has loss of joint motion, due to the lack of fluid when I was pregnant with him. The physical therapist usually doesn't start working with preemies until they're 32 weeks gestational age, but Fletcher's nurse thought he was ready to start now. When the therapist assessed him, Fletcher was able to do all the exercises without getting tired or overwhelmed, and she agreed that he was ready to start now. Fletcher will have physical therapy a few times a week. The therapist thinks that over time, his contractures will completely go away.

Friday, March 21, 2008 12:05 PM
1 Week 4 Days Old

Fletcher is having a lot more As and Bs episodes, which isn't abnormal in preemies, but they're mostly occurring in clusters. This concerns the neonatologists, so they might have to increase his oxygen level. The nurse told me that she had a long talk with Fletcher today about remembering to breathe, and she said, so far, he's been listening because he's had a lot fewer As and Bs today than yesterday.

The NICU orders head scans on most preemies born before 30 weeks. They do them a week after birth, and then a few weeks later. The scan checks for brain bleeds, and if present, the technician ranks the bleeds from one to four, according to the severity of the bleed. The scan also looks for any signs of brain damage, such as periventricular leukomalacia (PVL) or cerebral palsy (CP). PVL is the damage and softening of the white matter in the inner part of the brain that transmits information between the nerve cells and the spinal cord, as well as from one part of the brain to another. PVL shows up on head scans as white spots on the scan. CP is a group of chronic disorders that prevents the child from controlling their muscles normally.

I didn't even know about the head scans until Fletcher's nurse called and told me Fletcher's first scan came back clear. I told the nurse that I was thankful for that, but annoyed that no one told me about this test.

Understanding my frustration, the nurse went through Fletcher's chart and told me that his next head scan is scheduled for the first week in April. She also said he has an eye exam on April 3rd. A common issue that preemies have is retinopathy of prematurity (ROP). ROP is an abnormal growth of the blood vessels in one, or both, of the baby's eyes. The preemies have their first eye exam when they're about a month old, and continue to have them every two weeks while in the NICU. ROP has four stages and it's not unusual for preemies to have stage 1, 2, or even 3, and then outgrow it within a few weeks. Some babies need laser surgery to correct it, and some may need more invasive surgeries.

Friday, March 21, 2008 7:11 PM
1 Week 4 Days Old

Lee went to the hospital to see Fletcher this afternoon. I think it's his first time going since I was discharged. I know it's hard for Lee to get there because of work, but I also think it's hard for him to go back to the hospital. I hope he gets over it because I think it's important for Lee and Fletcher to bond with each other and have father-son time.

Lee said he would visit Fletcher again over the weekend, which made me so happy. I won't be able to go because I need the weekend to rest and regain my strength.

Saturday, March 22, 2008 1:00 PM
1 Week 5 Days Old

I just had a very scary episode. I got out of bed and couldn't breathe. I was literally gasping for air. After what seemed like an eternity, I was able to take shallow breaths. Lee was outside with the kids and couldn't hear me trying to call for him. I had read that back muscle spasms were common after long-term bed rest and they caused similar symptoms. I took a pain reliever and soon after, I was able to breathe again. I'm so tired of being sick and tired! I wonder how much longer it'll be until I recover.

CHAPTER 8

My new daily routine has left me no time to heal.

Monday, March 24, 2008 4:08 PM
2 Weeks 0 Days Old

When I went to see Fletcher, this morning, there was a note for me to page the neonatologist as soon as possible. The neonatologist was making rounds, so the physician's assistant came to see me. Because Fletcher's apnea and brady cluster episodes have increased, they decided to do a chest x-ray and the results were not good. The x-ray showed massive amounts of fluid in his lungs and that his lungs were deteriorating compared to the x-ray from a few days ago. The medical staff was caught off-guard by this, especially because of how great he was doing. They decided to draw blood to check for any infections, and they discovered Fletcher's hematocrit levels were dangerously low. Hematocrit is the part of red blood cells that help carry oxygen. The neonatologist thinks, and also hopes, this explains the fluid in his lungs and Fletcher's low oxygen levels.

The neonatologist started Fletcher on a diuretic to see if would help to get rid of the excess lung fluid. She wants to start him on a round of steroids, which I'm not happy about. There are many adverse side effects, including CP, but the neonatologist said the risk of not putting him on them outweigh the risk of giving them to him. She said she ordered the lowest dose of the steroids and will have him on them for a short amount of time. There's really no other option right now. The neonatologist also ordered another blood transfusion and thinks that will quickly increase his blood oxygen levels. I know all too well about low oxygen levels and needing blood transfusions. I thought that by me having to go through what I did during my pregnancy, it would save Fletcher from having to go through any of this. Obviously, I thought wrong.

I'm so upset and so scared. The physician assistant told me to expect Fletcher to have good days and bad; that having a child in the NICU is like riding a roller coaster. We've been so lucky up until now. At least the doctor thinks she's identified the issues and has a game plan. I just hope it works and works fast!

What's so strange is that Fletcher looks so great. He has perfectly pink skin, his eyes are clear and a wonderful deep blue, and he has shiny, soft, beautiful blonde hair. Seeing him look so good makes it even harder to grasp how sick he actually is.

Tuesday, March 25, 2008 11:29 AM
2 Weeks 1 Day Old

My mother-in-law flew in today for a few days. Hopefully she'll take me to see Fletcher every day. She can also give Lee a break and get the kids ready in the morning, drive them to and from school, grocery shop, and cook. I know it won't be fun for her, but it will be much appreciated.

Wednesday, March 26, 2008 6:09 PM
2 Weeks 2 Days Old

Cassie wasn't feeling well today so my mother-in-law stayed home with her. I needed to go and see Fletcher, so I drove myself to the hospital even though I haven't been cleared to drive.

Fletcher now has a primary day nurse that I absolutely love. She's so great with him. The NICU is over capacity so they've asked nurses to work more days. Fletcher's primary nurse will be with him for three days in a row, which is rare. She's worked in the NICU for over 16 years, but is my age. She has a loving, compassionate way with Fletcher and he seems to really respond to her.

Fletcher's been doing so much better since starting the diuretic. He's only had three brady episodes in the last 24 hours. He'll be given his last dose of steroids tonight and will have another blood transfusion this weekend. Then we all have to wait and see. The nurse keeps telling me not to worry, but that's impossible.

I was glad to be driving again. I cherished the time to myself and loved having some independence. I ended up running a few errands and definitely over did it. I have to realize that it'll be awhile until I'm completely healed so I need to stop pushing myself.

Thursday, March 27, 2008 9:10 AM
2 Weeks 3 Days Old

Fletcher had a terrible night last night. The nurse said he had clusters of bradys throughout the entire night and had a hard time breathing. We're all discouraged that the steroids and diuretics didn't work. His primary nurse said she's waiting for the neonatologist to make rounds and then she'll call me to tell me the game plan.

I wish I could spend the day with Fletcher, but I'm so sore and exhausted from yesterday that I need to stay in bed today. Lee told me that if I don't start to take it easy, I might end up back in the hospital. He's right, so I'll try to spend more time in bed.

Friday, March 28, 2008 1:42 AM
2 Weeks 4 Days Old

I called the NICU and spoke to the same nurse that Fletcher had last night. She said she can see a huge improvement in him compared to last night; his color is better and he's very alert and moving all around. She did say that she's been suctioning out his nose and throat every few hours because mucus keeps building up and she wants to avoid it going to his lungs. It's good that she's getting it out, but I wonder why he's producing so much.

She read me the notes in his chart and during the day Fletcher only had three bradys. Since her shift began at 7:00 PM, Fletcher has only had one, which he was able to recover from on his own.

I stayed in bed all day today and even took two long naps. I feel much better, so I'll definitely go see Fletcher in the morning. I haven't held

Fletcher yet and his primary nurse told me that he's ready to be held. I can't wait to hold him.

Fletcher is now 2 pounds, 7 ounces.

Sunday, March 30, 2008 5:15 PM
2 Weeks 6 Days Old

I got to hold Fletcher today! I really wanted to be alone with Fletcher when I held him for the first time. My father-in-law came down on Friday so he and my mother-in-law have been taking care of the other kids all weekend. Today they took the kids to the park, so I was able to go to the hospital alone.

As soon as I got there Fletcher's primary nurse asked me if I was ready to hold him, which of course I was. I sat down while she lifted him out of the isolette and then she placed him in my arms. What a moment! It's so hard to describe the emotions I was feeling. His body seemed so small and fragile, but at the same time, he filled my arms and my heart! I was aware of every breath, heartbeat, and movement he made. Fletcher's still so tiny, but acted just like a newborn; kneading my chest, twitching and jerking and making sweet noises. I was only able to hold him for a few minutes because he got over-stimulated quickly. I hated to put him back down, but his well-being and comfort come first. Preemies are so different because my other children wanted to be held all the time!

Monday, March 31, 2008 3:43 PM
3 Weeks 0 Days Old

My in-laws left last night and my mom flew back in to town today. She and my in-laws have been great, coming in every other week while I regain my strength. They're taking amazing care of the kids, but at the same time, I hate that I need them here. Having them here reminds me of how dependent I still am.

The neonatologist called and told me that the steroids and diuretics weren't working as well as she'd hoped. She ordered another blood transfusion, increased his dose of diuretic, and raised his oxygen level to

45%. I don't like that he needs to be on higher oxygen. Like the steroids, oxygen can have harmful, long-term side effects, such as eye problems, but once again we have no choice because the benefits outweigh the risks. The doctor hopes that as his systems mature, the apnea and brady episodes will stop.

Fletcher's now eating 23 ccs at a time and weighs 2 pounds, 11 ounces. The neonatologist asked who will be his doctor once he goes home, and I told her that we have a family doctor. Fletcher won't be allowed to leave the hospital without an actual pediatrician, preferably one who's worked with preemies.

Fletcher's primary nurse gave me the names of two pediatricians who see many of the NICU preemies once they're discharged. I set up appointments with them next week to discuss Fletcher and his potential health problems. I guess it's a good sign that the doctor wants me to secure a pediatrician for him.

Monday, March 31, 2008 8:58 PM
3 Weeks 0 Days Old

I had my two-week post-partum OB appointment this morning. I'm still very swollen and struggling physically. My OB asked if I was starting to get better and I told him that my body feels like that of a 95-year-old woman who's been hit by a train. He said my body was basically in the equivalent of a train wreck and that it'll take time to heal from the last few months. He told me he would bet that I'm doing too much, and said I need to take it easy.

I'm still anemic, so he gave me a prescription for iron pills. Hopefully they'll help with my heart palpitations and extreme fatigue. My OB scheduled an ultrasound for me in three months to check that everything has healed properly.

I'd been searching for an appropriate thank you present for my OB for everything he had done these last few months. When I was in the hospital, I had a huge bag of fruit shaped candies and my OB would always stop by and pick out the banana shaped ones. As a thank you to him, I brought him a five-pound bag of just the banana candies. He was so surprised that he gave me a hug, which was out of character for him. I'm glad he liked them.

Tuesday, April 1, 2008 9:44 PM
3 Weeks 1 Day Old

I just got some very bad news about Fletcher from the neonatologist. She said his oxygen levels are getting worse and they're not sure how to treat him since the steroids and diuretics don't seem to be working. The neonatologist is going to call the other neonatologists working in the area and see what they think. She's also going to call the head of Pediatric Pulmonary to come in for a consult and hopefully give her some ideas. Babies with lung issues are her specialty.

For now, another chest x-ray and more blood work has been ordered first thing in the morning to check Fletcher's thyroid function. Fletcher's oxygen has been increased to 55%, so the physician assistant warned me that Fletcher might be put back on the CPAP during the night. I hope this is only because Fletcher's system is so immature, but I know better. The fact that he's starting to get worse after all those medicines, and that the neonatologist is out of ideas about how to fix the situation, doesn't fill me with much confidence or hope. I'm glad she called the head of Pulmonary since babies with lung issues are her specialty, and I would think she's seen these cases thousands of times. I have to believe that.

Wednesday, April 2, 2008 2:45 PM
3 Weeks 2 Days Old

I'm not handling all the stress with Fletcher very well. To make matters worse, after telling Lee about the latest lung issues, his response was "Oh great! So Fletcher's going to have severe asthma and breathing issues his whole life?!" I wanted to scream at him and say that we should be grateful if that's all he has to deal with. Instead, I let Lee vent and then walked out of the room. Right now, I'm trying to deal with a struggling three week-old preemie.

I was going to wait until this afternoon to go up to see Fletcher because I knew he had x-rays and blood work done this morning, but I couldn't wait that long to speak with his doctor. The neonatologists start rounds around 10:00 AM, so my mom and I got to the NICU at 9:45 AM. Today there was a special staff meeting and they made rounds earlier this morning. I was so upset, but the nurse called the physician assistant to come talk with me.

His chest x-ray this morning was even worse than the previous one. The medical staff had hoped Fletcher's lung problems were typical preemie issues, but now they're convinced that he's struggling because of the lack of amniotic fluid during the pregnancy, which is a lot more serious. As Fletcher grows, his lungs have to work harder. Usually lungs grow with the rest of the body, but in Fletcher's case, they don't seem to be growing at all. This means at some point, he could outgrow his lungs and die. The neonatologist hopes Fletcher's lungs will start to grow, but at this point she has no idea if they will. If they do, they may not grow fast enough. It's so hard to wait, watch and see Fletcher struggling.

CHAPTER 9

I've read a lot about preemies, but there's nothing like learning through experience.

Wednesday, April 2, 2008 5:46 PM
3 Weeks 2 Days Old

I received a frantic phone call from Fletcher's physician assistant this afternoon telling me that he's been gasping and has not able to take deep breaths. They're going to run a bunch of tests to rule out an underlying infection, but they now have his oxygen level on the highest setting. I desperately want to drive back up to the hospital, but my mom and Lee won't let me. His test results should be back later tonight, so I'll call around midnight. I just hope he has an infection or something he'll outgrow. I thought the pPROM wasn't going to be an issue because he came out crying, and his first 10 days of life were amazing. Now, three weeks later, he's suddenly taken a turn for the worse.

Thursday, April 3, 2008 5:02 PM
3 Weeks 3 Days Old

Fletcher had a much better night than his day yesterday, probably because they increased his oxygen. The results of his urine culture haven't come back, but his blood work came back normal. Also, two out of three thyroid tests were normal. The third one takes a few days longer. Low thyroid levels can be normal in preemies, but abnormal thyroid levels can sometimes be indicative of developmental problems, or even cerebral palsy.

The night nurse said she had to suction out Fletcher's nose and throat every few hours. Each time she would get significant globs of mucous out. While that is great because those are the globs that keep getting in his lungs, it's not good that he keeps producing so much mucous. Even though I tested negative for cystic fibrosis in previous pregnancies, the NICU tested Fletcher and he is negative. Of course that diagnosis would've been life threatening, but it would have given the doctors a clear-cut way to treat him.

Fletcher had no desaturations at all, and his oxygen levels have been in the 90s all night long, which is great. Normal saturations are between 90 and 100. When levels fall below 85 there is cause for concern. Fletcher has consistently been in the mid-to-upper 80s, so this is the best he's ever been!

The nurse told me she's going to feed Fletcher more often than the typical two-hour schedule. She and Fletcher's other nurses have noticed that 30 minutes before his next scheduled feeding, he becomes extremely agitated and they believe it's because he's starving! This is a good sign. My body must be sensing that Fletcher needs to eat more often because my milk supply has increased dramatically. It's amazing that I can be so in tune with Fletcher, even though he's not here with me.

I was up all night crying and Lee was so supportive. He let me cry on his shoulder, something I needed to do for a long time. We're both frightened, but need to stay positive that Fletcher will outgrow these issues.

Friday, April 4, 2008 11:22 PM
3 Weeks 4 Days Old

My mom left on Wednesday, so I'm officially the one back in charge. The kids had off from school today, but I wasn't feeling up to taking them anywhere. I told them they could play on the driveway and I sat on a chair watching them. Cassie ran into the garage, climbed up on a chair and then started jumping on it. I yelled for her to climb down, but she ignored me. The chair started to wobble so I stood up and was about to run into the garage to catch her, but my legs buckled and gave out on me. I fell down, scraped my knees, hit my chin on the ground, and twisted my wrists. Thankfully, Cassie was able to catch herself and didn't get hurt, but I did. My body and my ego were badly bruised. The kids were frightened by what happened to me, so I quickly made a joke about it to get them calmed down. In reality though, all I wanted to do was stay on the ground and cry.

Saturday, April 5, 2008 2:00 PM
3 Weeks 5 Days Old

I'm still getting used to being home, and the kids are, too. They expect me to be able to do everything I used to do and don't understand that I still need time to heal. It's hard to explain to them that I'm limited in what I can do, and there have been more than a few tantrums when I've had to tell them no.

Lee took the kids to the beach this morning so I could rest. Rather than stay in bed, though, I wanted to rearrange my kitchen pantry, cabinets, drawers and closets. When I was in the hospital my mother-in-law rearranged items in the house in a way that made it easier for her to find things more easily, when cooking, cleaning and doing laundry. I appreciate how well she took care of everyone but now that I'm home I'm frustrated that I am unable to find things in my own house. I'll feel a lot better to have things back where they were before I was in the hospital.

Monday, April 7, 2008 10:59 PM
4 Weeks 0 Days Old

Fletcher's breathing troubles have been getting worse. Last night, they ended up putting Fletcher on a high-power oxygen machine, which is a step below the CPAP. I really hope he doesn't need to go back on the CPAP.

The nurse assured me that once preemies reach three pounds they really start improving at an exponential rate. I truly hope so since he already weighs 2 pounds, 15 ounces.

Fletcher is now starting to become more aware of his surroundings. He's making eye contact whenever I come see him and can distinguish voices. He's been lifting and turning his head, and moving his body all over the place. The nurse joked that Fletcher must really want out of his bassinet because he keeps scooting himself over to where the door is!

Tuesday, April 8, 2008 4:44 PM
4 Weeks 1 Day Old

I'm so proud of Spencer, Wesley, and Cassie and the way they're handling everything. They're thriving in school, looking out for each other, and being so loving to me. I'm glad they are doing so well, despite having to be in school all day and with me being so preoccupied with Fletcher.

Thursday, April 10, 2008 4:48 PM
4 Weeks 3 Days Old

I spoke to Fletcher's neonatologist today while she was making rounds during my visit with him. She said that while she hopes Fletcher has chronic lung disease, something he could outgrow, there's a real possibility he might have a fatal lung disease that he will die from within the next few months. She said a lung biopsy could help determine which disease he has, but it's a very dangerous procedure to do on such a small baby. The only thing we can safely do is to wait and see. She would not speculate on which she thinks it could be, but said we just have to think positively. Of course I'm devastated. I really thought once he was born and took his first breath that it would all be okay. At this point, it was all supposed to be ok.

Thursday, April 10, 2008 10:26 PM
4 Weeks 3 Days Old

Lately I've been experiencing sharp chest pains and difficulty breathing. It's been a month since the surgeries, so I finally went to my OB to get checked out. He sent me for a chest x-ray, to look at my heart and lungs, and an electrocardiogram (EKG), to record my heart's electrical activity. Thankfully the results of both tests came back normal. My OB thinks I have serum sickness, which is basically an allergic reaction to all the different blood I received from the blood transfusions. He said that although they match blood type, it's impossible to match things like gender, race, type of diet, and age. In addition, some of the blood and platelets were from universal donors or type O negative. He said that all these variables have caused my body to misinterpret these new proteins in the serum as being harmful and it has started to attack them. My OB said that as my own blood starts to regenerate over the next few weeks, I should start feeling better. I'm glad to have an answer, but I'm frustrated with all the setbacks and how long it's taking for my body to heal.

Friday, April 11, 2008 3:49 PM
4 Weeks 4 Days Old

Fletcher has another x-ray this morning and the neonatologist and physician assistant are having a hard time interpreting it. They said there were a lot of white patches and legions on his lungs, but don't know if they're from him being on the ventilator when he was first born, or are actually hypoplastic lungs caused by pPROM. Since he wasn't on the ventilator that long, the neonatologist thinks this scar tissue is from my having pPROM, which deeply concerns her. Preemies lungs can usually outgrow the scar tissue from being on the ventilator, but scar tissue from going without amniotic fluid for so long is a much more dire diagnosis. Fletcher's nurse said that it's way too early to know for certain, but hopefully they'll know more within the next few weeks.

I can't believe how stupid I was to think the pPROM issues were behind us! I'm still in the same situation as I was during my pregnancy; not knowing if Fletcher is going to survive or not. Holding him, seeing his sweet face, watching him, and getting to know him, but still not knowing if he's going to live or die is pure torture.

I asked again about doing a lung biopsy, but they reiterated that it's not an option for him, mostly because of having to put him under anesthesia to do the procedure. They said if he has to be put under, he'd have to be put on a ventilator and at this point, they don't think he's strong enough to come off the machine once they're done with the biopsy. The plan is to do another chest x-ray in three weeks.

Sunday, April 13, 2008 9:12 PM
4 Weeks 6 Days Old

I'm so distressed with everything going on. I'm tense and unable focus on anything. I lose patience easily with the kids and I'm completely miserable. My family is encouraging me to see a therapist, but I don't see the point. What could a therapist actually do for me? It's not as if he could change this situation, or give me any answers. There's been one person who's been able to keep me grounded, and that's Fletcher's nurse. She told me to be happy for today and not to project about what might happen, because no one ever knows what the future holds. It's a simple statement, and although my situation with Fletcher is different, I still need to cherish the time I spend with him.

Monday, April 14, 2008 2:25 PM
5 Weeks 0 Days Old

Fletcher's nurse must have told Fletcher's doctor about my struggles, because the neonatologist came over to me this morning and told me I need to stay more positive. She said that Fletcher can sense my feelings and he needs to know that I believe in him. I told her I'm positive about 10% of the time, but she said that wasn't enough! She's right and I will try harder, especially if it will help Fletcher.

The neonatologist said she'll do another chest x-ray in the morning and has ordered them once a week for the next few weeks, rather than wait to have another one in three weeks. She wants to monitor his lungs more closely, and said right now they're hoping his lung issues are not getting worse.

There has been some good news, though. Fletcher has gone two days without having any apnea or brady episodes, so we can introduce Fletcher to the bottle. The nurse asked me if I wanted to start now, and of course I said yes.

I was too nervous to hold him and try to feed him a bottle, so the nurse sat Fletcher on her lap and I watched. It was amazing that after all these weeks of not having to actually eat, Fletcher knew what to do with the bottle. He had his eyes closed until the nurse touched the bottle nipple to his lips and then his eyes opened wide and he poked his tongue out of his mouth. The nurse gently stroked his lips and suddenly Fletcher started sucking on the bottle. He was only able to suck for a few moments before he choked and then fell asleep, but the nurse said she was impressed by how well he did. She said Fletcher will still use the feeding tube, but they'll keep introducing the bottle to him once a day.

I was so glad that I was there to see this milestone. The nurse said next time I come to visit, I can give him the bottle. Even though I have three other children, I've never used a bottle before. The nurse said she would help me, especially because giving a bottle to a preemie can be challenging. Right now it's more about getting Fletcher to learn how to suck, swallow, and breathe, and not so much about actually eating.

Fletcher already weighs 3 pounds, 4 ounces and is eating a full ounce at every feeding.

Tuesday, April 15, 2008 8:46 PM
5 weeks 1 Day Old

Fletcher's x-ray this morning was exactly the same as his previous one; it showed no change. The neonatologist had hoped his lungs would show some improvement, such as lung regeneration, but she was happy that his lungs weren't getting worse.

The doctors have been able to lower Fletcher's oxygen pressure from five liters, the highest, to three liters. He had a couple of bradys overnight last night, but it's still a lot better than last week.

I had an appointment today with one of the pediatricians the NICU had referred me to. She was nice enough, but very blunt. After I filled her in on my pregnancy, and Fletcher's condition, she said that it sounds like Fletcher's lung issues are fatal. In her many years of experience with preemies, she said lung disease caused by pPROM often takes this same course and ultimately, the preemie catches an infection, or develops pneumonia, and never recovers. After saying that, there didn't seem to be any point in continuing the conversation. I thanked her for her time and cried the rest of the day. Lee has been dealing with work issues and is already so overwhelmed by everything going on, so I decided not to call him after the meeting. I didn't even discuss it with him tonight. I can't talk about it to anyone right now. All I keep thinking about is my poor, sweet little guy.

I really need to heed the advice of Fletcher's nurse and be grateful for every day I have with him, but it's so hard. I'm not good at ignoring the what-ifs, or being someone who can live in the moment and be happy for the here and now, without worrying about tomorrow, or the next day.

Wednesday, April 16, 2008 6:43 PM
5 Weeks 2 Days Old

In addition to being an emotional wreck, I'm still in a lot of physical pain. My stomach and legs are still very swollen, and I'm still weak and wake up sore every day. I found an on-line message board for women who have had hysterectomies and after reading through their posts, I felt better about my recovery. Most of the women said that at five weeks post-surgery, they spend most of their day in bed and only do minimal things around the house. As my mom pointed out, these people were not pregnant, nor were they on bed rest for seven months. They also didn't have their hysterectomies along with a C-section and another emergency surgery. I'm feeling a little less frustrated with the slow rate of my recovery now.

Thursday, April 17, 2008 8:53 PM
5 Weeks 3 Days Old

Spencer's been asking a lot of questions about Fletcher, so I asked him if he wanted to skip school and come with me today to meet him. He said yes. I was apprehensive about letting Spencer meet Fletcher, especially because of Fletcher's fragile health, but I decided I would feel more horrible if something happened to Fletcher and they hadn't met, even though Spencer had asked. I also thought that it would help ease Spencer's anxiety about everything going on, because he would no longer have to wonder about where I go when I leave the house and where his brother is.

When we got to the front desk at the NICU, I was told that a sibling visitation form had to be filled out by me and signed by a NICU staff member at least a week in advance. The front desk refused to let us go in. I was so upset no one had explained this to me. Spencer, sensing my anger and frustration, started crying and begged to go back home. There was no way I was going to leave without Spencer and Fletcher meeting, so I left Spencer in the waiting room while I went to get Fletcher's nurse. She was very apologetic and spoke to the admissions desk. After about ten minutes, Spencer and I were allowed to see Fletcher. The nurse got one of the medical staff to sign-off on the form, which is good for seven days. Now I know to fill out the form every week just in case Spencer asks to see Fletcher again.

Just as we were finally about to go see Fletcher, another nurse came up and screamed that Spencer had to put on a gown and a mask or else he would not be allowed to see Fletcher. Spencer started to cry again. I was so mad at the NICU for making this a horrible experience for Spencer. The NICU is intimidating enough for an adult, so imagine how it is for a five year-old. Instead of being warm and welcoming, they went out of their way to make this a traumatic experience. If Fletcher were to be discharged soon, I would've told the staff how horrible they were to siblings and that they needed to learn to show them compassion. Of course, Fletcher wasn't leaving anytime soon so I had to bite my tongue.

I finally convinced Spencer to put on the gown and hold the mask up to his face while we walked towards Fletcher's area. Spencer walked slowly, but asked a lot of questions, which I think was a good sign. Fletcher was sitting on the nurse's lap being bottle-fed and Spencer kept talking to me, not realizing we were standing in front of his brother. As soon as Fletcher heard Spencer's voice, he opened his eyes, pushed away the bottle, and turned his head towards Spencer. When Spencer went up to him, Fletcher stretched out his arm toward Spencer. I told Spencer to touch Fletcher's hand and there was an instant energy between them. Fletcher held onto Spencer's finger, and the boys stared at each other a few moments. It was magical. It was a moment I'll cherish for the rest of my life. On the way home, Spencer said he couldn't believe how tiny Fletcher was, but also said it surprised him how hard Fletcher squeezed his finger. What a wonderful day!

Friday, April 18, 2008 1:43 PM
5 Weeks 4 Days Old

Fletcher is now big enough to wear real preemie clothes. He looks so adorable in onesies, pants, shorts and t-shirts, even though they are a little big on him! He's been able to maintain his body temperature too, which is great. I started bringing him blankets his brothers and sister used when they were babies. The bad part is now that Fletcher is wearing clothes, the NICU expects me to do Fletcher's laundry at home and bring the clothes back every other day. The NICU also said I have to wash Fletcher's clothes separately from the rest of the family using a special detergent. It's exhausting and impossible for me to do, so I've asked Lee to take turns with me dropping off and picking up the clothes, blankets and bottles.

Friday, April 18, 2008 7:29 PM
5 Weeks 4 Days Old

I'm still in an enormous amount of pain and called my OB to refill my prescription pain medicine. I've only been taking it a few nights a week, but last night I ran out. I know I'm not healing as fast as I should be because I'm doing way too much. I want to go to the NICU as often as possible, and I also want to be here for my other kids. It's exhausting living this way and it's hindering my recovery, but there's nothing I can do about it.

Monday, April 21, 2008 5:10 PM
6 Weeks 0 Days Old

The hospital parking situation is a nightmare. It's hard enough finding a parking space under normal circumstances, but they've started construction on it, and every few days they close the garage completely. I've been parking in the other garage, which is attached to a different hospital wing. The problem is that it takes me an additional 20 minutes to get to the NICU, which is time I should be spending with Fletcher. Now I feel even more rushed because I also have to leave him even earlier. It's just an added stress that I don't need.

Friday, April 25, 2008 3:12 PM
6 Weeks 4 Days Old

Lee's been a huge help this week. He went up to the NICU three times this week and sat with Fletcher. I've been taking advantage of it and staying in bed most of the day. The nurse told Lee that she was able to lower the oxygen pressure to two liters and that he's been very stable all week. It's great news!

Sunday, April 27, 2008 2:03PM
6 Weeks 6 Days Old

Well, after a week of being stable, Fletcher has suddenly taken a turn for the worse. His oxygen pressure is back up to four liters. The neonatologist said he'd probably be put back on the CPAP tonight because even on the higher pressure, Fletcher is having a lot of desaturations. He had another chest x-ray this morning, but no one has interpreted yet. Fletcher's primary nurse will be back tomorrow and hopefully she'll have his results.

I'm so shocked! I had convinced myself that Fletcher was over the worst of it because he was finally improving. I feel so stupid for allowing myself to think Fletcher was on the road to recovery and might actually be able to come home next month. Now I don't know what to think or what to expect.

Monday, April 28, 2008 2:13 PM
7 Weeks 0 Days Old

Fletcher went back on the CPAP last night, but is still struggling to breathe and keep his oxygen levels up. The doctor put him on another round of steroids to see if that will speed up his lung development.

In the meantime, he had his second brain scan. The neonatologist casually mentioned to me that the scan showed some white spots on his brain, which could be possible PVL. That means he'll be mentally challenged, and/or in a wheelchair, for the rest of his life. She didn't have the time to discuss it with me, so she took out a piece of paper and wrote down the words "Periventricular Leukomalacia" and "Cerebral

Palsy" and told me to look them up on the Internet when I got home, and then moved on to her next patient.

I opened up Fletcher's medical chart to see if I could get more information. I found the head scan notes and was reading through them when a nurse saw me and snatched the chart away. She said charts are off-limits to anyone except medical staff. I couldn't believe this! I was just told that my son could have brain damage and this nurse is reprimanding me about reading my son's chart? I tried to remain calm and said this is my son and she had no right to interfere. She told me that not only did she have the right to stop me, but also she could have me kicked out of the NICU for reading my son's chart. Unfortunately, I learned from my experience in antepartum that she was telling me the truth, but that doesn't mean it makes any sense to me. The doctors and nurses don't seem to have enough time to give parents full details about medical tests and diagnoses, so it would make sense to allow the parents to read through their children's charts. This is a battle for another day, though. Luckily, I read most of the report and had enough information to do Internet searches, and I also found out there's another head scan scheduled for next Monday. I'll discuss all this with Fletcher's primary nurse later in the week.

Tuesday, April 29, 2008 5:48 AM
7 Weeks 1 Day Old

As soon as I got home from the hospital yesterday, I read up on PVL and CP and became physically ill. These are two very serious issues and I can't believe the neonatologist was so blasé about them. I feel lost and don't know where to turn. I understand that those who work in the NICU deal with these issues on a daily basis, but this is all new to me. These are serious, lifelong issues that affect the entire family. I'm getting more and more resentful of the NICU and their treatment of me and my family, but because they're the ones taking care of my son, I need to keep my feelings to myself for now.

Tuesday, April 29, 2008 11:20 PM
7 Weeks 1 Day Old

I met with Fletcher's nurse today and we talked about his head scan. She told me that the scan was inconclusive. Although the scan showed white areas, the technician said he couldn't tell if the spots were actually on Fletcher's brain or were shadows from the lighting on the machine. If the former is the case, then the spots are actually brain damage, which could mean he might be in a wheelchair, need leg braces, or have cerebral palsy. She said there's nothing to talk about until the scan is repeated next week.

Wednesday, April 30, 2008 9:13 PM
7 Weeks 2 Days Old

I discovered an on-line message board with families affected by PVL. I read through most of the posts and have asked a few questions. I've gotten a lot of responses and have learned so much from these amazing people. I'm so grateful that I found this group because, sadly, I've gotten more information from these strangers than I have from Fletcher's doctors.

Lee and I talked about the possibility of Fletcher having PVL and how that will change our family if he does. Lee's first response is that Fletcher is our son and we we'll love him no matter what. Lee's inability to cope with Fletcher's situation has made him appear cold in the past, so hearing this makes me feel relieved. That being said, Lee said he wants to wait for a definitive diagnosis before we get ahead of ourselves. He's still hopeful that the spots shown were shadows from the machine's lights. It struck me that I've been focusing on the worse case, while Lee is choosing to stay positive. I really need to be more like him!

Thursday, May 1, 2008 10:23AM
7 Weeks 3 Days Old

Fletcher's eye doctor left a note telling me that that he has level two ROP. I'm trying not to freak out because I've read that most preemies end up outgrowing it. He'll have another eye exam in two weeks and if he gets worse, we'll discuss treatments.

Thursday, May 1, 2008 9:51PM
7 Weeks 3 Days Old

I've been thinking a lot about how differently my OB and his staff managed me when I was in the hospital, and how the NICU medical staff is treating me. I miss the mutual respect and openness that I had with my OB. Since my OB's office is in the same building as the NICU, I decided to see my OB and ask if he would read Fletcher's chart and give me his opinion. I'm desperate for answers and I trust my OB to take the time and be honest with me.

My OB's office staff was so warm, sympathetic, and caring - such a difference from the NICU. They all got up to greet me and gave me hugs. I was so touched that I started crying. They told me my OB wasn't in his office, but they immediately paged him to come meet me. Unfortunately, after an hour of waiting and my OB never showing, I had to leave and pick up my kids from school. I left his office completely deflated. I was so disappointed, but his office assistant promised to give him all the information and have him call me. I trust him so much and feel like I have no one to talk to about all Fletcher's issues. It's pathetic that out of all the NICU medical staff, the only one I feel that would discuss everything with me is my OB! I hope he calls soon, but if he doesn't, I already feel better that he knows what's going on with Fletcher.

Friday, May 2, 2008 11:19AM
7 Weeks 4 Days Old

Fletcher now weighs 4 pounds, 3 ounces! His breathing has been slowly improving and was able to be taken off the CPAP this morning! Lee said he would go up to the hospital this weekend. I need the weekend to catch up on sleep, mentally regroup, and to hang out with Spencer, Wesley, and Cassie.

Monday, May 5, 2008 2:14 PM
8 Weeks 0 Days Old

I had a much-needed weekend with the kids, but felt guilty for not going to see Fletcher, so as soon as I dropped them off at school, I went to the NICU. I had completely forgotten that Fletcher's head scan was this morning. His nurse saw me washing my hands and ran up to tell me that Fletcher's head scan was clear! The spot was either just a lighting issue or a transient spot that was there and then resolved itself. If it's the latter, there's still some concern about possible brain damage so the neonatologist is going to schedule an MRI in a couple of weeks which will answer all the lingering questions. For now though, I'm going to think positively.

I had such a peaceful, bonding visit with Fletcher. I love being able to take him out of the isolette by myself and cuddle with him on the chair. I miss the one-on-one time that I was able to have with my other children. I'm doing my best to create our own moments together.

While I was holding him, a nurse I had never met came up to Fletcher and he gave her the biggest smile! She called him "Wolfie" and he started to coo and giggle. Apparently Fletcher is a popular baby in the NICU and already has a girlfriend.

Tuesday, May 6, 2008 3:23PM
8 Weeks 1 Day Old

I still haven't heard from my OB and am so distraught about it. I understand that once the OB delivers the baby, their work is done, but I thought after everything I went through with him during my pregnancy, he would have at least called me back.

Fletcher is still having a hard time bottle-feeding. He can't grasp how to breathe and swallow at the same time, so he's choosing to breathe, which I can't blame him for doing! I met with the speech therapist today that works with preemies that have lung and breathing issues. She said it's just going to take time for Fletcher to understand how to co-ordinate his eating and breathing. I've been told that white, male babies are the laziest in terms of using a bottle, and preemies with lung issues have a very hard time eating. He's sucking very well and blocking the milk from going down the wrong pipe, but he doesn't understand how to swallow and breathe at the same time. I've spoken to a few other moms of preemies and they all said they had the same issues with their babies and didn't think they would ever learn to eat properly. However, seemingly out of nowhere, they learned and it was as if they'd been doing it all along. I hope that happens with Fletcher, and soon.

When I talked about Fletcher's eating issue with the neonatologist, she said in preemies without lung issues, that usually is the case, but she blames his lung issues for why he isn't able to drink from the bottle. Since his lung issues are going to be chronic and long term, and we need him to drink from bottles in short term, I asked, "What are the options?" The NICU won't discharge him until he is able to eat, so if he can't drink from a bottle, she'll have to put in a gastrostomy tube (g-tube). The g-tube is a feeding tube that is surgically placed through the abdomen directly into the stomach for children who aren't able to take in their nutrition by mouth. It's a way for Fletcher to be able to get all his needed nutrition while bypassing his breathing issues. The neonatologist said to give Fletcher a few more weeks of trying to bottle feed before discussing the g-tube.

Fletcher was 4 pounds, 8 ounces at his weigh-in last night. He looks like a full-term baby!

Thursday, May 8, 2008 11:00 PM
7 Weeks 3 Days Old

I'm finally on a great breast-pumping schedule. It took awhile, but now it's become second nature for me. I pump first thing in the morning, bring my pump and use it while visiting Fletcher, take it with me when I'm out with the kids and/or when I get home in the late afternoon. I get in two more sessions before bed. I'm surprised with how easy it is to pump discretely, even out in public. The fact that my pump looks like an over-sized diaper bag definitely helps, too. The NICU told me to take advantage of not having to get up to feed the baby during the night. It took me a few weeks to allow myself that luxury, but once I stopped setting the alarm, I was able to sleep through the middle-of-the-night pumping session. I feel a little guilty about not getting up because I'd been using that time to call the NICU and check on Fletcher, but even the night nurse told me I should try to sleep instead. Since I have a freezer full of breast milk, and am getting enough milk each time I pump, I acquiesced.

Friday, May 9, 2008 3:45 PM
7 Weeks 4 Days Old

My mom and her boyfriend are coming to town this afternoon so I didn't spend a long time with Fletcher. I wanted to have some time alone before she arrived and the kids came home. However, while driving home from the NICU, I realized I missed my exit just as I drove past it. I lost it. I started bawling and screaming out loud about needing time to myself and asking out loud why this was happening. It took me an additional 40 minutes to get home and by that time I was completely frazzled. My body is tired, my brain is fried, and my nerves are shot.

Sunday, May 11, 2008 11:45 PM
8 Weeks 6 Days Old

It's Mother's Day. I'm thankful to be a mom, but right now I feel like a failure to all my kids. I'm not being the mom any of them deserve right now. I certainly don't feel like celebrating. The day dragged on for me, but I was glad to have my mom there as a distraction. I tried to make the focus more on her than on myself. I felt incomplete without having all four of my children with me. Although we all spent the day together, my heart was torn and my mind was with Fletcher. I was so absent that while I was chopping vegetables for dinner, I ended up slicing my finger. It hurt so badly and I wish it didn't happen, but I have to admit that part of me was glad to have a physical symbol of my emotional pain.

Lee had the foresight to know that Mother's Day would be hard on me, so at dinner, he handed me the most amazing present. It was a silver bracelet with five silver ovals, each engraved with the kids' names and the center one engraved with the word Mommy. No matter what happens, I will always be Mommy to Spencer, Wesley, Cassie, and Fletcher. The bracelet is so beautiful and the sentimental value is priceless.

Tuesday, May 13, 2008 2:34 PM
9 Weeks 1 Day Old

Our cat needed her annual check-up so I took her today, and brought the kids with me because they love the huge fish tank in the office. Today, in the waiting room, there was the sweetest kitten available for adoption. He was this bundle of black fur and we were allowed to take him out and play with him. The kids and I were instantly smitten. With so much tension at home, especially with me going back and forth to the hospital, I thought having a new kitten would be great for the kids. They begged me to call their dad and ask him if we could have the kitten, but Lee immediately said no. The kids all started crying, even though they had just met the kitten and it wasn't something we had ever promised them. I know their sadness wasn't really about the kitten, but more because of everything they've been dealing with these past few months.

We all went home feeling sad and I wished I hadn't taken the kids with me to the veterinarian. While I was making them lunch, our doorbell rang. Wesley looked through the window and yelled that it was Daddy at the door. I didn't understand why he wasn't at work and why he didn't use his key to let himself in. I was a little annoyed and asked Wesley to open the door for him. When the door opened, the little kitten from the vet walked in the house! The kids screeched and screamed with pure happiness! Lee thought about it after we called and agreed that a kitten would be a great idea. It was an amazing moment to hear the sound of laughter and see the pure joy in the kids' faces; something we haven't experienced in awhile.

Friday, May 16, 2008 10:11 PM
9 Weeks 4 Days Old

My OB finally called this morning and talked to me for a long time. First he apologized for not getting back to me sooner. He listened to me explain everything going on with Fletcher, my fears, and also what the NICU doctors have been saying. He ended up telling me a personal story about a family member who had triplets that were healthy at birth, but at 18 months of age two were diagnosed with severe autism. His point was that we never really know what's going to happen with anyone in the future. He said he was sorry that the NICU doctors weren't being forthcoming, but to try not to focus on all the tests and test results. He said that the worst-case scenario with Fletcher's lungs could be that he won't be able to run as fast when playing sports. We should only be so lucky. He ended up giving me his private office phone number and said I could call him anytime. I was glad he called.

Saturday, May 17, 2008 4:48 PM
9 Weeks 5 Days Old

Fletcher is now five pounds! The NICU made a huge sign for his crib. He's now one of the bigger preemies in the area. He's been breathing much better, too. The neonatologist has lowered his oxygen pressure to two liters.

The neonatologist was encouraged and scheduled a chest x-ray for this morning, hoping to see lung improvement and regeneration. However, there was no change from the previous x-ray. I have a meeting with the pulmonologist next week to see where we go from here, but I spoke with the neonatologist this afternoon. She said she's very concerned that Fletcher is still unable to breathe after he swallows and can't bottle feed. She thought by now he'd be able to do that. She reiterated that Fletcher wouldn't be allowed to leave the NICU without being able to take a bottle or having a g-tube. She told me to get prepared for him needing the g-tube, but we'll wait a few more weeks before making that decision. She did say that Fletcher's lung issues are more moderate than severe, so that's good.

We talked about his head scans. I asked about the last two scans and how one showed possible PVL and the next one was clear. The neonatologist explained that in her opinion, neither ultrasound was conclusive, but decided not to schedule him for an MRI. She said there's nothing that can be done if he does have PVL, or any brain damage, except to prescribe early intervention with physical and occupational therapy, which he's already started. If he has any issues, they'll emerge when he's around one year old. If or when he starts exhibiting signs of delay or symptoms of any brain injury, his pediatrician would order the MRI at that point. As much as I would like a definitive answer, and the unknown terrifies me, I know the doctor is right to cancel the MRI right now.

Sunday, May 18, 2008 10:31 PM
9 Weeks 6 Days Old

Lee's been handling things so badly. He's usually very calm and patient, but lately he's been snapping at the kids and not wanting to talk to me. I can't blame him. I feel so incredibly guilty and horrible for putting him and the kids through this. If only I didn't push having a fourth child, but how could I have known this was going to happen? Nevertheless…

Wednesday, May 21, 2008 11:23 PM
10 Weeks 2 Days Old

Fletcher's lung issues seem to have stabilized, so the NICU has put him on the discharge list, although he hasn't been assigned an actual date when he can come home. The neonatologist is waiting to see if his feedings will get better before we have to resort to putting in the g-tube. Either way, he'll be sent home with an oxygen tank and cannula, as well as an apnea monitor. The apnea monitor is a portable machine used to monitor the baby's heartbeat and breathing at home, similar to what the hospital uses, but much smaller and less complicated. She said Fletcher would need to use it for at least three months. There's no telling how long he'll need to be on oxygen.

Before preemies are allowed to leave the hospital, their parents must take an infant CPR and apnea monitor class. I took the class this morning and there was one other mother in it with me. She had given birth to her son at 25 weeks, and not only is he going home before his actual due date, he doesn't need to be on oxygen and he's bottle-feeding perfectly. It made me wonder if I should have delivered Fletcher earlier. I don't know. I hated that I was so envious of this woman. It was a rough day and I was ready for the class to be over.

The neonatologist also said before Fletcher could come home, his siblings had to be up-to-date on their vaccinations. There are a few I delay until the kids are older, so I have to make appointments for them to get these shots.

Even though it's been over two months, I feel as if the NICU is now rushing Fletcher out the door. I want him home, but don't want him to leave before he's medically ready.

Thursday, May 22, 2008 5:25 PM
10 Weeks 3 Days Old

Wesley and Cassie each had to get two shots today. They were very brave, especially when I told them the reason they needed them was so that Fletcher could come home soon. I hope that's true.

Chapter 10

I'll never give up on anyone, especially if he hasn't given up on himself.

Monday, May 26, 2008 11:24 PM
11 Weeks 0 Days Old

This is all so unbelievable. Fletcher went from being on the discharge list last week to suddenly becoming so sick that the doctors are telling me this turn for the worse could be the end of his life. Everyone is shocked. The medical staff thinks that Fletcher has aspirated, which means that liquid got into his lungs. Aspirating is bad in any circumstance, but for Fletcher, who is a preemie with BPD and other lung issues, this could kill him.

Fletcher is now on a higher dose of diuretics, more steroids, and back on the CPAP. He's having clusters of bradys again. He had three while I was holding him this morning. The third one took almost a minute for him to start breathing again, even with the nurse helping. He also has a hacking cough, which the doctor fears could turn into pneumonia. I remember what the pediatrician had said to me about her experience with preemies getting pneumonia and asked the nurse about her thoughts. She said, "Let's just hope it doesn't turn into pneumonia." I left the NICU scared, sad, and with a heavy heart.

Tuesday, May 27, 2008 11:23 PM
11 Weeks 1 Day Old

I got a call from the neonatologist a few hours ago telling me that Fletcher's blood tests showed his oxygen levels were dangerously low, and his carbon dioxide levels were extremely high, so she had no choice but to put Fletcher on the ventilator. They had to sedate him because he became so agitated.

The neonatologist decided not to wait for the pneumonia test results and started him on antibiotics. His x-ray showed increased lung hyperinflation and scarring, in addition to the aspiration.

Visualizing Fletcher lying alone, sedated, with a tube down his throat and not being able to do anything for him made me nauseous. This is beyond anything I can comprehend. I don't know what to do for him. I hate being so helpless and out of control, especially when it comes to my child.

Wednesday, May 28, 2008 12:26 PM
11 Weeks 2 Days Old

I went back to visit with Fletcher last night. I still can't believe what's going on. The night nurse was very kind and tried to calm me down by saying this setback isn't anything unexpected, but I don't believe her.

Poor Fletcher is sedated and on a high dose of pain medicine. He's been getting so agitated that they've already had to increase his sedation medicine. His feedings have been suspended, so he's on IV fluids. He has a PICC line so they can draw blood for tests easily and do a transfusion, if necessary. His arms are tied down to his bed because even on the sedative, he's thrashing around and trying to pull the lines out of his body.

The neonatologist ended up putting him on an oscillator ventilator. The oscillator is different than a regular ventilator because it keeps the lungs open with constant positive pressure, while vibrating the air at high pressure, in order to avoid damage to the lungs.

This is all beyond awful. Fletcher was doing well. I don't know how this got so bad, so fast. And the fact that he's up there in the hospital, alone, without me by his side, makes this so much worse.

Wednesday, May 28, 2008 11:26 PM
11 Weeks 2 Days Old

The neonatologist increased Fletcher's steroid dose as a last-ditch effort. Another neonatologist started his rotation today. He said that BPD only explains some of Fletcher's issues and struggles. He thinks that Fletcher is outgrowing his lungs. The lung hypoplasia is just too widespread and there isn't enough good lung tissue growing.

Fletcher looks horrible and from what the nurses keep saying about having to heavily sedate him, it seems that he's not doing well emotionally. His face and body are swollen and his coloring is off. Even his once-silky hair feels brittle. I knew Fletcher could die from BPD, but I thought since it's been almost three months, he would've started growing healthy lungs by now. He's beaten the odds so many times before, but the reality is, that even on the ventilator, Fletcher's lungs aren't pushing enough oxygen through his blood. His carbon dioxide levels are so high and his blood oxygen levels are so low that his body won't be able to sustain itself for much longer. The doctors want to see how Fletcher does over the next few days and hope that his lungs start to respond to the steroids.

Thursday, May 29, 2008 11:00 PM
11 Weeks 3 Days Old

Fletcher tested positive for pneumonia. Although I know pneumonia in a preemie could be fatal, I'm actually relieved to have a diagnosis, rather than simply blaming the development of his lungs. The neonatologist changed his antibiotic to one that specifically treats pneumonia.

Fletcher looks sickly and feeble. He's hooked up to so many IV lines and his face is so swollen that he looks disfigured. It's beyond distressing to see him this way. He's such a fighter, though. When I saw him this morning he was kicking all around and seemed agitated so I asked the nurse if she stopped sedating him. The nurse answered, "No, you're looking at Fletcher on sedation!" He's on the ventilator and his oxygen levels keep falling into the 70s. Normal levels are in the 90s. He's such a feisty little guy, but I wish he would stop fighting and try to relax, and hopefully his levels will normalize so he can start recovering.

Friday, May 30, 2008 2:28 PM
11 Weeks 4 Days Old

Even on heavy sedation, Fletcher is continuing to get agitated and thrash around. He pulled the ventilator tube out this morning and it took three nurses to get it back in. The neonatologist changed his pain medicine frequency from every four hours, to having a constant drip to keep him more comfortable. The neonatologist said he watching Fletcher and taking cues from him at this point. Right now he thinks things can go either way.

I'm trying to deal with everything as best as I can, but my nerves are shot. I'm mentally exhausted, tired, and worn out. I haven't fully recovered from my pregnancy, but I need to try to regroup and find more energy to keep fighting. It's even harder now because I'm still trying to physically heal while pumping and trying to maintain my milk. At some point, something is going to have to give, but I'm hoping that if Fletcher gets better, I will too.

Sunday, June 1, 2008 2:54 PM
11 Weeks 6 Days Old

It's my EDD today. June 1st was the day I would have been full term with Fletcher. Instead of celebrating his life, I'm being told Fletcher's condition has worsened. The neonatologist had hoped that once they started treatment for the pneumonia, that he would show remarkable improvement. But he hasn't. The neonatologist is out of ideas and set up a consultation with the pulmonologist tomorrow morning to get medical advice and possible treatments. The neonatologist said her main focus right now is to keep Fletcher comfortable.

Knowing that Fletcher might be dying, the NICU social worker asked me if I would like a Rabbi to come in to the NICU to meet with me and bless Fletcher. I'm not very religious, but thought that might bring us some peace, so I accepted her offer.

Sunday, June 1, 2008 11:12 PM
11 Weeks 6 Days Old

Last night when I approached Fletcher's area in the NICU, there were two nurses and the neonatologist trying to revive Fletcher because his oxygen saturation levels dropped way down and they weren't able to get his levels back up. They emergency paged the respiratory therapist, who came running with a handheld machine and was able to resuscitate him. I watched in horror knowing there was nothing I could do.

When they stabilized him, the neonatologist came up to me, handed me a phone and told me to call anyone who might want to say their goodbyes and/or be here with him. I called Lee and he said he was on his way.

The neonatologist asked me to sign a do not resuscitate order (DNR) because Fletcher is seriously ill. If he continues to crash and they keep intervening, it could leave Fletcher in a worse medical state than before.

He thinks it would be best not to use aggressive efforts, and to just let him go.

I've heard about DNRs, but actually signing one is so surreal. There are different parts to sign, such as "do not use chest compressions", or "only use oxygen", or "do not use any medication", or "do not tube feed". I didn't feel comfortable signing the blanket DNR, so the neonatologist and I reworded the document. It basically says to use medical means, but if he were to die, then I give permission for them to stop doing resuscitation and not to put him back on the ventilator. I felt more comfortable signing this DNR.

In the meantime, the neonatologist increased his steroids and diuretic dosages. They stopped all feedings and started him on an IV to keep him hydrated.

Lee came to sit with Fletcher and me. We're both unsure of what to do, but even if we thought of something, there really isn't anything we can do but be here with our son.

Monday, June 2, 2008 4:31 AM
12 Weeks 0 Days Old

The neonatologist gave us the option of transferring Fletcher to the hospital's hospice floor, or bringing him home. He explained that Fletcher's carbon dioxide level have remained at 105 millimeters of mercury (mm HG), which is more than twice the normal level. His chest x-ray was the worst one yet, with scarring throughout his lungs. He's having constant desaturations and bradys even though he's on the highest ventilator settings. His nurse told me that when infants get really sick, their faces tend to swell, and Fletcher is extremely swollen all over.

The neonatologist thinks Fletcher has reached the point where he's outgrown his lungs. He said that half of his lungs are nonfunctional because of the hypoplasia, and the rest has been affected by pneumonia. Now there's only a tiny bit of healthy tissue remaining, and it doesn't seem to be growing along with him.

Lee called his parents to drive down and say their goodbyes. We're going to meet with the neonatologist and pulmonologist tomorrow morning to discuss all the options.

Tuesday, June 3, 2008 11:31 PM
12 Weeks 1 Day Old

Lee's parents arrived at our house this afternoon, so Lee and I decided spend a few hours with Fletcher. Before we left, I collected all the saved breast milk, bottles, and my breast pump accessories and threw them out. Lee asked me if I was sure I wanted to do that and I said no, but I did it anyway. I'm not sure why I had that urge, but it was an impulse I couldn't control.

When we got to the NICU, Fletcher was actually showing signs of improvement. The night nurse said his carbon dioxide levels fell and were 90 mm Hg, and he was also a lot less swollen. Lee and I were delighted, but also so confused. Just hours ago the neonatologist told us to say our good-byes because Fletcher could die at any moment, and now the nurse doesn't understand our apprehension when she tells us Fletcher is showing slight improvement.

This can only be described as pure torture.

We sat with Fletcher for a little while, but I was so tired I asked Lee to take me home. I said goodnight to my in-laws and crawled into bed, still fully dressed. Lee talked to his parents and then I heard him go outside. He went through the trash and got out my breast pump, tubes, and bottles, and then sanitized them. He's not ready to give up on Fletcher. I need to follow his lead.

Wednesday, June 4, 2008 1:31 PM
12 Weeks 2 Days Old

An assistant Rabbi from one of the local synagogues met us in the NICU this morning. She asked me what I needed from her and which blessings I wanted her to say. I had no idea. I went with her to a private room to talk in more detail and she skimmed through her prayer book. I asked which synagogue she was affiliated with. All of a sudden, she started tearing up and told me that this was her last week at her synagogue because the main Rabbi is leaving and he chose not to take her with him. She cried and said that this time next week, she would be unemployed and was very upset and nervous about her future. I was shocked that she was having this conversation with me, making it about her, while my son was fighting for his life. I wondered if she forgot why she was meeting with me. The fact that she'll be alive next week, and that my son might not be, never even crossed her mind! Not only was it very uncomfortable for me, I was also getting angry that she expected me to comfort her. I stood up and told her to pick a prayer about peace, healing, and being watched-over, and left the room. She followed me out and we joined Lee and my in-laws at Fletcher's side. The prayers the assistant rabbi chose were perfect and while she said them, I was able to forget about her inappropriateness and could focus on Fletcher and the powerful words that were being said. These were blessings telling Fletcher that he is loved, that he doesn't need to struggle, and that he can live in peace, wherever that might be.

CHAPTER 11

Roller coasters are fun at amusement parks, but not so much in the NICU.

Wednesday, June 4, 2008 11:38 PM
12 Weeks 2 Days Old

Fletcher has made small improvements, but the neonatologist told me not to get too optimistic. Fletcher's original neonatologist is back on rotation and her opinion is similar to the previous doctor's. She said that half of Fletcher's lungs are dead and the other half has pneumonia. Today's x-ray showed dark white masses all over his lungs. She's unable to differentiate whether it's from the pneumonia, or is permanent scar tissue. If it's pneumonia, she hopes it will go away and not cause more scar tissue. If it's not pneumonia and it is actually scar tissue, then his lungs have irreparable damage and he'll eventually die from nonfunctioning lungs. The neonatologist told me this is a new situation for them, because most infants with lung hypoplasia never live for more than a few days after birth. Fletcher's lung issues are not so clear-cut. She said he definitely has hypoplasia and BPD, and that the pneumonia complicated an already disastrous situation. It doesn't look good for him.

Amazingly, even on the high dose of sedatives, Fletcher was awake when I visited him today. I got to talk to him and stroke his hair. He is such a strong little guy. This would almost be easier if he was sickly and weak.

Thursday, June 5, 2008 11:55 PM
12 Weeks 3 Days Old

Fletcher is still on the ventilator and probably will stay on it throughout the weekend, which means they have to keep him sedated. I hate that they need to sedate him. The physician assistant told me that the neonatologist, and everyone who has been working with him for the last three months, is distraught about Fletcher being so sick. I didn't realize Fletcher had so many people who care about him.

Friday, June 6, 2008 11:37 PM
12 Weeks 4 Days Old

Fletcher has officially stumped his entire medical team. This morning's x-ray still showed white patches on his lungs, but they're in different spots than they were on Wednesday's x-ray. The neonatologist called the pulmonologist, who said that she had never seen anything quite like this before and basically told the neonatologist to handle Fletcher how she thought best. I don't understand why the pulmonologist won't give any advice, especially since Fletcher issues all stem from his lungs. Both the neonatologist and I are completely stunned and frustrated by the pulmonologist's attitude.

The neonatologist told me she's going to try to slowly wean Fletcher off the ventilator and then take her cues from him.

Sunday, June 8, 2008 10:11 PM
12 Weeks 6 Days Old

Fletcher is doing exactly the same; he's not worse, but not getting better. I saw him tonight and his arms and feet were covered with bruises and scabs from all the IV line changes and medication injections. It's so excruciatingly painful to see him this way and know all that he's going through. I wish he would get on the road to recovery…and stay there!

Monday, June 9, 2008 11:48 PM
13 Weeks 0 Day Old

I just got off the phone with the NICU and the nurse told me that Fletcher became so agitated, that he grabbed the breathing tube from his windpipe and pulled it out, extubating himself off the ventilator. The nurse immediately called the neonatologist, but noticed that Fletcher's vitals remained stable, so they decided to keep him off the ventilator and under close observation. She said she'd still keep him sedated in order to keep his respiratory rate low.

I'm not sure how I feel about all this. I wish I could ask Fletcher why he pulled out the tube; was it because it hurts or is uncomfortable, or because he wanted to show that he could breathe on his own? Or is he trying to tell us all that he's done fighting? I want him to be able to tell me.

Tuesday, June 10, 2008 10:29 PM
13 Weeks 1 Day Old

Tonight was Spencer's Pre-Kindergarten graduation ceremony. I had heard that one of the mothers in his class was a nurse on the antepartum floor at the same hospital that I was in, but I never had a chance to meet her before I was admitted. A woman walked in behind me and I immediately recognized her and I could tell she recognized me as well, but she didn't stop to say hello. She was the antepartum nurse who had given me the wrong dose of one of my medicines and had argued with me about my MRI results. I wanted to be friendly, so I went over to say hello even though I knew it would be awkward. The first thing she said to me was that she was glad I came over to her because she's not allowed to approach any previous patients or talk to them about their hospital stay unless the patient initiates the conversation. I thought that was weird because I've been out of the hospital for a few months. I've also run into other antepartum nurses and they all approached me and initiated the conversation. I should have ignored her idiotic comment, but couldn't! I asked her point-blank, "If I didn't come up to you, what would you have done?" She said, "I would've ignored you." I stared at her and decided it wasn't worth my time or effort to talk to her any further. She tried to make small talk, but the ceremony was about to start, so I said good-bye and went to sit with my family. The strangest part was that she never even asked me about the baby.

Wednesday, June 11, 2008 1:16 PM
13 Weeks 2 Days Old

Today is the last day of school and I'm panicking! When we first put the kids in full-time I was so upset, but now I like my schedule. I drop them off at school, go see Fletcher and talk with the medical staff, rest for an hour, and then pick the kids up. Now I don't know when I'll be able to go see Fletcher and meet with his medical staff. I could go late at night, but usually by the afternoon I'm exhausted, in pain, and need to rest.

I want the kids to have a fun summer, but I know they won't get my complete attention. I'll be with them during the day, but I'll be thinking about Fletcher and trying to save my strength to get up there to see him. My friends keep telling me that Fletcher is being well taken care of and that Spencer, Wesley, and Cassie need me more, so I need to focus on them. Even though Fletcher might not realize what's going on, I do, and the guilt of not being able to see him daily just adds to my heartache.

Lee and I came up with a plan. He said he would go see Fletcher during the day a few times a week, and would come home early on other days so I can see Fletcher without having to drive there late at night. I already feel more comfortable and will start coming up with fun activities to do with my other kids.

Thursday, June 12, 2008 1:39 PM
13 Weeks 3 Days Old

Fletcher has started to regress. I wanted to go and spend the day with him, but Lee has to work and it wouldn't be fair to Spencer, Wesley, and Cassie for me to leave them with friends. At least I was able to have a phone meeting with the neonatologist while the kids watched a show on television.

The neonatologist told me that she wants Fletcher to have a tracheotomy. A tracheotomy is a major operation where they would open up his windpipe, or trachea, and insert a plastic tube through the opening. The tube would act like the windpipe, but the other side of the tube would be hooked up to the ventilator. She said the tracheotomy is the same as Fletcher being intubated, but without the dangers of him pulling the tube out. It would also be more comfortable for him. She didn't say it would help cure him, or help him with his lung issues.

Lee and I talked and decided that we're against the tracheotomy. Even though the NICU is acting as if the tracheotomy surgery and aftercare is no big deal, we know that's not the case. During my online research, I stumbled upon a support group for families with children who have tracheotomies. I met a member who lived a few miles from me and she agreed to meet with us.

She explained how her entire home-life has drastically changed. She has around-the-clock, live-in nurses that her insurance company won't pay for. She converted her living room into her daughter's room because she needed the space for the ventilator and all the medical supplies. She's had to learn when and how to suction the tube, when and how to clean the skin around the tube, when and how to change the tracheotomy ties, when and how to change the tube, what to do in a respiratory emergency, how to give oxygen through the tube, how to watch for infections, how to give medications, and where she can take her daughter and for how long. She explained how difficult it's been having strangers live with them and take care of her daughter, how hard it's been to give up the main area where the family used to hang out, how she had to give up her full-time job for this new full-time position even though the family relied on her income, and how caring for her daughter takes up most of her time. She's unable to give her husband and other children much of her attention. She said that her other children often act-out, especially when she tells them they can't have friends over because of the danger of germs being spread to her daughter. She has to constantly explain why she can't do activities with them, all the while feeling so extremely guilty. She said that she's had to call an ambulance at least once a month to take her daughter to the hospital and that her neighbors gossip about that, rather than ask if they can help. However, even after telling us the negative, she said it's all worth it because her daughter is alive and is expected to come off the ventilator in the next few months. Obviously her daughter's sickness is something very different than Fletcher's, but it was a relief to know that she would be there for us if Fletcher ultimately needs a tracheotomy.

On our way home, Lee and I both said we would be willing to do everything for Fletcher, if the doctors assured us this would help Fletcher's lungs start growing and working on their own. We would sacrifice anything if it meant Fletcher would have a full life, but the NICU isn't telling us that this procedure is the means to that end. The neonatologist even admitted to us that the tracheotomy would only take the place of the tube that is down his throat in order to make Fletcher more comfortable, but it wouldn't help with his lung issues.

We feel like the tracheotomy discussion is premature because Fletcher is too weak to undergo such a serious operation right now. He would need to go back on the ventilator and be put under general anesthesia. One of the anesthesiologists told me he wasn't confident that Fletcher would come out of the anesthesia once the operation was over.

After a long discussion with Lee, we decided against having it done. When I called the neonatologist back and told her our decision, she was extremely short with me and said if we didn't agree to the tracheotomy, she would have no choice but to discharge Fletcher because there's nothing else she can do for him. She said the NICU would make arrangements with Hospice to send Fletcher home with oxygen and medicines. She said he might improve, but more than likely he would pass away in a few days. She said someone from the hospital would be in touch with me later in the day. I feel like its Lee and me versus the NICU. I wish I had someone to guide me and help me figure out the best plan of action for our son! I hung up the phone and was astounded by the neonatologist's coldness. I wondered if this was a mind game she was playing with me, and had hoped I would call her bluff and give in to having the tracheotomy done. It's inconceivable that she would be playing games with my son's life.

I decided to call the NICU social worker and discuss the situation with her. Since she hadn't spoken to the neonatologist, she didn't want to give her opinion, but offered me another solution. She said we could move Fletcher to the Pediatric Intensive Care Unit (PICU). Fletcher would be reevaluated by a new set of doctors and have a private room where the entire family can visit and even sleep over. If the PICU doctors feel he's terminal, he can be moved to the children's hospice area on that floor. She told me to talk to Lee and then get back to her. In the meantime, she would speak to the neonatologist about Fletcher.

Before I had a chance to call Lee, the physician assistant called me to say that the neonatologist doesn't feel comfortable discharging Fletcher, and wants to set up a meeting with the pulmonologist to hear her thoughts before deciding if he's terminal. I told her I agree and that I didn't think having the neonatologist threaten me was professional or helpful. She apologized for how the neonatologist acted, but said it was out of love and concern for him. She said that this neonatologist rarely shows emotion over her patients, but that she has grown to love Fletcher and wants him to get better and thinks that the tracheotomy might help. I didn't want to argue and I was touched to hear that this doctor cares so much about my son. I thanked her for calling and told her I'd see her at the meeting this afternoon.

Thursday, June 12, 2008 6:39 PM
13 Weeks 3 Days Old

I called a friend to watch the kids. Lee was able to clear his schedule and join me at the hospital for the meeting.

When I arrived at the NICU, the social worker said she wanted to talk to me in private before the meeting. She thought it was the right time to tell me about a non-profit community organization that provides pediatric palliative or hospice care for children with life-long, severe chronic issues or terminal diseases. They also can act as advocates for the parents, as well as advisors. This community pediatric palliative care organization sounded amazing and exactly what I desperately needed. The social worker knew I would want to work them so she pre-arranged for them to come to the meeting and talk with me afterwards.

The meeting was very intimidating, but extremely productive. It included the neonatologist, her physician assistant, the head pediatric pulmonologist and her colleague, the NICU social worker, Fletcher's head nurse, the NICU respiratory technician, the medical doctor and two other team members from the pediatric palliative care organization, Lee, and myself.

The neonatologist started the meeting by telling us that because we're against the tracheotomy, we would have to meet with the hospital Ethics Review Board because we're not legally allowed to refuse Fletcher this operation unless the Ethics Review Board agrees. It's unbelievable. Obviously, Lee and I aren't medical professionals, but we don't feel like the NICU is giving us any concrete reasons why this surgery is medically necessary.

The pulmonologist, who is the head of Children's Pulmonology at the Children's Hospital, defused the tension in the room by saying the tracheotomy isn't an urgent surgery, so we don't have to decide about it right now. She said she reviewed Fletcher's chart and didn't think his lung issues were fatal. She said he's very sick and does have chronic lung disease and BPD, but thinks, in time, healthy tissue will eventually grow. She said if an adult's lungs looked like his, it would be terminal, but since baby's lungs develop and grow for several years, she's hopeful that Fletcher's will grow. She agreed that the hypoplasia caused much of his lung scarring, but if all his lungs were hypoplastic, he would've died soon after birth. She thought Fletcher's latest crash was due to the pneumonia. Even though he took himself off the ventilator, he needed to stay on it much longer.

This was the first time Lee and I had been told that Fletcher could actually grow healthy lungs. She convinced us to put him back on the ventilator for a couple of days to see if he improves. We will all re-group in a few weeks. The tracheotomy discussion has been put aside for now.

Lee left to go back to work and I took the pediatric palliative care team to see Fletcher and talk with them. I don't know why I wasn't told about this group before, but I'm so thankful to have them here now. Their doctor said she agreed with everything that was said in the meeting. The team plans on visiting Fletcher every few days, will get updates on his condition directly from the NICU, and will discuss any and all questions or concerns that I have at any time.

I feel like a load has been lifted off my shoulders and that I'm not alone in dealing with all of these medical decisions. This is a special group and a lifesaver for me. Now I have a team watching out for Fletcher and giving objective advice to us.

Friday, June 13, 2008 2:00 PM
13 Weeks 4 Days Old

When I got to the NICU this morning, it was closed and they weren't letting any visitors go inside. I found out the doctors were performing heart surgery on a preemie right there in the NICU! It's amazing how some seemingly serious issues, like heart defects, can be repaired so easily, but others, like lungs, can't be. There's been so much progress made in healing preemies' medical issues, except for their lungs and brains. Why is that? Why is it that the NICU can do a heart operation bedside, but can't figure out a way to heal, and grow, lungs?

Sunday, June 15, 2008 5:30 PM
13 Weeks 6 Days Old

It's Father's Day. Lee wanted to spend the entire day together with Spencer, Wesley, and Cassie, rather than split the day and have me go up to the hospital. Of course I felt so guilty about not going to see Fletcher today because Lee could be with our other kids. But today was Lee's day and he's right - the kids needed a day with the five of us staying together. Fletcher wouldn't know the difference, but the other kids would.

I called Fletcher's nurse throughout the day to check in. The nurse today was someone I'd never met before. She was very annoyed and angered that Fletcher didn't have a parent with him on Father's Day. The third time I called she told me if I wanted to know how he was doing, I could come up to the hospital and see for myself. I didn't want to argue with her, especially because a part of me felt like she was right. I should be up there with him. I hate that I feel so conflicted all the time, but I wish the nurses understood how hard this is on a parent with other children. I decided I would wait until the shift change to call and see how he was doing.

Sunday, June 15, 2008 11:51 PM
13 Weeks 6 Days Old

Fletcher's off the ventilator! The nurse said they took him off this afternoon. I shouldn't have let the nurse treat me that way because, had I kept calling, I would've learned this great news earlier. The night nurse said he's on the CPAP, but they hope to wean him back to the oxygen cannula within the next few days. I'm so happy and I'm sure Fletcher is too!

Monday, June 16, 2008 4:39 PM
14 Weeks 0 Days Old

The NICU primarily takes care of preemies that don't want to be handled or touched. By the time the baby becomes full-term, he leaves the NICU, so the staff isn't used to dealing with older, sick babies. Now that Fletcher is an older baby, he has different needs. He wants to be held, cuddled, touched, played with, and stimulated. The nurses don't have the time to constantly hold, cradle, and play with him, so they suggested I bring him a portable infant swing and baby bouncer seat. The kids and I went to the store and bought them this morning. They were so sweet, testing out each one to find the perfect ones for their little brother. We all brought them to Fletcher this afternoon. Luckily, cartoons were on in the waiting room, so I could leave the kids for a little while and see how Fletcher liked his swing and bouncer seat.

The nurse put Fletcher in the swing first, which wasn't easy because of the oxygen and feeding tubes, but she was finally able to get Fletcher in the swing. At first, Fletcher couldn't understand what was going on. He started to cry until he realized how much he loved the motion and being able to sit up and look around. It was so cute to watch his facial expressions. His eyes were wide open the entire time he was in the swing, and his head kept moving back and forth. It was a big deal for him, and after a few minutes he became over-stimulated and had to be put back in his crib. The nurse assured me that Fletcher's behavior was completely normal, and that she was certain Fletcher loved the swing. She promised that she would make sure all the nurses put him in either the swing, or seat, at least once during their shift. I was so glad I could be there to see Fletcher acting like a typical baby and having fun for a change. When I got back to the waiting room, all three kids were mesmerized by the cartoons and hadn't even noticed my absence!

Monday, June 16, 2008 10:23 PM
14 Weeks 0 Days Old

The night nurse told me that Fletcher stayed in the swing for quite awhile tonight. She's taken care of him before and said he seemed so happy being able to sit up and watch all the activity in the NICU while being rocked by the swing. I'm so happy for him, but at the same time, it makes me sad that I'm not the one holding and rocking him. When my other children were infants, they were held or worn in a sling most of the day allowing us to have constant interaction. Rationally, I know this is a very different situation, but emotionally it's very hard to comprehend that my baby is living this way.

After I visited this afternoon, the nurse was able to put Fletcher on a high-flow nasal cannula! What a great day Fletcher had today!

Tuesday, June 17, 2008 11:45 PM
14 Weeks 1 Day Old

Fletcher's CO_2 levels started climbing back up to unacceptable levels this morning, so he had to be put back on the CPAP. He had been acting up, too; screaming and crying a lot. Whenever he gets agitated, it's bad for his lungs, so the pulmonologist ordered him to be sedated again in order to give his lungs a break. I'm so disheartened. He had such a positive day yesterday and now he's back to lying in his crib, wearing a CPAP, and being heavily medicated. It's not fair to him. I want him to be a normal baby; happy and silly, and not have to struggle.

I didn't get up to see him today, but will get up there tomorrow night.

Wednesday, June 18, 2008 10:59 PM
14 Weeks 2 Days Old

Tonight, when I got to the NICU, the night nurse told me she'd heard that some of the day nurses have been talking about me. They said they didn't appreciate the fact that I'm constantly questioning the medical staff and were disgusted that Lee and I refused to allow the tracheotomy. They called me heartless because, in their minds, I don't want to do everything possible to keep Fletcher alive.

It's becoming clear to me that the goal of the NICU is to keep babies alive, and stable, long enough for them to leave the NICU. They don't seem interested in getting them well or trying to ensure a high quality of life. This revelation came to me tonight after hearing about the other nurses' comments. This seems to be the root of the tension between the staff of the NICU and me. Of course I want to do everything I can to keep Fletcher alive, but I'm also concerned about getting him well. I worry about the side effects of the procedures being done to Fletcher, and I also don't believe in doing an operation or giving medicine just because they're accessible. I want concrete reasons for why the doctors want to do certain procedures, and how they think it will benefit Fletcher. I don't think that's unreasonable. Until these nurses have gone through this with their own children, they need to keep their opinions to themselves. As soon as I got home, I snapped! I told Lee how the nurses were bad-mouthing us and that they had no right to judge us. But then I asked him if maybe I should stop asking so many questions and just allow the NICU to do whatever they want. Lee reassured me. He said that the only opinions that matter are ours and not to worry about the nurses. He told me that he respects and admires how I fight for our son by researching and asking questions, but the nurses perceive it as me questioning their expertise and take it as a personal criticism. It's hard enough having a child in the NICU without having to deal with gossiping and insecure nurses! I just need to remember that Fletcher is my one and only concern, and hearing Lee tell me that he's proud of me will help me ignore all the negativity.

CHAPTER 12

There are so many medical procedures to learn about, but too little time.

Thursday, June 19, 2008 2:43 PM
14 Weeks 3 Days Old

The pulmonologist said she thought Fletcher's lungs would've shown some growth by now, but his x-rays are still the same as previous ones. She told me she wants to do a bronchoscopy, which is a procedure where a bronchoscope is inserted down his throat to examine his airways, trachea, bronchi and lungs. She would also do a lung biopsy at the same time to check for infectious diseases. She specifically wants to check on his epiglottis, the flap of skin that covers the trachea and keeps food and liquid out of the airways. Her thought is that perhaps his epiglottis is weak, which is causing his lung aspirations and/or inflammation.

I'm not sure that Fletcher is strong enough to have this done, especially because he would have to be put back on the ventilator for the procedure. The pulmonologist thinks that Fletcher will probably have to be put back on the ventilator soon, so that shouldn't be a factor in my decision. I called pediatric palliative care doctor there agreed with the pulmonologist that he should have the bronchoscopy done. I'll talk with Lee about it tonight, but I think I'll allow them to do it.

Friday, June 20, 2008 3:18 AM
14 Weeks 4 Days Old

I went back to the NICU late last night and a new neonatologist, who was starting his three-week rotation, was making rounds. I wanted to get his opinion about Fletcher and he was very straightforward with me. He summarized Fletcher's condition and then said that things don't look good for him. He told me about a new type of BPD where the baby can live up to two years before outgrowing their lungs, when in the past, a baby with BPD would die within the first few hours, or days, of life. He told me that a baby at a nearby hospital just passed away at eight months old from this type of BPD. He said there's no way to know if this will be the case with Fletcher until it happens.

I asked his opinion of the bronchoscopy and lung biopsy. The neonatologist said he's against Fletcher having either procedure. The fact that Fletcher has some healthy lung tissue is only a small part of his overall condition. Aside from healthy tissue, lungs also need functioning alveoli. Alveoli are miniscule air sacs in the lungs that are responsible for the exchange of oxygen and carbon dioxide in the blood. In preemies, these don't open very well, mainly because they need a chemical called surfactant, which the lungs don't produce until later in pregnancy. Lung surfactant is a protein complex found in the lining of the alveoli that prevents the alveoli from collapsing during breathing, and protects the lungs from infections and injuries. He said the alveoli are so miniscule that they can't be seen during a bronchoscopy, and the results of the lung biopsy might not be conclusive. Another reason the neonatologist doesn't want him to have the procedure is because Fletcher would have to be put on the ventilator. He said Fletcher most likely wouldn't be strong enough to wean himself off of it.

The neonatologist doesn't think Fletcher's lungs are producing any surfactant. He said, since Fletcher is already three months old and still struggling, and the fact that I had severe oligohydramnios for so long during the crucial lung development stage of pregnancy, he believes Fletcher's lungs won't ever start producing it.

I asked him about the tracheotomy and he agreed with me that it's is a major operation that won't cure Fletcher's lung disease. The neonatologist said neither the bronchoscope, nor tracheotomy, would solve Fletcher's lung issue. Even though it was hard to hear, I felt like hugging him. This was the first time any of the doctors had been honest with me. He validated all my doubts, fears, and frustrations about all the different tests and operations, rather than regurgitate what the other neonatologist and pulmonologist recommended.

The last thing he said to me was, off the record, that if this were his son, he would not allow him to be put back on the ventilator. He said that could end up making matters worse for us. I wanted to ask him what exactly he meant, but he had to get back to the other babies. I took it to mean that if Fletcher went back on the ventilator and didn't get better, we would have to make a decision about taking him off of it, which is not only horrible, but would involve the entire hospital and ethics team.

I'm grateful to this neonatologist for being so open and honest with me, but I'm sick about everything. I don't want to believe that Fletcher's conditions are fatal, but what he said to me makes sense. I don't want to believe that the NICU isn't acting in the best interest of my son, but it seems like they want to do procedures knowing Fletcher won't benefit from them. I don't want to believe there are disagreements among the staff that is caring for my son. What I really want is for Fletcher to get better, and now I am not sure that he ever will.

Monday, June 23, 2008 11:07 PM
15 Weeks 0 Days Old

I saw Fletcher tonight and he was awake and alert. I was so grateful for that. I got to hold his hand and stroke his hair. It was so quiet in the NICU and I was able to sit and focus on him. There were no doctors around, and the nurse left us alone the whole time I was there. It was a beautiful night. The only thing that would've made it better is if I got to bring him home with me.

Tuesday, June 24, 2008 9:46 PM
15 Weeks 1 Day Old

The x-ray from this morning still showed that his lungs are still a horrible mess with no signs of regeneration. Everything else with Fletcher is perfect, why won't his lungs start growing? Please, start growing!

The neonatologist called the pulmonologist to try to set up another meeting with everyone in a few days, but I let the staff know that if there's any significant change in Fletcher before then, I would want a meeting as soon as possible.

Wednesday, June 25, 2008 9:23 PM
15 Weeks 2 Days Old

I had a follow up appointment with my OB today. He wanted me to have an ultrasound first to check that everything was healing properly. I told the technician that I'd been bleeding for a few weeks and suffering from constant pain in my lower left side. I told her it felt similar to the pain I had with my ectopic pregnancy. I could tell she thought I was being dramatic, but then she saw fluid in my left tube. Luckily it was just a ruptured cyst, but the technician noted that she was amazed how in tune I am with my body. I thought she would've known that by now!

After my ultrasound, I met with my OB. He asked about Fletcher and had no idea about everything that was going on. He was clearly upset and said he honestly thought that once the baby was born and could breathe, he would be fine. He added, "What a shame, given everything you've been through…" He's such an optimist and I hate that I took some of that away from him.

Of course I cried when I was telling him everything. He listened and then asked if I wanted a prescription for an antidepressant. I could feel my blood starting to boil and yelled at him, asking "Don't you think I am acting appropriately given the circumstances and what I'm going through right now?" He apologized and said he felt helpless and wanted to do something and that was the only thing he felt he could do for me.

He changed the subject. He brought up me having an HIV test because of all the blood I received. Although HIV usually doesn't show up in blood work until six months after being infected, he thought it would be a good idea to get a preliminary test.

My OB sent me to the lab, where they drew eight vials of blood to do a full blood work-up, including a CBC, hemoglobin, and HIV test.

I left his office feeling extremely heavy-hearted.

Wednesday, June 25, 2008 10:47 PM
15 Weeks 2 Days Old

The pulmonologist never called the neonatologist back. The respiratory analyst called her and the pulmonologist said she'd see Fletcher next week. She reminded the respiratory analyst that at the meeting she said she'd re-evaluate Fletcher in three weeks, and it's only been two weeks. Once she sees Fletcher, she'd get in touch with the neonatologist. I don't understand her bad attitude. Isn't it her job to work with the NICU? I know that was her initial plan but I thought she'd check on him sooner than that since he's not improving. I hate that I need her, but I do, so I'll wait until next week to hear more.

Thursday, June 26, 2008 2:52 PM
15 Weeks 3 Days Old

The pediatric palliative care organization doesn't only focus on the sick child; they act as a support for the entire family. This morning, one of their social workers came to the house to talk with the kids. She wanted to make sure the kids understood what was going on, and also to hear their thoughts. Cassie is too young to know what is going on, but she sat on my lap and listened the entire time. Spencer told her that he met Fletcher, and Wesley explained how I was in the hospital, now I'm home, but Fletcher is still at the hospital. The social worker listened to the boys and talked briefly about coming to the house a few times a month. She wants the kids to get used to seeing her because if or when Fletcher comes home, she'll be the person who makes the kids feel comfortable having a special needs brother. At first, the kids were unsure about her, but by the time she left, they seemed to like and open up to her. It's such a relief to have someone help with the kids and their emotional issues.

Monday, June 30, 2008 6:38 PM
16 Weeks 0 Days Old

Today started another neonatologist rotation. The neonatologist this month is the one who keeps pushing the g-tube, tracheotomy, and bronchoscopy. We're at a critical time for Fletcher and I wish he had a neonatologist who included me in the discussions of Fletcher's treatment, rather than giving ultimatums and pushing her own agenda. Having her on call this month makes me even more thankful to have the pediatric palliative care organization as my sounding board.

Tuesday, July 1, 2008 8:48 AM
16 Weeks 1 Day Old

The neonatologist called late last night and told me that Fletcher's vitals are weakening, so she had to increase the CPAP settings. She told me she scheduled the bronchoscopy for early next week. I didn't realize the decision was already made to have the scope done! I remembered my conversation with the previous neonatologist and asked her if this would show any information about the alveoli, hoping she would contradict the other doctor and give me a concrete reason for this procedure. She said it would not, but still wanted the scope done to see if they might find something to explain Fletcher's lung and breathing issues. I voiced my concern about putting Fletcher back on the ventilator, but she was dismissive and said we can discuss it before the test.

I know the doctor thinks that I'm just being a contrarian, but I'm not getting any answers that justify these procedures. I hate always questioning the medical staff and wonder if I should be more passive. I think I need to schedule another meeting.

Wednesday, July 2, 2008 9:25 PM
16 Weeks 2 Day Old

Today is Lee's birthday. I'm glad it's during the week and Lee had to work, because I didn't plan anything special for him. I doubt he even noticed because he's very preoccupied with Fletcher. Neither one of us can imagine celebrating anything right now. The kids, however, asked me to bake a cake, so I did. We just sang to Lee and I'm certain what he wished for as he blew out the candles.

Thursday, July 3, 2008 9:14 PM
16 Weeks 3 Day Old

Fletcher's condition is still the same. Fletcher's bad days are getting worse, and his good days aren't getting him back to where he was before he got pneumonia. I would give anything for his lungs to start growing and have a miraculous recovery. Every day I wake up hopeful, and every night I go to bed depressed and downhearted because he isn't showing any improvement. I'm completely drained.

Friday, July 4, 2008 10:23 PM
16 Weeks 4 Day Old

The country is celebrating Independence Day and I'm sitting here wishing for silence. My neighbors invited us to shoot off fireworks with them. I had to agree, for the kids' sake, but all I wanted to do was hide out at home. Unfortunately, things are tense at home, so I might as well be out. Lee is overwhelmed. Dealing with work issues and crises while your son is in the NICU can't be easy. I can't imagine, but I'm in no position to play the role of the loving, supportive wife. I'm completely tapped out, making sure the kids are having a fun summer, and handling everything going on with Fletcher. I feel badly that Lee is being neglected by me, but I don't have anything left to give right now. I have to hope he understands.

Saturday, July 5, 2008 4:36 PM
16 Weeks 5 Days Old

This afternoon, the nurse was able to take Fletcher off the CPAP and put him on the high flow cannula, which is a step in the right direction. But I'm finding I can't be happy when Fletcher has good days, although I still get depressed and frightened when he has bad days. The nurse said she could tell he's much happier with the huge CPAP mask off his face. I'm glad to hear that he's not fussing. The nurse told him he needs to keep his CO_2 levels down or else they're going to put him back on it. She told me she thinks he heard her.

The nurse said Fletcher is now 8 pounds, 1 ounce! She commented on his chubby cheeks, which amazes me! Even though he's below the average weight for his corrected age, the age he would have been if he was born on his due date, it's hard to imagine that he once weighed less than two pounds!

Fletcher's primary nurse is away for most of July, which is lousy, because that means he's going to have different nurses nearly every day. At least most of the nurses have either taken care of Fletcher before, or are familiar with him, because he's been in the NICU for so long. This makes me less nervous.

Sunday, July 6, 2008 12:48 PM
16 Weeks 6 Days Old

My friend had a house warming party last night. Her husband is a doctor at the children's hospital. One of the guests is a pediatric pulmonologist! I knew that I shouldn't bother him on his personal time, but I started running over to him before I could stop myself. I introduced myself and began to explain about Fletcher and his condition. He cut me short and I was thinking he'd tell me he didn't want to talk about work things, but instead he told me he one of the pulmonologists who had assessed Fletcher in May, and was the one who placed him on the discharge list. He told me he's been following Fletcher's case and didn't mind talking with me about him now.

We spoke for about 20 minutes, and although he didn't really tell me anything I already didn't know, I felt better after talking with him. I'm hoping that he might keep me in the loop going forward. He even told me he would try to go see Fletcher some time this week

One thing I directly asked him about was his thoughts on moving Fletcher to the PICU. He thought moving him would be a good idea, especially because the PICU is better equipped to handle older babies. I'm going to ask the NICU social worker about it tomorrow.

Monday, July 7, 2008 3:11 PM
17 Weeks 0 Days Old

I spoke with the NICU social worker to ask her opinion about moving Fletcher to the PICU. She said it wouldn't be a good idea, for a variety of reasons. She explained that even though Fletcher is an older baby, he still has characteristics of a preemie. He's easily irritated, doesn't like being held or touched, prefers his surroundings to be quiet and dimly lit, and doesn't handle stimulation well. She said I probably wouldn't like the PICU because they treat their patients much more aggressively in order to get the child home. He would still have the same pulmonology team, but they would insist on doing the tracheotomy immediately. She convinced me that, for now, the NICU is the right place for Fletcher. She said that if Fletcher was still in the NICU a month from now, it would be a good idea to have a meeting with the entire team and get their opinions on moving Fletcher to the PICU.

The pediatric palliative care social worker came back to the house this morning. The kids remembered her and kept asking why she came here again. She wanted to meet with just Lee and me, without the kids, to see how we were doing as a couple. We put on a cartoon video and went in to the other room. She told us that she constantly sees the toll that having a sick family member can take on a couple's marriage, and wants to make sure that Lee and I are communicating with each other and giving each other support. I had to be honest and say that Lee and I hadn't been acting much like husband and wife for a very long time. My main focus right now is Fletcher, and Lee's been trying not to deal with everything by concentrating on his job. She advised us to make the effort now, so that whatever happens in the future, we can give the kids a solid foundation at home. Lee and I both know she's right, but we also know how each of us copes during times of stress, which is to do our own thing. When things calm down we will make an effort to re-connect again.

Tuesday, July 8, 2008 9:21 PM
17 Weeks 1 Day Old

Fletcher's been back on breast milk for a few days. The NICU doesn't want to try to bottle feed him for a while, but they said Fletcher is very uncomfortable having the NG tube down his throat and keeps pulling it out. The neonatologist said it was time to put in the g-tube. She said it's a very common procedure and that he probably would only need it for a few years. She wanted him to have the surgery soon to make him more comfortable and to make sure he gets adequate nutrition because he wouldn't be able to pull the tube out. I asked her what the after-care entailed, and all she said was that I would get used to dealing with it.

Then, she mentioned she would have Fletcher's hernia repaired at the same time. I said I didn't know Fletcher needed a hernia operation! She said she was sorry I was just hearing about it, but since it's so common in preemies, no one had thought it was important to bring to my attention. Once again I'm blind-sided by the NICU not disclosing information about my child to me! What's insignificant to them is very significant to me! I've learned over the months that it's not worth letting them know how frustrated I am, but that doesn't mean I'm not angry about it.

Now I have go research all about g-tubes, including the after-care and what exactly I have to do for Fletcher at every meal, how to clean it, and anything else. More importantly, I need to decide if I want Fletcher to have these two surgeries right now.

Wednesday, July 9, 2008 9:35 AM
17 Weeks 2 Days Old

I don't know what to do. I don't feel that Fletcher can handle any surgeries. I don't think Fletcher should go under anesthesia because I don't think he'll be able to get off the ventilator once the surgeries are over. I desperately need someone to talk to me about this. I put a call in to the pediatric palliative care doctor and hope she calls me back before the NICU sets a date for the surgeries. I not only want to ask specifics about Fletcher's health, but also about how I care for Fletcher after he has the g-tube put in. Everything I'm reading is confusing me more and more, but one thing is very certain, there's nothing routine, ordinary, or uncomplicated about caring for a child who has a g-tube.

Wednesday, July 9, 2008 9:52 PM
17 Weeks 2 Days Old

Fletcher spiked a fever today. The nurse took blood work to check for any underlying infections, but everything came back normal. She thinks he might have an ear infection because he lies flat most of the time and fluid could be building up in his ear. She paged the ear, nose throat (ENT) doctor to come and check on him.

I wonder why Fletcher can never have more than a few good days without something else bad happening?

I'm still waiting for the pediatric palliative care doctor to call me, and in the meantime I put in a call to the doctor assigned to do Fletcher's surgeries. One of the NICU nurses mentioned to me that sometimes a surgeon could do these procedures with a spinal anesthetic that doesn't require putting the baby back on the ventilator, so I want to ask if that could be a possibility in this case. I know I'd feel a lot better about having the surgeries done if that was used instead.

Friday, July 11, 2008 10:52 AM
17 Weeks 4 Days Old

The reason for Fletcher's fever is because he has a urinary tract infection, which is an easy fix at least. The NICU never canceled the ENT and he ended up doing an examination and called me right after. He said Fletcher had a lot of fluid trapped in his ears, probably because he spends most of his time on his back. The ENT cleaned them out and put orders in Fletcher's chart for the nurses to clean them out once a day. I'm so sad for Fletcher because a baby his age shouldn't be spending so much time on his back. I wonder if the NICU is taking proper care of Fletcher. I keep thinking that if he were home, he wouldn't be having these issues.

The neonatologist scheduled the g-tube surgery towards the end of next week. I asked about the possibility of him having a spinal instead of general anesthesia, but was told they can't do a spinal because it won't be strong enough to get him completely paralyzed. It worries me to have him put under general anesthesia and be put back on the ventilator. The neonatologist said he'd be fine under general anesthesia, because the bronchoscope and g-tube surgeries are quick procedures so he wouldn't be under for very long.

She asked if I wanted Fletcher circumcised because she could have it done at the same time as the other surgeries. Her question took me by surprise because I've been so preoccupied with Fletcher's health issues that I completely forgot about circumcising him, which is not at all like me. When I was pregnant with my other boys, I researched Mohels and made sure each was circumcised on the eighth day of their lives. I knew Fletcher wouldn't be circumcised that early since he was a preemie, but after he was born, I never thought about it again. I was thankful that the neonatologist asked about it. I definitely want him to be circumcised and having it done while he's under anesthesia felt like the right thing to do for Fletcher because he's already experienced enough pain in his short life.

Friday, July 11, 2008 6:27 PM
17 Weeks 4 Days Old

I'm so uncomfortable with Fletcher having these surgeries right now and wonder if we shouldn't wait until he's a little stronger. I don't think he's healthy enough for any of the surgeries, but the NICU is adamant about getting them done. I wish I could trust that the NICU is doing what's in Fletcher's best interest, but it doesn't make sense to me to have these done right now. Why can't they wait a few more weeks? I don't know why they're rushing to do these operations. Not getting a straight answer from the NICU is making me question their intentions even more.

I finally spoke to the pediatric palliative care doctor and she said she thought it would be fine for Fletcher to have the surgeries. Even with this second opinion, I'm still not convinced, but I'm not a medical doctor and have no real reason to object to it.

CHAPTER 13

In the end, trust yourself to do what you know is right, regardless of how hard or difficult.

Monday, July 14, 2008 2:18 PM
18 Weeks 0 Day Old

Fletcher had a bad weekend. He's in such bad shape that even his neonatologist postponed his surgeries indefinitely. I'm relieved that the surgeries won't be done this week, but am upset about the reason why. I'm so tired out. It's becoming increasingly difficult for me to live this way. I'm trying to give my other kids a fun summer, but I'm dealing with my son fighting for his life in the NICU. When I'm out with my kids and meet other mothers who want to make small talk, all I want to do is tell them everything I'm dealing with. Of course I don't, but every now and then, when I meet someone who says they're having a bad day, I want to scream at them and tell them they have no idea. I find other peoples' issues so trivial and have no patience at all. I've been short-tempered with the kids for things that usually would not bother me. They feel my stress, which makes them act out and misbehave even more. I know that I am trying my best, but that's little comfort to the people who have to be around me and can't understand any of it.

Wednesday, July 16, 2008 2:53 PM
18 Weeks 2 Days Old

Fletcher's condition has gone from bad to worse. I know we've been here before, but this time feels different. I can't imagine him bouncing back and all of a sudden becoming healthy. I really think the end is nearing. His body and face are extremely swollen, and he seems to be in constant pain. He also has another urinary tract infection, which to me, means his body isn't functioning properly in general. I hate to think that I'm giving up on my son, but I think I need to start preparing myself.

I couldn't wait until Lee got home to go see Fletcher, so I ended up taking the kids to the NICU with me. I put them in front of the television in the waiting area so I could sit with Fletcher for a few minutes. I needed to touch, see, smell, and be with him. I interweaved his fingers with mine and just stared at him. There's nothing I can do for either one of us except for this.

Thursday, July 17, 2008 10:55 AM
18 Weeks 3 Days Old

Although Fletcher's still in very bad shape, the neonatologist called and said they scheduled Fletcher's surgeries for tomorrow morning, so I need to sign consent forms this afternoon. I don't understand the urgency, especially because none of these procedures will repair his lungs.

Now I need to drag the kids back to the NICU with me so I can sign these papers. I wish I could stay in the NICU through the night, but I don't have anyone to watch the kids. I already need to call around and see if anyone will watch them tomorrow so I can be in the NICU during his surgeries.

Thursday, July 17, 2008 4:56 PM
18 Weeks 3 Days Old

Lee came home early to talk to me about Fletcher. He was adamant about not allowing the surgeries. He said he agreed with me that Fletcher isn't strong enough to endure the surgeries, and even though the medical staff said it was fine, that we're his parents and have the final say. I was so relieved and glad Lee put his foot down and made this decision. He called the NICU and told the neonatologist we would not be signing the consent forms, and to cancel the surgeries for tomorrow. She was not pleased and asked if I would meet her first thing in the morning.

Friday, July 18, 2008 3:28 PM
18 Weeks 4 Days Old

I had my meeting with the neonatologist. She was disappointed that we canceled the surgeries and told me that Fletcher really needed to be put back on the ventilator or else he wouldn't be alive much longer. I told her to go ahead and put him back on the ventilator, but she reminded me of the DNR letter I signed in June. I told her she should have called me, but she explained that the DNR also prohibited her from even discussing it with me and that she could get in a lot of trouble right now, but she had a feeling I didn't realize the DNR was still in effect.

I couldn't believe it. This whole time I assumed the DNR expired and was only valid for the time period he had pneumonia! The neonatologist explained that until I write different orders or revoke the DNR, they're not allowed to put him back on the ventilator.

As she was telling me this, I realized why the NICU was pushing the surgeries. They wanted Fletcher back on the ventilator, but weren't allowed to broach the subject with me because of the DNR. If I consented to the surgeries, it would over-ride the DNR and allow them to re-intubate him.

I can't believe that a misunderstanding could've caused Fletcher to pass away. How was I supposed to know about these rules? There should be some sort of NICU handbook for parents to learn about these issues and deal with the politics there.

I signed a new order allowing them to put Fletcher on the ventilator. I'm not sure if it was the right decision, but don't want him to struggle, and I don't want to be the one who decides when his treatment is over.

The neonatologist took a huge risk meeting with me today, which definitely brought us closer. I finally feel like we've a made a connection, and going forward I'll be more trusting of her.

Friday, July 18, 2008 11:19 PM
18 Weeks 4 Days Old

The night nurse told me they put Fletcher back on the ventilator fifteen minutes after I left the NICU this afternoon.

Sunday, July 20, 2008 6:54 PM
18 Weeks 6 Days Old

I spent most of the day with Fletcher today. He's really struggling and he looks completely drained and worn-out; definitely not the way a four-month-old should look. I don't think he has much fight left in him. I sobbed and told him it would be okay if he stopped fighting. I told him he's the strongest person I've ever met, and if he let himself be at peace, it wouldn't be him giving up, it would be freeing himself from these struggles. I told him I didn't know why this was happening to him and that he didn't deserve any of it. I kissed him over and over, and then had to get a towel to wipe off all my tears that had fallen on his little body.

I don't understand any of this. I'm grateful I could spend the entire day with him, but that's not enough. It's never enough time.

Monday, July 21, 2008 11:45 PM
19 Weeks 0 Days Old

I received a phone call early this morning telling me the gastroenterologist would be doing the bronchoscope at 3:00 PM this afternoon, without having to put him under anesthesia. I called Lee and asked him to be home by 2:00 PM, so I could be at the NICU while the scope was being done. Lee ended up being stuck in a meeting and got home at 2:15 PM. I was determined to be at the NICU, even though the hospital is over 30 minutes from my house, and parking is always a problem. I found a spot at 2:55 PM, jumped down the stairs and ran through the hospital. I got there at 3:05 PM, and no one was around Fletcher. I asked the nurse and she said the gastroenterologist had come by earlier and said Fletcher was too sick and unstable for him to perform the scope.

I sat there in disbelief. I was so angry that no one called to tell me that they canceled the scope. They all knew how difficult it is for me to get to the NICU, and that I always have to make arrangements well in advance, especially if I have to be here during the day. But I was much more upset to hear that Fletcher's too sick to have the scope done. I wonder what the gastroenterologist's thoughts were on the likelihood for Fletcher getting well. I wish I could've been here when he assessed Fletcher.

I stayed with Fletcher for a few hours and got home just in time to kiss the kids goodnight.

Wednesday, July 23, 2008 8:01 PM
19 Weeks 2 Days Old

The gastroenterologist performed the scope this morning, even though Fletcher's condition hasn't changed. I received a call from the nurse after it was done, which was just as well because I wouldn't have been able to get to the NICU today.

He diagnosed Fletcher with mild-to-moderate tracheomalacia. Tracheomalacia is when the walls of the trachea are weak and flaccid, making them collapse and cause airway obstruction. This makes it difficult for Fletcher to breathe. The neonatologist was hoping the tracheomalacia was severe enough to be blamed for most of Fletcher's breathing difficulties. I wish the results were more conclusive.

However, since tracheomalacia was present, the neonatologist and pulmonologist want him to have the tracheotomy. Lee and I don't agree, but don't feel like we have a choice because there's no way to know if his tracheomalacia could be contributing to Fletcher's breathing difficulties. The neonatologist didn't promise the tracheotomy would cure Fletcher, but said she's optimistic Fletcher would only need it for a few years. I want to hear that the tracheotomy will enable Fletcher's lungs to grow and make him healthy, but so far, neither the neonatologist, nor the pulmonologist, has said that.

Thursday, July 24, 2008 4:59 PM
19 Weeks 3 Days Old

The NICU staff was too aggressive with the ventilator settings and now Fletcher has a collapsed lung. His carbon dioxide levels are starting to rise again, even while on 95% oxygen, and he's having clusters of apnea and brady episodes. He's been back on the ventilator for almost a week and is still deteriorating. It's obvious to me that his lungs aren't functioning, which is why I am so baffled that the neonatologist is still pushing to do the tracheotomy! I asked for a meeting with Fletcher's entire medical team for early next week to hear everyone's opinion on what the best course of action is for Fletcher. In the meantime, the NICU moved Fletcher to his own private room. The nurse said it's because Fletcher couldn't handle all the noise and activity, but I think part of the reason is for the parents of the other patients. It's frightening to see an infant like Fletcher.

Saturday, July 26, 2008 9:55 PM
19 Weeks 5 Days Old

Today was another surreal day. Some friends invited us to their house for a party. My kids had a great time running around with the other kids. I tried to be social, but in between meeting new people, I was fielding phone calls from Fletcher's neonatologist, physician assistant, nurses and the pediatric palliative care team. I must have come off as being extremely arrogant and rude to the other guests because I was on the phone so much. I tried my best to be social, but all I wanted to do was drive up to the hospital.

The phone calls were about Fletcher's poor blood test results, horrible x-rays, and his struggles to breathe, even though the ventilator was on the highest settings. I had to hang up the phone after hearing devastating news and make small talk with a bunch of strangers. It was exhausting and I couldn't wait to go home and cry. I told the NICU staff that I would be up there first thing in the morning to talk with the neonatologist.

Sunday, July 27, 2008 7:00 PM
19 Weeks 6 Days Old

There's a new neonatologist assigned to Fletcher this month. I've never met him before. He came to talk with me and told me the outlook for Fletcher was grim. He said that Fletcher's CO2 level is over 100, and even on high doses of morphine, he seems to be in pain. He tried nitric oxide inhalation treatments on Fletcher this weekend. He said it's used as a last resort because there are conflicting studies about its safety. He said if it were going to make a difference, it would have by now.

He asked the pulmonologist to come in and assess Fletcher, but he thinks there isn't anything else to do for him and I should start thinking about when to take him off the ventilator.

What do I do? What do I do? Fletcher's primary nurse called in while I was in the NICU. She's still out of town, but has been calling in every day. The nurse handed me the phone and she's straightforward with me. She explained that she has seen other patients act this way before. When babies near the end of their lives, they get sicker, and other parts of their body start to break down, causing infections and other issues that weren't a problem before. She brought up Fletcher's two urinary tract infections, and that his heart is under tremendous stress because it's overcompensating for his lung issues. His apnea and brady episodes mean that his heart is starting to fail as well. She said she'd arrange a meeting with the medical team on Tuesday morning, and I should prepare myself to hear that it's time to take Fletcher off the ventilator. She's still scheduled to be on vacation, but promised me she would come to the meeting.

I knew this day was coming, but I hoped that it wouldn't. It was hard to sit alone with Fletcher, knowing that his end was near. I probably should have sat with him longer, but I couldn't. I needed to get home and talk with Lee, and also be alone for a while to think about everything.

Lee thought I was exaggerating when I told him what the neonatologist and nurse had said. He said he wanted to wait and hear from everyone personally, so he'll wait until Tuesday before he believes that Fletcher is going to die. There was nothing else for us to talk about until then.

Monday, July 28, 2008 10:01 AM
20 Weeks 0 Days

The meeting is scheduled for tomorrow morning. Almost everyone who's taken care of Fletcher will be there, including the original neonatologist, Fletcher's primary nurse, two physician assistants, the respiratory technician, the pulmonologist and her team, and the entire pediatric palliative care team, along with Lee and I. I don't know how I'm going to handle hearing from everyone that my son is going to die. I don't know how Lee is going to handle it either.

The neonatologist told me I should call any family members who want to say goodbye to Fletcher. Lee called his parents and they're going to drive down tomorrow. My mom can't get a flight on such short notice and is extremely upset. She was crying to me on the phone but honestly, I have no desire to comfort her when Fletcher is going to die soon. I wish she would try to comfort me right now. I'm so tired of having to console my mom, defend myself to my in-laws and family, take care of my children, fight with the NICU, try to be a wife to Lee, and somehow take care of myself. I don't have the energy.

Monday, July 28, 2008 12:29 PM
20 Weeks 0 Days Old

Fletcher's primary nurse got home from her vacation yesterday and went straight to the NICU to check on Fletcher. After reading his chart and speaking to the other nurses and doctors, she called me. She told me that Fletcher is terminal. The pulmonologist assessed him yesterday, and wrote in his chart that the odds of Fletcher ever leaving the NICU are grim. She also noted to tell the family that they have the option of taking him off the ventilator. Hearing that the pulmonologist put that in writing was really all I needed to hear.

The nurse prepared me for what to expect at tomorrow's meeting. She said the neonatologist is going to tell me to take him off the ventilator, most likely right after the meeting. Even though I knew this was coming, it's still so unbelievable.

I tried to talk to Lee about this, but he said he refused to believe it until he hears it directly from the doctors. "We've been here before," he says. I tell him, "It's different this time." He tells me, "You've said that before." So, once again, I have to deal with this news alone, and yet, I understand exactly how Lee feels. As stupid as it sounds, I keep hoping Fletcher will shock us all and suddenly make a dramatic recovery.

Monday, July 28, 2008 7:51 PM
20 Weeks 0 Days Old

Fletcher's original neonatologist called me a few minutes ago and told me that Fletcher is indeed terminal. There's no more hope; nothing more can be done for him. She isn't even on rotation at this NICU this week, but received a call from the other neonatologist because he knew how attached she'd become to Fletcher. She went over to the NICU and read what the pulmonologist had written in his chart. She told me that Fletcher's lungs are too diseased, and that what little healthy lung tissue he did have has stopped growing. He has literally outgrown his lungs.

She told me the reason for the meeting tomorrow would be to discuss the logistics of taking Fletcher off the ventilator, and how to keep him tranquil and serene while we let him go. She warned me that it could take anywhere from a few seconds, to days, for Fletcher to pass once he's taken off the ventilator. I'm listening to her but my mind keeps telling me this is not for real. I can't believe I'm having this conversation. I can't believe any of this and I'm wondering if this is really happening. I can't believe that I'm on the phone making plans for my son to die.

Tuesday, July 29, 2008 2:24 AM
20 Weeks 1 Day Old

I can't sleep. I'm literally sick to my stomach. I don't want tomorrow to come. I'm having severe chest pain and palpitations. My body is shaking, and I'm trembling and sweating.

The only thing going through my head is the Rick Astley song, "It Would Take a Strong Man"...

My heart starts breaking
When I think of making
A plan to let you go
I keep thinking maybe tomorrow
I'm gonna let you know
But when I think about leaving
I think about losing...
Every time I think of you
My heart starts aching
My hands keep shaking
And you know, you know, you know
It would take a strong, strong man
To ever let you go 'to ever let you go
To ever let you go

My heart's been hurting...
I keep thinking maybe tomorrow…
Every time I look at you
My heart starts aching
My hands keep shaking
And you know, you know, you know
It would take a strong, strong man
To ever let you go 'to ever let you go
To ever let you go…
When you're gone all I ever do is miss you
Anyone in love would know
Anyone with half a heart
Could never let you go…

My heart starts aching
My hands keep shaking
And you know, you know, you know
It would take a strong, strong man
To ever let you go 'to ever let you go
To ever let you go
I'll never let you go

Tuesday, July 29, 2008 10:11 AM
20 Weeks 1 Day Old

Lee, the kids, and I drove to the hospital this morning. We worked it out with the hospital to have a volunteer watch the kids while Lee and I went to the meeting. Once the meeting was over, all five of us would spend time with Fletcher. We drove two cars so that Lee could take the kids home and wait for his parents to come, and I could stay by Fletcher's side.

Attending the meeting were two neonatologists. One of them was the neonatologist who was there when Fletcher was born. She was the most involved with him, and fought the hardest for him.

She's the one who was called the other day to tell her about his condition even though she isn't even working in the NICU this month. Ironically, the second neonatologist was the one who came to talk to me when I was 25 weeks pregnant in the antepartum room in the hospital. She started the meeting by saying, "I'm so sorry. We've done everything we can for him, but he's not responding to any treatments, and there's nothing more we can do for him." Lee and I started crying, even though we knew that's what she was going to say. The other neonatologist also started cry and had to leave the meeting because she was so distraught.

The pulmonologist never bothered to show up. She told the neonatologist that because she'd already written her diagnosis in his chart, there was no reason for her to be at the meeting. Personally, I would've liked to speak with her in person, especially because her diagnosis is the one that sealed Fletcher's fate. I can't imagine why the pulmonologist wouldn't do at least that much for us.

The neonatologist said the plan was to take Fletcher off the ventilator this afternoon, as soon as Lee's parents got here to say their goodbyes. They would then go to our house to watch the kids so Lee could get back to the hospital.

I told them we brought Fletcher's siblings here to kiss him goodbye. At least Spencer was able to visit Fletcher a few times before, but for Wesley and Cassie, it would be their first and last time seeing him.

The NICU only allows one sibling to visit a patient at a time, and only lets them stay for a few minutes. The social worker actually tried to enforce that rule and asked us which child would go in first. I couldn't believe she was going to stick to protocol right now, knowing that Fletcher was about to die. I was about to lose it when Fletcher's primary nurse told her that, in this case, there should be an exception made. The social worker realized her mistake and allowed all of us to go in. She even said we could stay as long as we wanted.

CHAPTER 14

The brief moments of having my husband, our four children, and me together have to last me the rest of my life.

Tuesday, July 29, 2008 2:29 PM
20 Weeks 1 Day Old

Lee carried Cassie while we walked into Fletcher's room. Spencer saw Fletcher and said he couldn't believe how much his brother had grown. He kept telling Wesley about when he last saw Fletcher, and how different he looked now. Spencer wanted to know why Fletcher couldn't come home with us, especially since he's growing. I tried not to cry, but it was impossible. I tried to explain that Fletcher's lungs weren't growing, and he couldn't come home with us. Spencer stared at me blankly, and then walked away to stand near Wesley. Wesley keep bouncing back and forth between Lee and myself, asking a lot of hard questions about why he'd never see Fletcher again, and why Fletcher wasn't getting better, and why he couldn't come back to visit Fletcher another day. Lee and I just looked at each other and hoped that one day the boys would understand. Cassie wasn't sure what was going on, which I actually appreciated. I needed to have that innocence in the room with us. She was more interested in the sink and all the beeps and lights than with Fletcher.

I tried to focus on the kids and how happy they were to be allowed in Fletcher's room to spend time with him. Fletcher was awake most of the time the kids were here and seemed to love and appreciate having us all around him. I think, and hope, it brought him some peace; I know it did for me. The nurses kept taking pictures of the six of us, and of my four kids together. It was disruptive to have all the camera flashes going off, but I knew that one day I'd appreciate having the pictures of my entire family together.

It was so hard to hold back my tears while the kids were in the room, but I tried hard to stay in the moment. The kids were so happy to be allowed in Fletcher's room and have us all together. Although the kids were playing and laughing, Lee and I were so heavy-hearted, knowing that in a matter of hours that Fletcher would be gone.

One of the NICU staff brought stuffed animals for Spencer, Wesley, and Cassie, and told them they were gifts from Fletcher. Spencer received a dinosaur, Wesley's was a giraffe, and Cassie's was a rainbow lizard. All of them were truly delighted that their brother bought presents for them, but Wesley was confused and asked how in the world Fletcher was able to go shopping. It was adorable and painful at the same time. We never answered him.

After an hour, the kids were getting restless, and I could tell that Fletcher had enough, so Lee left to take the kids home. As they left, I realized we were one step closer to taking Fletcher off the ventilator. I wanted time to stand still, but I knew the inevitable was coming.

I felt badly that Lee had to be responsible for taking the other kids home but there was no way I could, or would, leave the room until Fletcher was gone.

Tuesday, July 29, 2008 3:40 PM
20 Weeks 1 Day Old

Lee's parents finally got to the hospital and said their goodbyes. I probably should have given them time alone with Fletcher, but there was no way I was going to leave him. I'm not sure what they said to him, but right before they left they hugged and kissed him and told him how much they loved him. It was so sad.

They could only stay for a few minutes because Lee was waiting for them to get to the house and stay with the kids so he could come back to the hospital.

CHAPTER 15

After all these months, I can't believe it's the end.

Tuesday, July 29, 2008 6:00 PM
20 Weeks 1 Day Old

While we waited for Lee to return, Fletcher's nurse told me she called the NILMDTS photographers to take pictures of Fletcher for us. She hoped I didn't mind; I didn't, but wondered what they were going to do. They weren't able to come until 4:00 PM, which worked out well, because Lee didn't get back until around the same time. Fletcher's nurse brought me a white outfit and asked if I wanted to put Fletcher in it for the pictures. I love that her heart was in the right place, but I told her that would make me uncomfortable to dress Fletcher up for his final pictures. She agreed, but wanted me to know that she had been thinking about this moment. I love that she loves Fletcher so much.

She handed me two white plaster plates and a porcelain jar. She told me that she took imprints of Fletcher's hands and feet, and cut a lock of his hair for me to have as keepsakes. They were beautiful, and I know I will treasure them one day. But for now I need to soak in these last few moments with my son.

Lee got back at 4:00 PM, a few minutes before the photographers came. I asked him if it was okay for them to take pictures. He initially didn't like the idea because he thought it was weird to have a photo shoot knowing our child was about to die. I agreed with him, but said that the pictures will be all we have of Fletcher and, eventually, we'll cherish them.

The photographers took pictures for about ten minutes. It was so gut wrenching. The photographers started by taking pictures of all

Fletcher's equipment, wires and IV lines, and then started taking pictures of him alone. We decided to have him wear nothing but his diaper, which seemed appropriate. They took pictures of his ears, legs, hands, and feet as well.

Fletcher was handed to Lee and more pictures were taken with Lee, Fletcher, and me, together, and alone. It was beyond difficult to do, and after a few minutes, Lee was getting angry. I told him that we can never get these moments back and even though it was completely bizarre, I will appreciate having these pictures.

As the day went on, Fletcher was more and more uncomfortable, and by this time, his pain was becoming unmanageable, even though the nurses were giving him extra boosts of morphine. We all knew it was time.

We decided to allow the photographers to stay and take pictures even after we unhooked Fletcher from the ventilator. I realized I didn't have any pictures of Fletcher's face without wires or oxygen tubes, except for the ones when he was a few days old.

At 4:40 PM, the respiratory therapist took out the breathing tube connected to the ventilator and the physician assistant and nurse removed all the IV lines, except for the one giving him his pain medicine. Then the ventilator was turned off. The photographers took a lot of pictures and we all sat in silence and motionless.

The photographers took Fletcher and placed him on his bed, but I had enough. Knowing time was against him, I panicked and yelled out not to let Fletcher die alone on the bed! His nurse jumped up, checked his vitals, and said it wouldn't be long. I told the photographers to please stop and asked to have Fletcher placed in his father's arms.

The neonatologist promised me he wasn't uncomfortable and explained to me that the carbon dioxide levels were rapidly increasing in his system, putting him in a relaxed, dream-like state. I believed her because Fletcher looked so tranquil. When Lee was holding him and I started stroking his head, Fletcher opened his eyes and looked at us.

A few moments later, Fletcher died. It was 5:35 PM, a mere 55 minutes after removing the ventilator tube.

CHAPTER 16

Sometimes there are no answers and no reasons why.

Tuesday, July 29, 2008 11:59 PM
20 Weeks 1 Day Old

After seven months of pregnancy, and four months and 19 days of hoping, praying, loving, hating, hurting, yearning, aching, pain, and tenderness, Fletcher was gone.

Lee and I held Fletcher until the funeral home director came at 8:00 PM. In the meantime, nurses and other medical staff from all over the NICU came in to say their goodbyes to Fletcher and all left sobbing. I can't believe how many lives Fletcher touched. Everyone who came in the room hugged him and cried, saying how much they would miss him.

The funeral home director took off Fletcher's blanket and handed it to me. Fletcher was still wearing his diaper, and I kept thinking that he would get cold without his blanket on. The funeral director lied Fletcher down gently in a basket. He said he was sorry for our loss, and then walked out a back door of the NICU. A stranger took my son. Some random guy took my son. He took my son and I never even got his name! Lee and I just stood there in shock.

Staff members hugged us and the social worker handed me a card of the funeral home and told me to call them tomorrow. Then Lee and I walked out of the NICU and headed home.

What a day. What a tragic day. I'm dreading tomorrow; a day and a life without Fletcher.

FLETCHER'S EULOGY

I always felt there was someone missing from our family. I loved and wanted Fletcher long before he was born. When I got pregnant with him in September, I was so happy and immediately felt that our family was complete. In October, when we were told we only had a 10% chance that the pregnancy would be viable, I was crushed. I couldn't believe it, but I prepared for the worst. Three weeks later, to everyone's amazement, the baby was growing! There was a heartbeat! From that point on, Fletcher grew under the most adverse conditions. Even before he was born, he wanted so much to live. When I was hospitalized during the pregnancy, I was never alone. We fought together!

And during the pregnancy, hundreds of people from all over the world "met" him and cheered him on. Many grew to love this little boy. Phone calls and letters poured in.

Oh! And when he was born – and came out crying – that was such a wonderful day! I finally felt at peace and hopeful that, finally, after so much work and sacrifice, we'd have our little boy and our family would be complete. Even some nurses in the NICU said Fletcher would be a feeder and grower, and would be home before his due date.

When he was two weeks old, he experienced his first setback. But I was told that Fletcher needing to go on oxygen was to be expected. He remained feisty, and strong, and a fighter. A few months later, he was put on the discharge list, two weeks before his actual due date. But suddenly, he crashed and had to be put on a ventilator. We were told to say our goodbyes. There were more tears and more heartache. Fletcher had contracted pneumonia but after a week of antibiotics and other medicine, he started getting better! Hope returned. No one could believe it. This boy was a fighter. Then, six weeks later, he crashed again, but this time he couldn't recover. His lungs had too much scar tissue and were no longer growing. They could no longer support his 10 pound, 4.2 ounce, beautiful, perfect body. Perfect except for his horrible lungs. His condition was diagnosed as fatal. Even with his strong will, Fletcher's fight was over.

He couldn't win, but he didn't lose, either. We took him off the ventilator at 4:40 PM Tuesday, July 29, 2008 and he died at 5:35 PM, 55 minutes later.

I truly believe he will live on in all of us. He will always be Lee and my son; Spencer, Cassie, and Wesley's little brother. We'll always be a family of six.

Fletcher will also live on through all of you; through his relatives, through all who took care of him, who tried every single thing to get him well; all of our friends; all who love us; all who loved him just because of hearing his story; all of you who have talked about him to your family and friends. All of you! And for that I cannot thank you enough. Thank you all for your support, love, optimism, prayers, positive thoughts, and hope. All of it has helped us get through this last year. And will continue to help us going forward.

I'm asking for just one more thing from you. Yes, I know it's more than selfish, but it's for Fletcher. Please remember him. Remember his strength and determination. Smile when you think of him. Keep him alive by remembering him every now and then. We love you all. Fletcher loved you all.

A friend said to me that Fletcher came early because he knew his time here would be limited. I really believe that, so I am even more thankful for the extra three months we got to be together and know him.

EPILOGUE

I wish I could say every year since Fletcher's death has gotten easier, but it hasn't. There isn't a day that goes by when I don't think about him. Sometimes hours pass when he's not on my mind, but soon after, everything comes rushing back to me, and in that moment, I relive everything all over again.
Some days I can't believe it all really happened; that I gave birth to a son who ultimately died far too soon.

People still try to convince me that it gets easier over time, but I can't imagine it will ever will. I constantly think about how my family would be different had Fletcher lived. When I see kids the age that he would have been, I have to hold back the tears. When my other sons fight with my daughter, I think that if Fletcher were here, he would play with, and include her. When extended family gets together over holidays, I realize my core family will never be together again.

I talk about Fletcher with Spencer, Wesley, and Cassie, but I'm so grateful when they initiate conversations about him.

Sometimes they ask me why he can't be here with us, and other times they make family pictures and draw him next to them. My favorite was one that showed him playing in the mud while the other kids were on the swings. Even though it's painful for me, I always allow the kids to talk to me about Fletcher whenever they want.

Every year for Fletcher's birthday, I make a cake shaped in the number of how many years old he would have been. The kids insist on making him cards, and we get balloons to attach the cards to them, and send up to him. Buying balloons is especially hard because most people see them and smile, assuming I'm going to birthday celebration. I always avoid making eye contact with others while holding the balloons, and I rush to my car to avoid any questions about who's getting them. But every year

I do this; for my kids, and for Fletcher. At first, Lee thought it was weird to make a cake and send balloons to Fletcher, because he said birthdays are to celebrate someone living another year. I explained that we're doing this to acknowledge and remember that Fletcher was born, his actual birth day, because even though he won't ever be a year older, his birthday is forever.

The anniversary of his death is a lot harder for me to commemorate. I simply light a candle for him because that's all I'm able to do right now.

When I meet new people, I get asked how many kids I have and if I would ever have more. I usually decide how to answer them in that moment. Sometimes I say I have three children and am unable to have anymore, but there are times when I feel I'm betraying Fletcher, so I say I have four children, but one has passed away. I talk about him even to strangers I'll never see again. I need to figure out when to share his story with people and when it's okay to not. There are times I end up having to console the other person, which just makes me mad. This is still a learning process for me. I never asked to be in this situation, and I'm still learning how to live with this, day by day.

The most important thing to me is that my children know Fletcher's story and realize they have a younger brother. I hope they keep their brother's memory alive, and when they have their own family, they'll tell their children all about Fletcher, who loved them very much.

GLOSSARY

Alveoli - are tiny air sacs in the lungs that are responsible for the exchange of oxygen and carbon dioxide in the blood.

AMA – advanced maternal age refers to a woman 35 years or older at the time she gets pregnant, or delivers a baby.

Amniocentesis – a procedure where amniotic fluid, which contains fetal tissues, is taken from the uterus and tested for genetic abnormalities.

AFI - amniotic fluid index – a rough estimate of the amount of amniotic fluid in the uterus. A normal AFI is about ten centimeters. An AFI less than six is low, and called oligohydramnios. An AFI greater than 20 centimeters is called polyhydramnios.

Apgar – an acronym that stands for Appearance, Pulse, Grimace, Activity, and Respiration. When babies are born, doctors use Apgar scores to assess newborns. The Apgar score is determined by evaluating the newborn baby on these five criteria, on a scale from zero to two, then summing up the five values, with ten being the highest. The assessment is taken at one minute, and at five minutes after birth.

Aspiration of lungs- an inflammation of the lungs and bronchial tubes caused by breathing in foreign material.

Betamethasone - a corticosteroid that's been shown to help an immature fetus's lungs produce a compound called surfactant. The betamethasone helps to speed up preemie's lung development.

BPD - bronchopulmonary dysplasia - the abnormal development of lung tissue. It's characterized by inflammation and scarring within the lungs. It develops most often in premature babies, who are often born with underdeveloped lungs.

"Broncho" refers to the airways (the bronchial tubes) through which the oxygen we breathe travels into the lungs. "Pulmonary" refers to the lungs' tiny air sacs (alveoli), where oxygen and carbon dioxide are exchanged. "Dysplasia" means abnormal changes in the structure, or organization, of a group of cells. The cell changes in BPD take place in the smaller airways and lung alveoli, making breathing difficult, and causing problems with lung function. Babies who are born prematurely, or who experience respiratory problems shortly after birth, are at risk for bronchopulmonary dysplasia (BPD), sometimes called chronic lung disease. Although most infants fully recover from BPD and have few long-term health problems as a result, BPD can be a serious condition requiring intensive medical care. A child is not born with BPD. It's something that develops as a consequence of prematurity, and progressive lung inflammation.

BPP - biophysical profile – measures the health of the baby by assigning points of either zero or two to the baby's muscle tone, movement, breathing, and the amniotic fluid, and sometimes the results of the NST, resulting in a maximum score of 10.

Bronchial Tubes – airways to the lungs.

Bronchoscopy – a procedure where a bronchoscope is inserted down the throat and into the airways to examine the airways, trachea, bronchi, and lungs. A lung biopsy can also be done to check for infectious diseases.

CBC – complete blood count - a blood test that usually measures WBC, RBC, and platelets in the blood.

CP – cerebral palsy. CP refers to a group of chronic disorders that prevents the child from controlling their muscles normally. CP affects the brain and nervous system functions, such as movement, learning, hearing, seeing, and thinking.

CPAP – continuous positive airway pressure - comprised of tubing, a facemask and air oxygen machine. The tube is connected to the oxygen machine that gives constant oxygenated air pressure into the baby's nose, and into the lungs.

CVC - central venous catheter. The CVC is a catheter placed into a large vein in the neck, and is a quick way to give medicine, check blood levels, and have more control over the patient in an emergency situation.

D&C - dilation and curettage is when a doctor widens the cervix and surgically removes part of the lining of the uterus.

Ectopic Pregnancy – an abnormal pregnancy where the fertilized egg implants outside of the uterus, usually in the fallopian tubes, and must be terminated.

EDD – estimated due date.

EKG – electrocardiogram – a non-invasive test that records the heart's electrical activity.

ER – emergency room.

g-tube - gastrostomy tube - a feeding tube that is surgically placed into the stomach through the abdomen.

hCG - human chorionic gonadotropin hormone that detects early pregnancy. A level measuring over ten mIU/ml is indicative of a woman being pregnant.

Incubators – where preemies sleep. The incubator helps keep a baby in a clean environment to avoid infection and control temperature. The incubator also keeps noise levels low, and can shut out light by throwing a cover over the top. Preemies are very sensitive to noise and light.

Jaundice –excessively high bilirubin levels.

L&D – labor and delivery.

Lung Surfactant - a protein complex found in the lining of the alveoli, which prevents them from collapsing during breathing and protects the lungs from infections and injuries.

MRI - magnetic resonance imaging – a non-invasive technique to get detailed images of internal structures

Mucus plug - substance that blocks the opening of the cervix and prevents bacteria from entering the uterus. For some women, this signals the start of labor, for others it could still take weeks before labor begins.

NICU – neonatal intensive care unit.

Nifedipine - a medication primarily used to treat angina and high blood pressure, but has been clinically proven to relax the uterus, preventing contractions.

NILMDTS (Now I Lay Me Down To Sleep) - an organization of professional photographers who generously volunteer their time and services to provide beautiful remembrance pictures for families who are suffering the loss of a baby.

NST - non-stress test- a non-invasive test to check that the baby is getting enough oxygen by monitoring heart rate and movement. It consists of two belts; one belt has a sensor that's wrapped around the stomach to measure the baby's heart rate. The other belt checks to see if there are any contractions. The NST usually lasts about thirty minutes, and charts the baby's heart, and how it reacts to movements and/or contractions.

NTT - nuchal translucency test - measures the clear space and fold in the tissue at the back of the baby's neck. Babies with abnormalities tend to accumulate more fluid at the back of their neck during the first trimester, causing this clear space to be larger than average.

Oligohydramnios – having too little amniotic fluid in pregnancy, with an AFI less than six centimeters.

OR – operating room.

Palliative care – medical and comfort care for patients facing life-long illnesses to improve their quality of life, as well as to provide support and resources for their families.

Perinatologist - a high-risk OB.

Phototherapy – a light treatment for jaundice that rids the baby's body of excess bilirubin through light waves. These waves absorb into the skin and blood, and transform bilirubin into compounds that are excreted through urine and stools.

PICC Line – A peripherally inserted central catheter similar to an IV line, but can stay in for longer periods of time, up to 30 days.

PICU – pediatric intensive care unit.

Placental issues in pregnancy:

> placenta previa – when the placenta attaches to the lower part of the uterus and covers the cervix.

> placenta accreta – an abnormally deep attachment of the placenta into the uterine wall that does not penetrate it.

> placenta increta – a deeper attachment of the placenta into the uterine wall.

> placenta percreta – the most severe placental issue where the placenta goes through the entire uterine wall and can attach to other organs.

Polyhydramnios - having too much amniotic fluid in pregnancy, usually having an AFI over 20 centimeters.

pPROM – preterm premature rupture of membranes.

Progesterone - a hormone that, in pregnancy, is produced by the ovaries to sustain the pregnancy until the placenta takes over. This happens near the start of the second trimester.

Pulmonary Hypoplasia - a malformation characterized by incomplete development of lung tissue.

PVCs - premature ventricular contractions - when the heart skips a beat and then resumes beating normally a few seconds later.

PVL - periventricular leukomalacia is the damage and softening of the white matter in the inner part of the brain that transmits information between the nerve cells and the spinal cord, as well as from one part of the brain to another. PVL is frequently associated with neurological and developmental problems in growing babies, usually during the first to second year of life. As the baby grows, the damaged nerve cells cause the muscles to become spastic, or tight, and resistant to movement. Babies with PVL have a higher risk of developing cerebral palsy, spasticity (tightness, or increased muscle tone) in the legs, and may have intellectual or learning disabilities.

RBC - red blood count - a decreased number of such can signal internal bleeding, anemia, and other disorders.

Rh – rhesus factor in blood. When Rh negative blood is exposed to Rh positive blood, the Rh negative person starts to product antibodies to fight the invading blood. In pregnant women, if the mother has antibodies to the Rh antigen, those antibodies can attack the baby's red blood cells. This can lead to complications to the baby including anemia, jaundice, and other blood related problems, and possibly even miscarriage. Rh immune globulin shots are given to prevent issues in future pregnancies.

ROP - retinopathy of prematurity is an abnormal growth of the blood vessels in one, or both, of the baby's eyes.

SCH - subchorionic hematoma is a clot situated between the uterine wall and amniotic sac. SCHs can be small, medium, and large, with small being the least worrisome. The bigger the SCH, the more bleeding it can cause.

Surfactant - a protein complex found in the lining of the alveoli that prevents the alveoli from collapsing during breathing, and protects the lungs from infections and injuries.

Terbutaline - a bronchodilator medicine that's typically used as an asthma treatment, but is often used as an off-label drug to stop contractions in pregnant women.

Trachea - the windpipe that connects the larynx to the lungs, allowing for the passage of air.

Tracheomalacia – a condition where the trachea walls are weak and flaccid, causing them to collapse obstruct the airway.

Tracheotomy – an operation where the windpipe, or trachea, is cut creating an artificial opening, called a tracheostomy. A plastic tube is inserted in the trachea that helps with breathing.

WBC - white blood count - a high number can indicate infections or other diseases, and a low number can also indicate other types of diseases.

www.ingramcontent.com/pod-product-compliance
Lightning Source LLC
Chambersburg PA
CBHW050522260626
47157CB00004B/1436